McFADDEN'S WAR

Jeff & Melonie!

Blessings,

Mac

Other books by Craig MacIntosh

The Fortunate Orphans
(Beaver's Pond Press, 2009)

The Last Lightning
(Beaver's Pond Press, 2013)

McFadden's WAR

By Craig MacIntosh

PUGIO BOOKS

ISBN: 978-0-9913611-0-6

Cover design by Kent Mackintosh
Book design by Mayfly Design and typeset in Janson Text

Printed in the United States of America
First Printing: 2014

18 17 16 15 14   5 4 3 2 1

Published by Pugio Books
13607 Crosscliffe Place
Rosemount, MN 55068
cjmacintosh.com

ACKNOWLEDGMENTS

I spent my teen years in Hawaii, and sharing high school life with Filipino-American classmates planted a curiosity about this Asian nation. Then in 2009 I read a fascinating book entitled *Imperial Grunts: The American Military on the Ground* by Robert D. Kaplan. In one chapter, the author visited the small U.S. Special Forces garrison in Zamboanga City on the island of Mindanao. The selfless American soldiers serving on this southernmost island in the Philippines faced every challenge imaginable. My initial curiosity about the Philippines combined with this inspiring book and others, and the seed of a story was planted.

During the process of creating a cast of characters for my novel, I was introduced to America's elite warriors: those serving in our Special Forces. Thanks to U.S. Navy SEALs Kenneth Bulahan, William Hellman, and Chuck Wolf for their enthusiasm. I am equally grateful to Green Beret colonels Bill Coultrup and John Alexander—patriots who spent many years at the tip of the spear and yet were gracious enough to review my manuscript. I am particularly indebted to these gentlemen for their willingness to read my first draft. They offered encouragement and the occasional correction on tactics, culture, language and weaponry. They shared their experiences in the Philippines with me, giving my story the credibility every author wants.

Friends Commander Roger Herman, U.S. Navy (Ret.), Ken Wolf, and Marcia Herbster gave my book its first read. Thanks also to Tim Peters, Dave Bacig, and Dr. Tim Dirks. As usual, my editor, Cindy Rogers, kept me focused on the craft of writing. Though readers will not detect her hand, her excellent advice is evident to me on every page. Without proofreader Molly Miller's discerning eye, my words would not have the clarity she brings to every page. My brother Kent created the striking cover, as he does for all my books. Designer Ryan Scheife not only added his skills to the interior layout, a key contribution, but shepherded this project to its completion.

No acknowledgement would be complete without giving my wife, Linda, her due for supporting my desire to write.

—Craig MacIntosh,
Rosemount, Minnesota

For Chuck Wolf, Navy SEAL,
patriot, warrior, raconteur, and friend.

THE
PHILIPPINES

PACIFIC
OCEAN

✦MANILA

SOUTH
CHINA
SEA

SULU SEA

MINDANAO

ZAMBOANGA

PROLOGUE

The Global War on Terrorism has forever changed the face of our world. The attacks of 9/11 clearly demonstrate that America can no longer isolate itself from terrorist violence. After more than a decade of war Americans everywhere, especially those living abroad have come to realize there is no global safe haven. The nexus of terrorism and organized crime—connected by the Internet and other means—has made the world a very small place indeed. As global violence escalates, American expats, who once enjoyed the promise of foreign shores, now find themselves increasingly at risk.

Living amidst the turmoil of unstable communities where governments are unable to protect them, Americans find their own security a personal responsibility. Dreams once thought inviolable can be destroyed in an instant. Those who suffer most are often innocent bystanders in this global tumult. Americans, who for generations have shared their lives with people of the Philippines, today find themselves facing the challenge of mutual survival.

—Captain Chuck Wolf, U.S. Navy SEAL (Ret.)
Alexandria, Virginia, 2014

". . . may disaster hunt down men of violence."
—Ps 140:11

CHAPTER 1

Southwest of Mindanao, June, two years ago

Empty save for a lone southbound trawler laboring through gentle swells, the Sulu Sea shimmered like silk, changing from the color of newly minted silver coin to turquoise in the morning sun. Scattered flocks of woolly clouds cast their shadows across the placid surface. Trailing a thin curl of oily smoke in its wake, the battered trawler was invisible to all but the most trained eye . . . or radar.

Eight miles east of the plodding fishing boat, a Philippine Navy patrol boat cruised south at a steady fifteen knots. Despite its blunt, pig-snout bow, the aluminum hull, driven by dual-thrust jets, effortlessly planed the swells. The crew—one officer, four sailors and eight heavily armed Philippine Marines—had been hunting since dawn. Adding to the crew's firepower were two U.S. Navy SEALs. Acting as American eyes assigned to the JSOTF-P—Joint Special Operations Task Force-Philippines—the SEALs were aboard as advisors.

The boat's captain, Lieutenant Carlos Guzman, a tough ten-year navy veteran wore his usual scowl and an armored vest bulging with thirty-round magazines. Poking his head from the crowded bridge, he pointed west and bellowed at the taller of the two Americans on the open deck amidships. "We have contact, sir."

Bracing himself against the cabin roof, Commander Thomas Wolf crouched at Guzman's ear. "Say again." Repeating his message, the captain added details on range and compass heading. "Gonna take a look?" asked Wolf. The lieutenant nodded. Calling the ranking enlisted marine to the bridge, Guzman ordered his men to gun positions and gave his coxswain a new heading. Clapping the Filipino officer on the shoulder, the American smiled, flashing a thumbs-up.

With twenty years in the navy and multiple tours in Latin America, Iraq and Afghanistan, Wolf was on top of his game. Six-two, 190 pounds, he still looked the surfer he had been growing up in Santa Cruz, California. His stance and sun-bleached blond hair buzzed short had American military written all over him—a liability in some parts of the Philippines, but not today, and definitely not to the crew closing in on a suspect vessel fleeing south across the Sulu Sea.

Wolf worked his way across the open deck to the second SEAL, Chief Petty Officer Dennis "Preacher" Hackett, a wiry Minnesotan thirty pounds lighter and six inches shorter than Wolf. An odd duck, Preacher was a perpetually grinning, Bible reading prayer warrior who eschewed sailors' profanity and carousing, yet loved combat. Pound for pound, Preacher was Wolf's equal in a fight, if not in weight or rank. Singled out during Great Lakes basic, Preacher had thrived during brutal BUD/S training in Coronado and had racked up eight years with the teams. His love affair with guns and explosives was matched only by his ferocity in firefights.

Towering over Preacher, Wolf passed the news. "Contact! Five miles! Bearing two-six-niner! Guzman wants a looksee!" No sooner had he spoken than the patrol boat picked up speed, carving a tight starboard turn. Preacher steadied himself on the slanting deck. Sweeping the western horizon with binoculars, he spotted a trace of dirty smoke, nothing more. It was enough. He handed the glasses to a grim-faced Wolf, who studied the horizon, then returned the binoculars. Both men patted their web gear, double-checking equipment and ammo. Preacher chambered a round in his M4 Colt Commando and flipped on the safety, then checked his holstered 9mm SIG Sauer. Wolf mimicked Preacher's moves.

On the horizon, the blossoming smoke grew larger with each passing minute. Accelerating to twenty-five knots, the patrol craft flew across the sea. Leaving a harnessed man at the controls, Guzman scrambled topside, loaded M4 in his hands. Wolf and Preacher donned Kevlar helmets and stalked across the open deck where sailors manned M60 machine guns mounted behind steel shields. A third crewman scrambled aft to his post at the big .50 caliber gun. Eight marines spaced themselves along the railings.

On the open deck behind the bridge, Preacher raised binoculars and followed the greasy plume to its source—an ugly, battered wooden-hulled trawler with a high curved bow and a wheelhouse set well forward. Tiny figures crabbed across the boat's cluttered deck in panic. "What are you seeing, Preacher?" asked Wolf.

"A bunch of scared rats, Skipper."

"I'd be running around too if I were them."

"No doubt," said Preacher, the glasses glued to his eyes. "Hey, they just tossed a kayak overboard. Like we wouldn't notice. What's that about?"

"Did you say kayak?"

"Affirmative. Bright-yellow one. One of those sea-going kayaks tree-huggers use. Seen em in Hawaii. Tried one in Savannah once. Yep, definitely a kayak."

"Odd," said Wolf. "What are they doing now?"

"Looks like we got ourselves a Chinese fire drill in progress."

"How many?"

"So far I count a dozen on deck."

"Okay, stand by, Preacher. Remember, this is Guzman's show."

"Roger that. Just so you know . . . I hate playing traffic cop."

"No choice. I don't need a firefight when I'm about to pull the pin."

"I hear you, sir. Thirty days and a wake-up, right?"

"You got it, Preacher. After this party I'm done. Paperwork's already in the pipeline. You ready to rock and roll?"

"Aye, aye, sir. Lord, please let one of our little brown brothers try something stupid."

Shaking his head, Wolf laughed at Preacher's impromptu battle prayer. Circling like a hawk closing in on prey, the boat jumped the trawler's wake and ran parallel, staying out of RPG range as a precaution. Guzman had his gunner fire six .50 caliber rounds across the wooden boat's bow. Message received. The fishing boat slowed, then stopped, wallowing in place. Guzman put on a show with his boat, jetting in a circle to underscore the craft's power and maneuverability in case the other pilot decided to run. Using a hand-held megaphone, Guzman ordered the trawler's crew to assemble at the bow. The patrol boat came alongside. A squad of marine commandos leaped aboard the fishing boat. Two marines held the knot of crewmen at gunpoint while four cleared the bridge and main cabin. Despite Wolf's caution that he stand off from the trawler, Guzman drifted closer. Two marines mounted the bridge's catwalk to cover the sullen crew gathered on the bow. The remaining four marines pulled back a hatch amidships and went below, flushing three more crew, prodding them topside. Guzman relayed the discovery to the SEALs. "Commander. They found a prisoner, a foreigner, below deck. He's in bad shape. We'll bring him on board."

"Right," said Wolf. "You may have interrupted a kidnapping."

Preacher stepped to the rail. "I could give Guzman's marines a hand, sir."

"Rules of engagement, Preacher. Let them handle it."

Grumbling at the caution, Preacher strained at the leash, his weapon ready.

"Hey, not my choice either, but I'm days from being a civilian and you might do something dumb. Besides, I feel better having you over here in case it hits the fan. These routine stops sometimes turn out to be anything but that."

Grinning, Preacher swept his eyes across the trawler's deck. "Roger that."

Guzman nudged closer, the hulls kissing. Crossing to the other boat's stern, two more marines disappeared below to help with the prisoner. In minutes, they climbed back on deck, an emaciated, bearded figure sagging between them like a wilted scarecrow. Wolf and Guzman took the handoff, steadying the glassy-eyed man. Guzman and a sailor shepherded the gaunt figure below decks.

"Was he talking, sir?" asked Preacher.

Wolf shook his head. "Incoherent." Pointing at the drifting trawler, he said, "Guzman thinks we have something else going on here. He's sending his marines below for another look."

"Huh, I've got a funny feeling, sir."

"Instinct?"

"Yeah," snorted Preacher, "something like that." He backed from the trawler's gunwale.

A shadow behind the ladder in the open hatch moved. Spotting a gunman raising an AK47, Wolf roared, "GET DOWN!"

Preacher dropped, rolling across the deck to his left, firing quick bursts into the hold. Wolf drilled six rounds in the shooter's torso. No contest. Crumpling, the man fell back, his rifle clattering to the splintered deck.

At the sound of gunfire, two of the captive crew made a suicidal leap at the guards on the catwalk above. The marines cut down both men. One of the M60 gunners fired a short warning burst over the heads of the huddled sailors. The cowed knot of crewmen folded in the face of the firepower.

Guzman raced on deck just as the last shots were fired. The marines who had been rushed doled out payback among the prisoners with their boots. Guzman watched but did not interfere.

Pushing from the deck, Preacher crouched, staring at the open hatchway, his blood up. Peering cautiously into the gaping opening, he aimed his M4 at the lifeless gunman. His wish for a fight fulfilled, Preacher watched a pair of Guzman's marines drag the bullet-ridden body topside. They dumped the corpse in the sunlight and returned below. In minutes, they were back at the top of the ladder, asking Guzman to send them another crewmember.

The Filipinos began manhandling wooden crates topside. When they were finished, one dozen boxes of contraband sat scattered on the deck. The searchers pried open lids with a Ka-Bar knife and held up, in turn, M16s, RPGs, launchers and a pair of M60 machine guns. Ammo cans filled with thousands of rounds littered the planking. Each crate bore an AFP—Armed Forces Philippines—stamp. A marine passed an M60 to Preacher on the patrol boat.

"They look brand new," snarled Preacher, running a finger along an M60's glistening barrel. He passed the weapon to Wolf. "Someone in the food chain got some splaining to do, Boss."

Guzman, at a loss for words, gripped the rail, staring at the arsenal, furious. He radioed a Philippine Navy cutter patrolling an hour away for assistance. While awaiting its arrival, he began a preliminary interrogation of the trawler's crew with Wolf at his side. To a man, the prisoners refused to talk.

Once the cutter arrived and took the recovering stranger onboard—along with the trawler's crew—Guzman conferred with superiors on board the larger ship. An hour passed before he came back over the side to brief Wolf and Preacher. After the prisoners had been separated, two had babbled freely. According to the pair, the nom de guerre of the man Wolf killed was Abu Bakr, a second-string holdover from Abu Sayyaf's infamous days in the headlines. The other two dead were fodder. More erstwhile pirate than jihadist, Abu Bakr and his rag-tag collection of bandits had boarded the fishing trawler two days earlier with the prisoner and contraband arms when their own boat had lost an engine and had begun taking on water. The fishermen had been beheaded and thrown overboard after surrendering their boat.

"So much for the Good Samaritan legacy," quipped Preacher.

"We cannot be too careful out here," declared Guzman. "Really, who can we trust?"

"And this white guy?" asked Wolf. "Was that his kayak they tossed?"

It was, said Guzman. Two months previous, dispersed by a sudden squall, a group of western kayakers had been scattered throughout a nameless necklace of islands off Mindanao's Zamboanga Peninsula. Finally reunited, the Frenchman's companions assumed their missing friend had drowned. It had been the man's misfortune to come across an Abu Bakr desperate for money. The Frenchman found aboard the trawler had been a winning lottery ticket to cash and notoriety, or so the pirates thought. Dehydrated and suffering from exposure, their prisoner would not have lasted another two days, according to the cutter's corpsman.

With the rescue, Guzman's star soared. On the way back to base, Guzman told how his crew's actions had been lauded by the commander of naval forces–western Mindanao who, luck would have it, was aboard the navy ship called to the scene. Commendations, perhaps a promotion, were sure to follow, crowed a pleased Guzman as they headed northeast.

Wolf and Preacher were having none of it. In keeping with their training, limelight was something to be avoided. When they returned to the navy pier at Zamboanga, Guzman's prediction of official approval had preceded them. Philippine media, hand-fed by government flacks, had a field day over what the press, with the navy's encouragement, had dubbed "Mini-Trafalgar on the Sulu Sea." Along with Guzman and his crew being lionized for their bravery, special mention of Navy SEAL Thomas Wolf's killing of Abu Bakr played large in Manila's tabloids. Though the details were wrong, leftist mouthpieces and anti-American rabble-rousers rode the issue for weeks. The gruff American commander, cast as a noble symbol of the two nations' cooperation in some quarters, was vilified in others. Preacher, grateful to remain incognito, avoided the same fate for his role in the affair.

Unbeknownst to Wolf—the price of being a short-lived darling of the Philippine media was to be anointed a marked man.

CHAPTER 2

Mindanao, April, present day

Traffic in Zamboanga, the Philippines' sixth largest city, flows in a constant unbroken stream. In this teeming city of 800,000, rush hour is never finished, the cacophony of horns never silent, the streets never empty. Jeepneys, motorcycles, three-wheeled cyclos, SUVs, bicycles, and delivery vans jockey with tanker trucks in a hazardous ballet. Pedestrians, confronted by lanes of weaving vehicles, bunch into a critical mass at traffic lights and force their way across white-striped crosswalks. Braver individuals make mid-block suicidal rushes into the same unyielding traffic.

A white van joined a continuous queue passing the ancient

stone parapets of Fort Pilar overlooking the turquoise sea. Traffic wound along the shore's concrete esplanade where early risers haggled with fishermen perched on lava rocks, displaying their morning catch.

Parked at the foot of the battlements, the driver of a fire-red Honda XR200 motorcycle checked his watch as the white van passed. Nodding to a rider straddling the rear seat, he threw a leg over the saddle, kicked the engine to life, and joined the line of traffic heading into the city. Muscling their way into the flow, the duo challenged more cautious motorists for position. The bike flew around a line of motorized cyclos carrying commuters cocooned next to the drivers. Drifting to the right, the Honda worked its way to within two car lengths of the white van and stayed there. Anonymous behind his helmet's tinted eye shield, the bike's driver risked a red light to stay with his white target.

Perched on the Honda's rear seat, a woman, round brown face framed by a black shoulder-length hijab, eyes hidden by mirrored sunglasses, leaned against the driver. Knees locked around his hips, the unsmiling woman kept her right hand buried in a black nylon bag balanced on her thighs. To fellow cyclists the pair was just a typical young jean-clad Muslim couple heading to jobs or perhaps playing hooky from prayers at the mosque.

The white van signaled a right turn. Two trailing vehicles, a hulking SUV and an over-crowded taxi, continued on. Turning in the van's wake, the Honda bike accelerated, driver and rider leaning into the turn to keep the white vehicle in sight. Ahead of them, the van slowed, its driver searching for a parking spot. Throttling back, the bike's driver let the distance grow.

One more block and the van pulled to a crumbling curb next to an outdoor flower market. A small, wrinkled mahogany man in khakis slid from behind the wheel and hurried to the rear door on the passenger side. He bowed slightly as a tall porcelain-skinned, long-haired Filipina exited. A second, younger woman, pony-tailed, shorter than her elegant companion but equally beautiful, reached for the taller woman's hand. Laughing at some intimacy, the pair linked arms, said something to their driver, coaxing a smile from the taciturn chauffeur.

A flower vendor, more alert than her competitors, spotted the new arrivals and bustled toward her potential customers, fiery bouquets in hand. The seller pushed past a cyclist who, distracted by the stunning women, dismounted, his morning ride interrupted. The bike's owner, a westerner wearing a sweat-soaked blue T-shirt, baggy shorts, and baseball cap, walked his bicycle along the sidewalk, his eyes fastened on the striking women.

At the end of the block, the rider on the Honda slapped the driver's helmet and got a nod in return. The motorcycle accelerated. Pulling a pistol from the bag on her lap, the shooter raised her right hand and opened fire mid-block when the motorcycle drew abreast of the white van. POP! POP! POP!

Startled by the gunfire, the chauffeur and his passengers turned. The driver took three bullets in his chest and fell, dead before he hit the balding strip of grass.

Vaulting his bike, the man on the sidewalk dove at the women, shouting, "DOWN!"

Pushing the tall woman to the ground, the blond stranger instinctively crouched, covering her body with his. "STAY DOWN!" A bullet meant for the lady nicked his arm. He reached for the other woman. Too late. Four bullets hit the pony-tailed girl in the face and shoulders, shattering a collarbone, showering her cowering friend and would-be rescuer with gore. Standing on the motorcycle's foot pegs, the assassin emptied the weapon's magazine, spraying the last shots in a wild coup de grace. Two bullets struck the stunned flower vendor, who fell to her knees, bloodied bouquets scattered across the concrete.

Drawing a Sig Sauer P226 from under his T-shirt, the cyclist wormed his way between two parked cars, rose to one knee, and fired, hitting the assassin twice. Crying in surprise, the shooter slumped against her driver, the empty pistol clattering on the pavement. Roaring away, the Honda rocketed to the corner and disappeared into a river of traffic.

Buyers and vendors in the market found their voices, the screaming chorus multiplying. The tall woman who was spared, her white blouse and pants splattered in blood, crawled to her friend's side, futilely staunching the dying woman's wounds with a silk bandana. A tardy policeman, pistol in hand, appeared, cellphone to an ear, babbling for help. Training his gun on the westerner, he barked at the cyclist to surrender his weapon and raise both hands. The man did as ordered. Passersby flooded from the flower stalls to do what they could. Stunned, the useless curious gathered. A teary repairman in overalls, abandoning a company van in the street, hovered over the dead chauffeur, holding the little man's hand in a hopeless last gesture. Ambulance and police sirens wailed in the distance.

A vendor ventured from the market to help. Ignoring the nervous policeman who kept his pistol pointed at the cyclist, the seller wrapped the stranger's forearm with gauze to stop the bleeding. "Just a flesh wound," the muscular westerner insisted.

His impromptu nurse was insistent. "You so brave. You could have died, sir."

"Yeah, it was close," he admitted. "Thank you."

Tires squealing, strobe lights pulsing, a fleet of white police cars arrived, late but welcome. The crowd of blue shirts and camouflage uniforms grew as police officers and army brass converged on the scene. Snapping a blizzard of commands, they ordered the scene cordoned off, the curious pushed back. Radio calls went out with sketchy descriptions of the shooter and driver.

A solicitous high-ranking policeman tried to comfort the tall woman in bloodied white. Two of his men gently pried her from the pony-tailed victim on the ground. Coaxing what information he could before shock set in, the senior policeman eventually surrendered the survivor to medics who examined her, certain she had been wounded given the amount of blood on her clothing. She resisted, shooing them away. Instead, she imperiously parted the sea of officers, asking the stranger, "Your name, please. What is your name?"

"Sam."

"Surely you have a last name, Sam."

"Sam McFadden," he answered as the medics finished. "And you?"

"Regina. You are American?"

"I am."

"Military?"

He nodded. "Yes, once."

"Thank you, Sam McFadden," she mouthed, tear-filled green eyes never leaving him.

Mesmerized by her beauty, the American smiled despite the carnage. "Wait," he said. "Your full name?" He didn't get an answer. Two uniformed men hurried her to an army jeep and she was gone in a burst of sirens.

Surrounded by men furiously scribbling notes, the dead lay where they fell. Rapid flashes: someone was snapping pictures of the crime scene. A policeman began McFadden's interrogation anew—taking name, contact information, and a brief initial statement. The new cop handed McFadden to two officers higher in the food chain who marched him to a white van. "You will come with us to police headquarters." It was not a request. McFadden insisted his bike be loaded in the van. Shrugging, a senior police commander told a corporal to honor the American's request. McFadden spent the next four hours reciting his story before he was released. Surprisingly, his handgun was returned to him when he was dismissed. Declining a police escort, McFadden retrieved his bicycle and battled a river of traffic on Governor Lim Avenue to reach home.

For the policemen still at the scene there were families to notify, calls to be made, facts to be sorted. Interviews were done with television and newspaper reporters who descended, drawn by the scent of blood. The highest-ranking police commander on the scene huddled with his army counterpart who was given an unenviable task: calling retired general Pablo Rosario with news of an assassination attempt on his eldest daughter. Not yet noon and the air steamed with humidity. War seemed more certain than ever.

CHAPTER 3

Peddling steadily, McFadden dueled traffic all the way from police headquarters on Valderosa Street to his neighborhood— on city maps, a triangular island in Zamboanga's Barangay III district. From the air, the community was a sea of rusting corrugated metal roofs, bounded on the north by Governor Lim Avenue, Veterans Avenue on the east, and Pilar Street running southeast to northwest.

Turning down a familiar road of broken macadam shaded by leafy banyan, palm, and banana, McFadden weaved past high concrete walls wearing graffiti and tops of jagged glass shards and barbed wire. Along the way, he picked up a posse of giggling children. They trailed him for a block before tiring of the chase. Riding deeper into a labyrinth of houses jammed shoulder-to-shoulder behind walls of corrugated iron, cement block, and scavenged planks, he coasted through an intersection to a point where the road split before the blunt weathered prow of a ten-foot-high cement wall. A scarred metal gate crowned with iron spikes was set in a flat face of masonry where the walls met. McFadden dismounted and pulled on a cable connected to a hidden string of copper bells. In seconds, footfalls sounded and the gate creaked open. A wizened one-armed groundskeeper peeked from behind the barrier, his good right hand resting on a well-oiled .45 caliber Colt holstered on a belt cinched at his narrow waist.

At the sight of McFadden, a relaxed smile broke across the man's brown face. "Hey, Major Sam. You gone long time. How was the ride, eh?"

"Interesting, Eddie."

Eddie spotted the bandage on McFadden's arm. "Eh, what happen? You fall?"

Walking his bike across the tiled driveway, McFadden tossed an answer over his shoulder without looking as the gate was locked behind him. "No falls," he said wearily. "Just a scratch. I'll tell you later, okay?" Cradling his wounded arm, McFadden let the small man take the bike.

The Filipino locked the BMX behind an elaborate wrought-iron grill where a pick-up truck, motorcycle, and polished black Mercedes sat in a carport tucked under the main house. In a locked cage next to the vehicles was a washer, dryer, and well-ordered workbench where McFadden maintained his livelihood's collection of scuba gear.

"Eddie, how's the work on the guest house coming along?" The property's previous owner had neglected a second cottage behind the main house and McFadden had plans for it.

"We clean it out today. Tomorrow I fix the windows and my nephew puts new tiles in the bathroom just like you ask."

"Outstanding. I'll help with the painting when the bathroom's done."

The old man waved away the offer. "Hey, I do that too. You got the boat to fix, right?"

"Yeah. But we're coming along on that project. That's my worry, not yours. But the cottage is important. I want to make sure everything is done in two weeks, right? I'm expecting company. An old friend will be coming to stay here with us for a while."

"Hey, no problem. You don't worry. I fix everything just right."

"I'm sure you will, Eddie."

"You go to work on the boat later, Major Sam?"

"Not today, Eddie. I'm going to take a dip in the pool and hit the sack."

"Okay. You rest. My wife making coconut chicken curry for you tonight."

McFadden allowed a smile. "Good. My favorite. A swim and rest for me now, okay?" Waving him ahead, the groundskeeper shuffled past the columned entrance of the two-story concrete house and headed for the larger of two caretaker's cottages. The smaller homes nestled in a grove of bamboo towering over the wall enclosing the property. Behind the main house, a screen of hedge, pierced by a flagstone walkway, hid a lap pool and lanai. The swim would wait. Exhausted, Sam McFadden shouldered open a heavy wooden front door set in a deep, arched alcove and mounted a set of wide polished marble steps to the home's second level.

McFadden lived in a walled, trapezoid-shaped lot at the junction of two narrow alleys. Leased three years ago from a bankrupt Australian ex-pat, the furnished home was a refuge, the monthly rent reasonable. Squatting on six reinforced concrete pillars the size of well-fed men, the main house's second level consisted of two bedrooms, a den-turned-office, two bathrooms, gourmet kitchen, dining room with a massive teak table, large living room, and wraparound screened porch—"good high ground," said McFadden when he signed the lease. Though the master bedroom and den had A/C units set high in the nine-foot walls, ceiling fans kept the other rooms cool.

Along with the property, McFadden inherited the owner's Mercedes and, more importantly, husband and wife Eddie and Rose Delgado, caretaker and cook. The couple, promised the Aussie's agent, would take good care of both the house and its new occupant. Eddie, a one-armed army veteran of campaigns against Moro jihadists, may have lost a limb, but not his vigilance and honor. During McFadden's first year in his new home, Eddie foiled two attempted robberies. In gratitude, the former Green Beret armed the old soldier with one of his handguns, the vintage Colt M1911A1 he now carried. The day he received the pistol was a proud one for the old Filipino soldier. The year before, a nephew had come to live with them. Like most victims of the last botched raid ordered by the Moro National Liberation Front's warlord, Nur Misuari, the nephew had fled a burning home during the government's retaking of the city. McFadden had welcomed the refugee.

Eddie's rail-thin wife, a devout Catholic who never missed Sunday mass, proved an excellent cook and housekeeper. McFadden thought the woman mute the first months but she won the American's trust—keeping his home spotless. Only McFadden's den remained off-limits.

Despite the obvious dangers of living in the midst of a city known for sectarian violence, random crime, petty thievery, bombings, kidnappings, and sporadic jihadist reprisals like Misuari's failed attack, McFadden felt at home. For two years, Mc-

Fadden had watched and listened, only responding when asked for his opinion by neighbors. His tactic of reticence, drawn from Special Forces training, worked. Now well-known to his fellow citizens, McFadden had won their trust as a stabilizing force, joining the neighborhood's Filipino elders to quell petty disputes, raising funds to provide school supplies for needy families, and contributing to the local parish's annual fundraiser. McFadden was also careful to avoid becoming a walking American ATM. Working hard at being an encourager, not an enabler, his efforts paid off. Now in his third year in the city, McFadden had settled in, felt accepted and respected in the community. But his morning heroics, driven by instinct and training, were about to change everything.

CHAPTER 4

As McFadden did lazy laps in his pool, a Philippine Army colonel arrived at the seaside estate of retired General Pablo Rosario. Northwest of the city, a stone's throw from the emerald greens of the Zamboanga Golf Club, the general's seven-hectare retreat was more armed compound than retirement home. A West Point graduate, Class of 1985, Rosario, once a fast-rising star in the military, lived in opulent exile. Though he kept a low profile, he wielded a subtle, practiced hand in politics and his beloved army. Cordoned off from prying eyes by high stone walls running all the way to the beach, his two-story, twelve-room refuge sat in a well-groomed forest of acacia, banana, mango, and stately palms. Two smaller homes sat well back from the main house. Blanketing the property's security walls, undulating waves of blood-red Bougainvillea hid razor-sharp iron spikes. Draping the interior stonework, morning glories softened what visitors would otherwise think were penitentiary grounds. During the day, a pair of groundsmen in mufti discreetly watched the grounds while doing chores. Dobermans in hand at night, a sentinel made rounds, safeguarding the general from enemies real and imagined.

Shortly after noon, an army jeep rolled to a stop at a cottage serving as the estate's gatehouse. At the checkpoint, a sentinel in khakis circled the vehicle, checked the passenger's credentials, and nodded to another guard behind tinted glass in an ivy-covered booth. Massive wrought-iron gates parted and the jeep followed a gravel road to the main house where a woman wrapped in a rainbow sarong waited. The jeep parked, and the passenger, a stoic army colonel in camouflage fatigues, followed the woman down a flagstone walk sheltered by a stone archway. Passing through two massive mahogany doors, she ushered the officer inside and down a tiled hallway lined with oil portraits of Filipino patriots: Rizal, Bugallón, Calderon, Aquinaldo, and Sakay. Stopping respectfully before another set of dark, polished doors, she stepped back as the colonel entered.

The room was a long, high-walled rectangle cooled by a trio of lazy fans. Light poured through a set of wide French doors. A pair of couches, low table, and paired armchairs faced a large desk of Philippine mahogany lined with ruler-straight stacks of folders, a large magnifying glass serving as a paperweight.

Hands clasped behind his back, Rosario greeted the nervous messenger without looking. "Santos, good of you to come. Bad news has preceded you. Not an hour ago I spoke to your commanding officer. I trust you have additional news?"

Rosario finally turned, waving his guest to an armchair.

"Sir," began the colonel, "I am sorry to be a bearer of bad news."

"Yes, Santos, I know. My daughter's friend, Margarita, a lovely girl. A pity, of course."

The colonel coughed, his eyes on the file in his lap. "And your driver as well, sir."

Steepling his hands, Rosario sighed. "Ah, yes. Tomás, good man. A chauffeur can always be replaced, one's daughter not as easily. Wouldn't you agree, Colonel?"

"Most certainly, sir. Regrettable about the driver. But your daughter is safe."

"No thanks to the police, I understand."

Shifting awkwardly, the officer braved a feeble defense. "There was a policeman nearby, sir, but the attack was so sudden, completely unexpected."

A fleeting smile crossed Rosario's face. "Your defense of your counterparts is admirable, Colonel. I only suggest that vigilance is the handmaiden of prevention."

"Of course, sir."

"I understand a noble soul intervened, Colonel. An American, correct?"

"Yes, sir. He was apparently cooling down from an early morning bike ride in the city when he happened by just as the shooting started."

"The hand of God, it seems," mused the general.

"Undoubtedly, sir. Most fortunate for your daughter."

"What do you have for me? More details that your dear chief deems fit to share, I hope."

Rising slightly from his chair, the guest handed paperwork to Rosario and returned to his seat. "All the available information is contained therein, sir. Any new discoveries will be forwarded immediately to you as soon as they are uncovered."

Ten minutes passed. "Hmm, good," purred Rosario, shuffling through the paperwork in his hands. "The notes say this American is former military. That he was wounded defending my daughter. A warrior's actions. Commendable."

"Most commendable, sir," parroted Santos.

"Was his weapon returned to him as I requested in my phone call?"

"As you instructed, sir. He had permission to carry. It was returned with a caution."

"Good." Rising, Rosario tucked the file beneath an arm, his guest springing to his feet as well. "Most instructive, Colonel. Good work. I appreciate your taking the time to notify me with these details. I shall go over it again." Tapping the report against his leg, Rosario, boomed, "I will meet my daughter's savior. This . . . Sam McFadden. Courtesy demands it."

"Of course, sir. God certainly put him there this morning."

"Most assuredly."

Santos found himself being ushered to the door. A salute was offered to Rosario and the general returned the officer's gesture. "Thank you for coming, Colonel. I will remember this."

"My pleasure, my duty, sir."

Holding the door, Rosario nodded to the woman in the hall. A final click of polished boots and the colonel was marching behind the general's wordless servant to the entryway where his jeep waited. The retired general tossed the file on his teak desk and returned to the large window with its view of the banyan and the sea. *So, you have struck the first blow. War has often begun over more trivial things*, he thought, *but this is different. You will feel my anger in good time. I will choose the hour, not you.*

CHAPTER 5

Circling each other warily, two fighting cocks, orange manes erect, hurled themselves at each other. Exploding in a cloud of feathers, the birds tumbled in the dust. Each fowl drew back, looking for an opening. Prodded by their pacing handlers, the birds closed in furious combat, each slashing with two-inch ra- zor- sharp spurs fastened to their left legs. Roaring enthusiasti- cally, the crowd of sweating men pressed against the ring. An ear-shattering chorus of bloodlust drowned out the frenzied squawking of the combatants. Stabbing wildly in a short, vio- lent blur of wings, the big red champion drew first blood. The second cock, a high-stepping crowd favorite, took a blow in its spotted breast and backpedaled to escape the enraged red. The crazed bird pressed its attack, forcing its opponent to retreat from a flurry of blows. Another quick flashing of the silvery spurs and it was over. A howl went up from the assembly. Step- ping in to rescue his vanquished bird, the loser's handler car- ried the bleeding, torn fowl from the ring. Declared victor by the koyme—ring referee—the dazed winner was gathered up and held aloft to cheers. The champion's owner, Davido Clem- ente, worked the crowd, accepting handshakes and pats on his back. Fistfuls of pesos changed hands under the watchful eyes of a squad of kristo—bet takers who had already forgotten the match and were busy seeking wagers on the next contest.

His bird's victory was doubly sweet for Davido. Having spotted his former father-in-law in the stands across from him, a gloating Davido flashed a wide grin and tipped his straw hat at Gilberto "Sonny" Rosario. Ignoring the insult, a reddened Ro- sario pretended not to have noticed the younger man's gesture. Shouldering through a raucous scrum to the exit, Rosario hailed his driver lounging against a white Mercedes sedan. Snapping an address at his chauffeur, the former senator climbed inside. Gambling, once a pleasurable pastime for Rosario, was becom- ing a problem. Like betting on the wrong bird, his third wrong pick in as many days at yet another sabong—cockfight. Rosa- rio's losses were mounting, his winnings much too infrequent.

To add insult to injury, today's money, lost by betting on the losing bird, had gone to Davido, a disgraced ex-son-in-law he loathed. Rosario's mood was dark. After ten minutes in the city's claustrophobic traffic, the Mercedes delivered the politician to his favorite haunt, the Blue Orchid Hotel, one of Zamboanga's newest "in" spots.

With fifty plush rooms, a well-heeled business clientele, and trendy poolside bar, the hotel was Rosario's home away from home, a refuge from his troubles. A high-maintenance wife reluctant to leave Manila added to his woes. A former Miss Philippines, his spouse thought Zamboanga "provincial" and had spent exactly four months there before fleeing to the capital and its nightlife. A joyless political union from the first, Rosario's deteriorating marriage had paralleled his declining importance to the ruling party's political fathers. Rosario's last campaign, a vicious fight for re-election sabotaged by media exposés of his dealings with members of the Moro Liberation Front, had crippled his value. Whispers of alleged drug use, secret arms sales, and illegal logging profits sealed his fate. Once a rising figure being groomed as a possible presidential candidate, Gilberto "Sonny" Rosario was no longer the "bright shining star" Manila tabloids had trumpeted. Only sizeable investment loans from his brother and political kingmakers who still thought him useful had allowed Rosario to stay afloat. He ran—a figurehead only, some said—one of Zamboanga's largest import companies. Staffed by professionals installed by the real owners, the import business was successful despite Rosario. Behind the scenes, his gambling was hemorrhaging his partners' business interests and with it, his future.

Rosario dismissed his driver and headed for the Blue Orchid's bar. A friendly nod from the bartender and several familiar faces briefly cheered him. Taking his usual corner booth, Rosario traded small talk with two regulars who wandered by to pay their respects. Light-skinned, blessed with sensual B–movie star looks, the politician also projected an unflappable air about him that drew admirers. A comely bar girl, new to the hotel, brought him a tumbler of Tanduay rum and retreated, her place taken by a tall, elegantly dressed woman in a gray pantsuit—Regina Rosario. Carrying a sheaf of folders and arching an eyebrow above a faint trace of a smile, she tapped her papers on Rosario's table. "Uncle Sonny, up to your usual tricks? You look like a man who has wagered and lost. What was it today? Golf, casino, or sabong?" Propping a fist against her hip, she waited for the excuse.

Ignoring the slight, Rosario purred solicitously. "My favorite niece. How are you, dear Regina? I heard about your narrow escape two days ago. So sorry to hear about Margarita and your chauffeur."

"Did Father call you?"

"No, I have friends in the police. By God's grace you were spared."

Her brow furrowed, Regina Rosario settled in the booth opposite her uncle. "Though God didn't seem disposed to spare Margarita's life, did he?"

"You must not think like that, my dear. It was God's will."

"I think not, Uncle. Though I will grant that it was God's will to send an angel, however."

Rosario sipped his rum. "Ah, the American. Yes, I heard. Remarkable."

"Not that his presence did Margarita any good."

"A great loss. Have you taken any new precautions?"

"Father thinks I should move back home after Margarita's funeral."

"Not a bad idea. You never know. It could happen again. The next time your guardian angel may not be there to spare you, eh?"

Pushing aside the folders, Regina laced her fingers together, her smile gone. "It's good you came by. We need to talk." Shrugging, Rosario did not respond. Waiting for the lecture he suspected was coming, he sat silently, turning the glass in his hand. He did not have to wait long. "You know, Uncle, as my father's brother you have always been welcomed here at my hotel."

Rosario replied icily. "Oh, when did the Blue Orchid become your hotel, Niece?"

Brushing aside the rebuke, Regina finished her thought. "You know very well what I mean, Uncle. For the two years since we opened, you have come here day after day, meeting your business partners, drinking my best rum, running up a bill in my dining room . . . which I know you have no intention of paying . . . perhaps because you think since I am family I will not expect you to pay . . . and . . . you chase girls on my housekeeping staff when it suits you."

"You forget yourself, Niece," interrupted Rosario. "Anyone other than myself would be insulted. I bring my business here to help build your clientele. I am well known. I add to this hotel's reputation. Perhaps you are distraught because of your close call and because you have lost a dear friend. I forgive your impertinence because of your loss. Or perhaps it is the American in you that is showing. But do not think you can talk to me like this with impunity. I will speak with my brother if you continue your insolence."

"I wish you would . . . speak to Father. Though he is much more forgiving than I, he would tell you the same thing. I would not feel deprived if you took your business elsewhere, Uncle. I work hard to make this hotel a success. Father trusts me to make this place a good investment for him. I do not need, nor do I want, bad feelings between us. But . . . and this I mean most sincerely . . . I think you have worn out your welcome here. I ask you to consider taking your business elsewhere. If you ask Father, he will be of the same mind."

Bristling, Rosario downed what remained of his rum and pushed from the booth. "I do intend to speak to Pablo about this. I come to show my concern over your brush with death and you are rude enough to make light of my efforts?"

"Let us at least be frank. You came for the free rum and to look over my new bar girl."

Maintaining his calm facade, Rosario smoothed his thick oiled hair, called up a theatrical wounded look that had worked before. "I wanted only to enjoy a single drink, to see friends . . . and yes, to talk business if my companions desired to do so. Really, Regina, have you no respect for family, your elders?"

She did not answer. Her unflinching eyes stayed on Rosario, a deliberate breach of etiquette. Infuriated, he brushed past her without looking back, his bill unpaid as usual. Regina slowly exhaled. After a few moments, she gathered her paperwork and rose. Putting on her best diplomatic face, Regina Rosario headed for her office; she had a hotel to run.

CHAPTER 6

Two days later, with dawn a sliver of rose in the sky, McFadden loaded a wooden crate of tools and a generator in his pickup. He drove down Veterans Avenue to Valderosa and then to Corcuera Street where he turned toward Zamboanga's waterfront. Caught in the wake of a small van bulging with early risers, McFadden passed a pair of shuttered banks, a sleeping post office, and the city's blue-roofed coast guard station. McFadden tailgated the van to the concrete expanse of the ferry dock where a cavernous white-hulled ferry nestled against an L-shaped pier. Despite the early hour, the big boat's crew readied a ramp, lights glowed in the lounges and bridge, and clusters of passengers milled about the city's ferry terminal. A caravan of jitneys arrived, delivering more sleepy Manila-bound fares. Driving beyond the swelling crowd, McFadden made a wide turn, aiming for a corner of pier jutting into a bay fronting the nearby Lantaka Beach Hotel. Anchored fifty feet offshore from the hotel's gritty, dark sand beach, a cluster of frail-looking dinghies, a quartet of fishing boats, and several large bancas—the Philippines' ubiquitous outrigger boats—bobbed in high tide.

McFadden parked alongside a sixty-foot steel-hulled trawler wearing a fresh coat of light blue paint trimmed with two white horizontal stripes. Surveying the boat through his windshield, he smiled. *Beautiful. Even at this stage, she's beautiful. Another month and she'll be ready. We'll both be ready.*

Beauty was in the eye of the beholder. Compared to the huge sleek ferry, the forward deck of McFadden's project was littered with jumbled piles of lumber, tarps, and sealed wooden crates. A Medusa's tangle of snaking hoses led to an air compressor jammed against a cluttered workbench. Welding equipment set up beneath a catwalk girding the bridge spoke volumes about unfinished tasks. Yet for the last three months, under McFadden's guiding hand, the boat—his dream—was undergoing a metamorphosis from working vessel to a live-aboard dive boat. Thanks to Zamboanga media entrepreneur Felix Cataldo's 60 percent investment share, McFadden was close to realizing his lifelong ambition: running a scuba operation in the Philippines. Added to McFadden's 40 percent ownership, the savings of his close friend, former Navy SEAL Tom Wolf, provided enough funding to make the dream a reality.

His work-in-progress was moored astern an ugly, rusting barge bulging with fifty-five gallon drums filled with something dubious. A pair of barge crewmen cocooned in rope hammocks on the barge's fantail showed no signs of life despite a lightening sky and McFadden's pounding of the truck's horn to announce his arrival next door.

Sliding from behind the wheel, McFadden lowered the truck's tailgate and bellowed at an open hatchway on his trawler's stern. "Sal, Andy, you up?" Shrugging, he nimbly stepped aboard a wooden gangway leading from the quay to the boat's stern. Straddling a pile of PVC, McFadden poked his head in the hatch and repeated his greeting. A face like a crumpled brown bag with gold teeth appeared at the bottom of the ladder. "Morning, Sal," said McFadden.

"Hey, morning, Sam. Me and Andy finishing breakfast. You want some?"

McFadden imagined the fare. "Nah. I've eaten, thanks. Give me a hand when you're done. I brought the truck. Got a generator with me. I'll need help unloading."

"Okay, be up quick enough." The wrinkled face disappeared. McFadden worked his way forward through a nearly completed galley to the unfinished main salon. The framing for the cabin had been finished days ago. Most of the overhead teak paneling and recessed lighting was in place. Bulkhead storage lockers built under the bench seating had been completed. McFadden imagined paying guests lining the upholstered seats for meals or gathering in the salon, sipping drinks while viewing videos from a day of diving. Supports for what would be the main dining table were firmly anchored to the deck and in two days, a crew of six laborers would be sanding and painting throughout the boat. *Things are looking good,* he thought. Taking the spiral staircase below decks, McFadden roamed the length of a finished teak-lined passageway, inspected five staterooms with their individual water closets, and took a close look at the engine room crowded with a massive Cummins diesel. He ran his hand along the gleaming muscular machinery, a faint scent of oil in the air. Dodging saw-horses, McFadden stuck his head in the cramped crew's quarters forward of another ladder leading to the main deck.

Sal and Andy, his live-aboard ship's carpenters, looked up from their breakfast remnants. "So, how you like it so far, Sam?"

Nodding, McFadden grinned, rubbing his hands together. "I like it very much, Sal. You and Andy are national treasures. When you're done I'm going to call Malacañang Palace and personally tell the president how pleased I am with your work." Christened Andy by McFadden due to his indecipherable last name, Sal's younger, shaggy-haired, bow-legged partner broke into toothless high-pitched giggles. McFadden joined in the laughter, then scrambled topside, the men following him on deck. The three offloaded a generator and tools from the pickup. That done, McFadden spread a blueprint over a sheet of plywood and went over the day's tasks. A Kiwi ex-pat was due in the afternoon to finish wiring the bridge. McFadden, who knew something about electricity, wanted to be there to help if needed. "I think another three weeks at most, eh, Sal?"

"No problem, Sam."

McFadden chuckled. "Why am I not convinced?"

The two Filipinos pretended to be hurt. "Gee, but . . . you don't think we going finish on time, or what?"

Rolling up the blueprint, McFadden grinned. "There's a right way, a wrong way, an army way, and . . ." On cue, both men finished his thought. "And a Zambo way." The three roared at their familiar shared joke.

"You have the list, Sal?" asked McFadden. A daily ritual by now, the list in question was a folded sheet of paper Sal pulled from his pocket and handed to McFadden.

"Just a few things, Sam." More laughter. "Few" was a relative term. Confident his boat was in good hands and the work close to schedule, McFadden headed to the local marine hardware supplier for the supplies Sal needed.

The morning ferry was easing from the pier as McFadden got in his truck and drove from the dock. Threading his way through the parking lot, he passed the now half-empty terminal. A pair of helmeted motorcyclists in matching black nylon jackets watched McFadden cruise by and kicked their engines to life. Doing wheelies from the lot, the two pulled behind his pickup truck. Despite thickening traffic, the two bikes stayed with him for ten minutes, the riders studying the American at the wheel. Just short of an intersection in town, the two peeled away in a burst of speed. Oblivious, McFadden had failed to notice, his mind wrestling with the goal he had set—finishing the dive boat in time for an inaugural mid-June run to Sulu Sea reefs. If everything went well he had sixty days to fulfill his dream.

CHAPTER 7

At day's end, drenched in sweat, McFadden extinguished his welder's flame, shut down the acetylene and oxygen tanks, and, along with tools, locked everything in a metal bin on the boat's bow. Pleased with his handiwork, he studied the main deck's newly anchored port and starboard boat davits. Positioned just forward of the main cabin, the angled steel arms would easily handle a pair of eight-man inflatables he planned to use for trips on the reefs. McFadden wearily climbed into his truck perched on the edge of the adjacent pier and drove home.

Barely had he left the waterfront when he spotted a tail, a lone biker staying forty meters distant. Eyes glued to the rider trying to blend in with the heavy traffic, McFadden replayed the recent shooting in his mind. When the bike accelerated, as if to draw alongside, McFadden whipped his truck into a tight right turn, causing the motorcycle to shoot past him. *Amateur,* he sneered.

Squeezing through an alley, McFadden doubled back in a series of right turns. Emerging from between a noodle shop and a tailor's storefront, he plunged back into streaming traffic, his foiled pursuer nowhere in sight. To shake any further chase, he altered his route through neighborhoods, arriving at his walled home twenty minutes later with a blast on his horn. The steel gates swung open, Eddie on duty as usual.

McFadden parked, unloaded tools, and briefed his caretaker about the motorcyclist. Taking the warning to heart, the old veteran promised renewed vigilance. Upstairs, a small pot of sautéed vegetables and rice simmered on the stove. He discarded the old bandage on his arm; the wound was healing well. He showered quickly, dressed, and padded to his balcony, calling to Delgado pacing below. "Eddie, thank Rose for my dinner, please." His thanks was acknowledged with a wave. Beyond his villa's gates, the barrio came alive with music, a chorus of children's shouts, neighbors' gossip, and scents from a hundred cooking fires.

After dinner, McFadden put the day behind him. For the next two hours, he scribbled notes in a ledger, reviewed a dog-eared set of boat plans, and bounced around the Internet, checking his investments and national and world news. A Manila cable channel rehashed the capital's politics, celebrity sightings, murders, robberies, and kidnappings—all flawlessly delivered by a Filipina newsreader wearing a distracting low-cut floral number. Aside from the previous day's over-hyped report of a westerner's intervention in a senseless Zamboanga murder, McFadden was relieved to know his role had not been mentioned since—an oversight for which he was grateful. The last thing he wanted was to be noticed in the nation's notorious tabloid press for doing what he thought right.

As much as he struggled to put the attack behind, the image of the beautiful woman stayed with him. *Face it; you would like to meet her again. How odd. Fate? A chance encounter that turns deadly for two victims. I heard their names but I've already forgotten them. But the survivor,* McFadden told himself, *that's different. I know who she is.* Remembering the woman he had saved, and the lecture a senior policeman had given him, he recalled the admiring officer whispering, "There is now a debt you are owed." McFadden knew the exaggerated Filipino sense of honor would have to be satisfied. *I suppose,* he mused, *something like this can change . . . no, disrupt things, but I would just as soon nothing had happened. Still, I would like to see her again . . . this Regina Rosario. Maybe just once. To talk. To ask how she is doing. Forget it. Not going to happen.*

Killing the lights, McFadden sat in the dark, trying to clear his thoughts of the tall woman in bloodied white. His efforts failed. So did his attempt at sleep.

CHAPTER 8

McFadden did not like surprises. Hated them, in fact. Surprises were for the other guy—those caught at the right time, in the wrong place, doing the wrong thing. In Iraq, it had been the Mahdi Militia with their AK47s, arrogantly strutting through Najaf's garbage-strewn streets; in Afghanistan, outside nameless mud-walled villages, it had been thermal images of Taliban descending like avenging wraiths in the night. During his career in Special Forces, it was McFadden who had done the surprising. Not today.

The sudden appearance of a black SUV barreling across the ferry terminal's deserted lot toward his moored dive-boat caught McFadden off balance. Whoever it was, they were coming straight for him. Patting the holstered SIG Sauer underneath his denim shirt, McFadden shouted a warning down the ladder to Sal and Andy below decks. "We got company!"

Easing onto the bridge's catwalk, well above eye-level with the dock, McFadden watched the hulking car nose next to his gangplank. Tinted windows hid his visitors. *Probably another government remora looking for a gift in exchange for a permit I suddenly need. Maybe a required document conveniently misplaced? A mid-level functionary's missing signature from some official inspection report?* Suffering them all in turn since beginning his project, McFadden had reached the end of his patience with the notorious Philippines bureaucracy.

Then again, it might be more red tape bullshit from the shooting, he thought. *After all, hadn't his handgun been returned to him a bit too easily?* He gave a passing thought to tossing his pistol in a drawer but opted to keep it with him. *Better to ask forgiveness than permission. And always better not to be surprised.*

The front passenger's door opened. A stocky, bull-necked man built like a Manila nightclub bouncer, unsmiling and wearing immaculately pressed khakis, slid from the seat, his eyes hidden behind the ubiquitous mirrored sunglasses hired Filipino guns seemed to favor. Instead of a weapon, the visitor carried a single dainty envelope as if it were toxic.

McFadden, the SIG Sauer behind his back, filled the bridge's doorway. "Can I help you?"

The messenger removed his dark glasses, glanced at the trawler's bridge, saw McFadden, and waved the envelope. "Major Samuel McFadden?"

"You found him."

"I'm to deliver this to you." The visitor shot a skeptical look at the sagging gangplank and hesitated. Sal and Andy, covered in paint chips and sawdust, emerged from the engine compartment and began slinking along the rail, huge wrenches in hand as if to repel all boarders. The man on the dock was unimpressed by their show of bravado.

Backing down the ship's ladder to the deck, McFadden pushed past his hired help, meeting the messenger at the top of the gangplank. He took the envelope.

Mission accomplished, the man in khaki scanned the dive boat-in-progress, shook his head, and retreated. Without a word, he climbed in the car and drove away.

"Trouble, Sam?" asked Sal.

"Doesn't look like it." Elegant script trailed across the front of the envelope. In place of a return address there were two white stars embossed on a field of red. McFadden returned to the main cabin and took the spiral stairs to the bridge. Sal planted a foot on the first rung as if to follow. McFadden growled. "I'll tell you about it later . . . when you knock off for the day." Sal shrugged and returned below, his curiosity blunted.

McFadden ran a blade along the seal and pulled out an invitation printed in a graceful font.

My dear Major McFadden, Please accept a grateful father's thanks for your actions of last week. Your courageous intervention saved my beloved daughter's life. My apologies for not writing earlier but I have been preoccupied since that unfortunate event. My daughter, Regina, spoke most admiringly of your bravery. As a soldier, I appreciate the risk you took on her behalf. If you are agreeable, I extend an invitation for dinner next week at our family home. Please do plan to attend. Regina adds her appeal to mine.

Most respectfully, Maj. Gen. Pablo Rosario

McFadden read the letter twice. Included was the general's card and a time, RSVP, telephone number, and map printed on a separate sheet. The note, though warm, was formal and direct like one a military man might compose. The invitation to dinner was part cordiality, part summons. In McFadden's experience, generals, retired or not, did not pursue audiences—they granted them. Intrigued by both Rosarios, he knew immediately he would accept the offer. The beautiful Regina was the draw, though her father would be interesting to meet.

Something of a mystery, Rosario was an invisible man. An alleged Manila puppet master, political éminence grise, and charismatic soldier with deep roots in the ranks, Rosario was an enigma. McFadden, like any American stationed in Zamboanga in the last decade, knew of the general's reputation, his bravery in the fight against Islamic rebels in the south, and his role as a junior officer in ousting Marcos. One of the first of the Western Mindanao commanders, Rosario retired as a two-star, lived in self-imposed exile, and proved a staple of gossip among the Philippine military. If those in power knew reasons for his banishment, they weren't talking.

CHAPTER 9

On the appointed day McFadden quit the boat early and returned home. He swam laps and dressed for dinner with the Rosarios, choosing a traditional embroidered, long-sleeved barong shirt and dark trousers. Taking the Mercedes, he followed the coastal Labuan-Limpapa National Road northwest from the city. After passing the Zamboanga Golf Club's deserted fairways, he turned toward the sea, taking a paved road running between large homes hiding in lush foliage. McFadden ran out of road at a locked iron gate bathed in blinding floodlights set on a high stone wall. Two sentinels—a large man with one hand on a holstered handgun, the other a frowning gnome wielding a long, L-shaped pole with a flat mirror attached to the short end—approached the Mercedes, one man on each side. Lowering the driver's window, McFadden surrendered his invitation. "I'm to dine with the general this evening."

The man with the pistol glanced quickly at the offered note. "Of course, Major McFadden. You are expected. One moment, sir." He stepped back, watching the mirror being swept beneath the car. That done, the guard announced flatly, "Good evening, sir. Please lower your lights and drive to the main house." McFadden doused the Mercedes's lights and the gate opened. He drove slowly along a gravel path outlined in muted lighting. Drawing up to the big house, McFadden killed the engine and got out. Two greeters, a tiny woman and a robotic guard nodded politely in welcome. Motioning for him to follow, the woman led McFadden down an arched walkway, the security man several steps behind. Entering a tiled, circular, two-story foyer dominated by a glowing chandelier, McFadden trailed his guide into a large living room filled with leather couches. Beyond the furniture, a set of French doors framed a dying sunset and a luminous Regina Rosario in a simple ivory-colored gown. She dismissed the little woman with a nod. "Thank you, Amihan." The servant retreated and Regina, smiling, glided toward McFadden, extending her hand. "Welcome to my father's home, Major."

Mesmerized, and unable to hide it, he said, "Thank you, Señorita. My pleasure. And please, plain Sam will do."

"If you insist, Plain Sam." She laughed, tossing back her long black hair. "Please call me Regina. After all, we have met before."

"Regina it is. Yes, I'm sorry for the circumstances, but not the chance to meet you." Her green eyes narrowed for the briefest of moments and McFadden immediately regretted his words. She ushered him to a sideboard crowded with crystal decanters, wine bottles, glasses, and a silver ice bucket. McFadden followed the faint scent of sweet jasmine drifting in her wake.

"May I offer you a libation, Major? Tanduay rum or perhaps Lambanog, an excellent local coconut wine? We also have fruit drinks. Or do you prefer California wines?"

"Thank you. What would the hostess suggest?"

Arching an eyebrow, she shot McFadden a bemused look. "Your hostess guesses you are a San Miguel man."

He shrugged. "You are correct. A fine beer. Am I that easy to read?"

"You are."

"In that case, perhaps the Lambanog just to mystify you."

She poured the wine, handed it to her guest, and lifted a glass of the same to her lips. "Are you one of those who follows the rule of when in Rome . . . or, when in the Philippines, I suppose."

"Possibly. Though, tonight might be the right occasion for wine, not beer." Raising his glass, he said, "To long life, Regina."

"Thank you, Plain Sam. Though it's I who should be toasting you."

"All in the line of duty, ma'am. Sorry I wasn't quicker on the draw."

Another moment of awkward shared silence passed. Regina cast her eyes at the carpet, and then recovered. Affecting a practiced pained look, she said, "My father will be with us shortly."

McFadden smiled. "I know the drill. I've met many generals during my career."

"Is his behavior that obvious?"

"A general's rank entitles him to make others wait, m'lady."

"Personally," she whispered, "I've always found it a bit rude. Please don't be put off. If it's any comfort to you, Father's an equal opportunity offender, regardless of rank or standing."

CHAPTER 10

On cue, footsteps echoed in the doorway. The major general, his face creased in a wide smile, marched, not walked, into the room, a beautiful Filipina on each arm. Breaking from the women, he thrust a hand at McFadden. "Ah, the courageous major. Welcome to my home, Sam McFadden." The two men shook hands, each taking measure of the other.

Behind the general, the older of the two women cleared her throat. Rosario turned in mock embarrassment. "Ah, yes. Forgive my lapse in manners. May I present Señora Frances Yadao, a close family friend." A pale beauty, with powdered, flawless shoulders set off by a heavy gold necklace and jeweled cross, offered her hand. McFadden tilted his head in a bow and took her hand. Wearing a traditional Philippine–style gown, black hair swept high and held in place with jeweled clasps, the handsome woman captivated him. *A younger version of the legendary Imelda Marcos*, he thought. *Haughty, beautiful, but with a calculating aura.*

"Your presence honors us, Major," purred Frances Yadao. "Like others, I was awed by the story of your bravery. The way you so fearlessly saved Regina's life."

McFadden blushed. "Happened to be in the right place at the right time."

"You are much too modest," she said.

General Rosario gestured to the other woman. "Allow me to introduce my daughter, Ivy."

Smiling demurely, the second Filipina who had adorned the general's arm stepped forward. "Regina said you were magnificent, like a knight to her rescue."

Hooking her arm through McFadden's, Regina cocked an eyebrow at him in warning. "Don't let my younger sister's words fool you, Sam. Ivy may be a primary school teacher leading impressionable children about, but she's also a beautiful, notorious flirt, equally at home in a classroom or a presidential palace."

"While leading impressionable men about," deadpanned Rosario.

Circling McFadden, Ivy took his other arm. "Don't let Regina spoil your impression of me, Major. You know how older sisters can be sometimes . . . so selfish . . . so territorial." The siblings shared laughter. McFadden reddened. *The wine or the attention?* He wasn't sure.

Shaking his head in mock solemnity, the general sighed. "I fear you are besieged, Major. Now you know what I have to endure. I'm outnumbered by these lovely ladies."

Glancing at Frances Yadao and the sisters, a self-conscious McFadden added, "There are certainly worse fates. You are to be envied."

An hour of polite probing followed with the general guiding McFadden's questioning while deftly avoiding revelations of his own. During the interrogation, a possessive Frances Yadao never left the general's side. As McFadden recited his story, Rosario's daughters floated about, Ivy refilling his drink, Regina hovering at his elbow. The wine was excellent, the night air like silk, the laughter contagious. No stranger to cocktail chatter from his days in officers' clubs, McFadden nonetheless felt outmaneuvered by beautiful women—a warm, seductive feeling. It had been years since his emotions had been similarly tapped.

"This trawler you convert," asked Rosario. "Certainly an expensive project. Have you business partners, backers who believe in what you do?"

"There is a local investor as well as an acquaintance from my service days who has agreed to invest, General. My friend is due to arrive soon. I hope to persuade him to stay and help me run the dive business."

"Fascinating, Major. You'll have competition, of course, but there surely must be demand for such a service. If you're willing I should like to see what you're doing."

"Father has many interests," Regina added. "Many fingers in many pies. Hotels, restaurants, real estate. He's done well for a soldier. So many investments, so little time."

Frances Yadao scolded her. "Don't mock your father's accomplishments, Regina my dear. Remember, you benefit from the fruit of his labors."

Rosario's daughter covered her embarrassment with laughter. "We all enjoy Father's success. He is extremely generous to family . . . and friends."

Seemingly oblivious to the tension between the two women, Rosario waved away his daughter's comments, saying, "True. But what choice do I have? How else am I to support so many women?" The five of them laughed.

McFadden said, "I'd be honored to have you come for a tour of the boat, sir. Perhaps in another two weeks we will have made enough progress that a visit would be worth your while."

"I accept. And I applaud your entrepreneurial efforts. It benefits our people."

From another room, a bell sounded.

Regina put a gentle hand on McFadden's back. "Saved from more of Father's questions, Major. Dinner is served." Rosario and Frances Yadao led the way to the dining room, the general's daughters following on the arms of the guest of honor.

For the next two hours, the party traded witty repartee across a floral centerpiece of sampaguita and orchids while dining on the region's famous red crab cakes, a salad, a meat dish, fish, rice fried in garlic, and breads. The meal ended with coffee and two dessert options chosen by Regina, both samples of Zamboanga's street confections: sweet, skewered Saba bananas and sticky rice mixed with coconut milk and brown sugar. McFadden tried both. When coffee was served, she presented McFadden with a beribboned tin of hand-pressed cookies from Cebu.

When General Rosario and the ladies finally retired from the table, it was past midnight. After profuse thanks, McFadden bid his hosts good night. Besides memories of an extraordinary evening, he carried with him the tin box of rosquillos, a promise of a round of golf with Rosario, and the general's permission to call upon Regina.

CHAPTER 11

Condemned to a painful death as an object lesson, the weeping man played his last card. Arms tied behind him, the trembling thief tearfully promised to faithfully serve the man before whom he knelt—his judge, jury, and executioner.

Flipping a razor-sharp balisong knife inches from the prisoner's face, the malevolent Buddha-like figure filling a large rattan chair savored the moment. Gangster Eugenio Clemente was in high dudgeon. Playing the part of feared godfather holding another's life in his hand was a role Clemente enjoyed. By any standards, the gang boss was ugly. A shaven pate, jowls dotted with fatty tumors like cockroaches burrowing in his flesh, sloping tattooed shoulders, and a wrestler's torso balanced on stumpy piano legs added a bizarre comedic touch to his carefully cultivated mobster image.

Folding the butterfly knife, Clemente tossed it to one of his watching goons. "I've decided to spare this worthless dog. Untie him. Return him to his family."

Sobbing, the reprieved prisoner flooded the rough boards beneath him with tears. Rising from his rattan perch, Clemente spoke without looking at the groveling man. "Reynaldo, if I hear one word of you selling drugs anywhere in the city"—the big man paused for effect—"without my permission . . . I will have you brought here again"—another pause—"and cut you into one hundred pieces which I feed to the fish."

"Thank you, Papa Manong. Forgive me. I give you my life. I serve you."

"Of course you do. Now go back to your ugly wife before I change my mind." Backing from the windowless room, a trembling Reynaldo Nato groped for the door, and when he reached it, fled.

Pleased with himself, Clemente dismissed his guard dogs. The third witness, Clemente's son Davido, stayed behind. Rubbing his chubby hands together, Clemente, now playing the businessman, tapped his shaggy-haired son on the shoulder. "So, I hear you humiliate Sonny Rosario at a sabong, eh?"

"Who told you that?"

"A little bird, my boy."

His son sneered. "You mean a little dead bird."

Clemente laughed. "Ah, very good. Yes, a dead bird. How much you win from your former father-in-law?"

"Enough to make him abandon the remaining matches."

Wagging a finger in rebuke, Clemente said, "I am not sure that is wise."

The two left the cavernous warehouse and climbed stairs in a wooden tower where Clemente's office overlooked a wharf and lumberyard serving as his fortress-kingdom. "You should not toy with Sonny Rosario. He knows too many things. For me, is nothing worse than a former partner scorned. For you, nothing worse than a father whose child has been shamed. You should have stayed married to his daughter, Maria. The union was one of strategy. It bound our families as one."

Scowling, Davido muttered a protest. "Why must you always remind me? I hate that. You wanted the match, not me. I'm happier without being tied to her and the Rosario family."

At the top of the stairs, a huffing Clemente poked a finger in his son's chest. "And now with the Rosario family as enemies we have to play the game even more carefully. Learn from this or you will not succeed."

The tower, fitted with two floors of offices, dominated the harbor compound. From the tower's large windows or its outside catwalk's commanding view, Clemente could scrutinize every delivery, monitor every loafing employee, or spot incoming freighters and prowling government patrol boats. The room was simple: two desks, a bank of security screens, and assorted furniture—a couch and six chairs around a conference table. Clemente settled into a leather chair behind a desk sinking under piles of paperwork.

Sprawling in a chair, Davido took a cell phone call, babbled a few minutes, and rang off with, "Yes, I'll tell him. Perhaps you should have doubled the rate. No, it's done. Next time . . ." He shut the phone. "Joseph at the dive shop said there was an American who rented one of our pump boats for a week. He's asking a lot of questions about the business."

His nose buried in bills, Clemente mumbled, "So? How

much money our boats make just sitting there? Is there a problem?"

"Perhaps. The American asked him about tourists. He says this one looks like he might be military." Mildly interested, Clemente put away his folders. "Not unusual. They are here, of course. So, if you think we may have a problem, solve it. Call Joseph and get a name. When he comes back to pick up the boat tell Joseph to be extremely helpful, perhaps send one of his boys along as guide. If this guy is gone within the week, no problem."

Davido punched keys on his phone. "And if he stays around?"

"If he stays, he has a reason. If he stays, you will find out what he wants."

After a minute, his son snapped the phone shut. "He's not answering."

Clemente slapped his desktop. "Do I have to think for both of us? GO! Find Joseph and talk to him. And when you get back, ready your crew for next week. We have one hundred logs coming. I want you here to handle the delivery when I'm away in Davao City."

"Ah, nights are for going to the clubs with my boys."

Frowning, Clemente shot back, "Not until we take the logs. For seven days you will keep your pants on. Your whores will have to do without until those logs are unloaded and hidden. It's your job to make sure this is done. You are my eyes and ears while I'm gone." Nose back in his paperwork, Clemente arched an eyebrow at his son to make sure his message had been heard. "You have two tasks. You will complete them both to my satisfaction. Questions? I didn't think so. GO! Humor me. Find out who this American is."

Pushing himself from the chair, the younger Clemente shrugged in defeat.

Slouching down the stairs, he thought, *If I cannot go to the clubs, perhaps the clubs can come to me once he leaves for Davao City. But first, the American.*

CHAPTER 12

Under the bored eyes of an off-duty policeman, a wary McFadden trusted his Mercedes to a red-vested parking valet at the entry of the Blue Orchid Hotel. Casually dressed in a floral shirt, linen jacket, and jeans, McFadden strolled past a doorman giving directions to a pair of Asian suits. In the lobby, a woman manning the front desk intercepted him. "Sir, Señorita Rosario will be with you momentarily." Grinning, McFadden thought about the general's tardy entrance at dinner a week ago, *Like father, like daughter.*

Looking more like a schoolgirl than concierge, the gatekeeper approached from behind the desk wearing a crisp white blouse and angelic smile. "May I offer you bottled water, a coffee, perhaps?" Declining, McFadden took a seat at the edge of a planter crowded with flowers and surveyed the lobby. As Regina predicted, he was impressed. Despite its proximity to the heart of Zamboanga, the Blue Orchid offered privacy behind a perimeter of lush, towering foliage walling off the city's bustling river of traffic. Regina Rosario was running a classy operation. It may have been her father's money, but McFadden's initial impression of her obvious touch was favorable.

Spotting Regina in her business uniform—dark pantsuit and ivory blouse—he rose to his feet, took her hand in his. "You were right."

"About what?" she asked.

Gesturing at his surroundings, McFadden said, "This place.

You talked it up and I have to admit you were right. It's a lovely spot. And quiet."

"I prefer to think of it as an oasis of muted elegance."

"I agree. Your hand at work, I assume."

"Throughout. I've worked hard to have my way in every detail."

He smiled. "Well done. It shows. Now let's give your chef a trial run. You invited me to lunch, remember?"

"So I did. You won't be disappointed." She led him through a dining room just beginning to fill and continued to a tiled outdoor space set with tables shaded by huge umbrellas. For the moment, they were the only patrons. A waitress appeared immediately and retreated with drink orders.

"Today it's my turn to ask questions . . . if you're game," he said. "Your family gave me the third degree last week."

"You acquitted yourself well," she replied. "I feel as though I know you." Returning with drinks, the server scribbled their menu selections and withdrew. "Ask what you want, Sam. However, I reserve the right to lie," she said coyly.

Leaning forward, McFadden said, "I'm curious. That evening your father made several remarks about 'your American showing.' What was he referring to, exactly?"

"Oh, that." Regina laughed, brushing back her hair. "It's just his way of saying he disagrees with something I've said."

Puzzled, McFadden asked, "I don't understand. As an American, was I being insulted?"

"Certainly not, Sam. Father often refers to my 'American' half. My mother is American, a California girl from one of Silicon Valley's founding families. Mother took a different turn in life. She served in the Peace Corps in Davao City. That's where my parents met. He was a captain then. Handsome. A charmer. One of the army's rising stars. They fell in love. She stayed. They married. Ivy and I came along but the army always came first.

One doesn't get promotions for being a good father. Mother was bored, missed America. Nine-eleven happened. The Islamists. I'm sure you must know some of my father's history."

McFadden stifled his surprise. "Every American who does a tour here knows a little something about the general but none of us knows everything. I certainly did not know about your mother . . . being American, that is."

"You're disappointed to find out I'm only half-Filipino, Sam?"

"On the contrary. It explains the green eyes and your independent nature."

"Shows what little you know. All Filipino women are feisty."

Their food arrived. McFadden continued his questions between mouthfuls. "I take it your parents are divorced."

Dismissing his presumption, she said, "Oh, no. He's a good Catholic soldier. Wouldn't think of a divorce scandal. It's a long story, complicated. I won't bore you with all the details. Mother left when Ivy and I were in our teens. We had a choice, of course. But we were born here, raised here, and wouldn't think of living anywhere else. It's home."

"That your Filipino side talking?"

Reaching across the table, she nonchalantly dabbed the corner of McFadden's mouth with her napkin, an intimate gesture. "You're catching on, Sam. Anyway, it's a stalemate of sorts. Father hasn't pressed, and Mother, bless her, is content with the arrangement. Ivy and I fly to LA once a year to see her."

"And Señora Yadao?" Regina rolled her eyes and McFadden wondered if he had probed too deep.

"Part of the charade. I can't believe I'm telling you all these family secrets."

He held up a hand. "You don't have to say a thing. I didn't mean to pry."

"Yes you did. But not to worry. Turnabout is fair play. The

whole arrangement is public knowledge at the same time it's supposed to be hush-hush. I love my father but, in a way, I find it all so hypocritical. It's not as if their relationship is a closely guarded state secret."

"So . . . Frances Yadao is . . ."

Regina sighed in resignation. "My father's mistress. Her husband was a fellow officer who was killed. My father and Frances have long been involved, even before her husband's death. My father's generation—men of his age, station, and wealth—all indulge this particular flaw. It's their failing, a national pastime. I assume you've been with local beauties yourself on occasion."

Blushing, McFadden locked eyes with Regina. "It's not that I haven't been tempted . . . ."

"Of course you've been tempted, you're a man. We Filipino women are beautiful, Sam . . . and available. I'm not judging you if that's what worries you."

McFadden suddenly lost his appetite and voice. They finished lunch in silence and she changed subjects. "Did you approve of your choice, Sam?"

"Outstanding, thanks."

"Just to be clear," she said disarmingly, "I was speaking about today's lunch."

Reddening, McFadden stammered. "I knew that."

"Oh, of course you did." Laughing at his discomfort, she waved their waitress to the table. Repeating McFadden's words, Regina told the server to pass on her guest's compliments to the chef. When the woman left, Regina reached for McFadden's hand. "Sam, we're both adults. As an army man, a Green Beret at that, I assume you've probably lived up to your calling's reputation. That's all I'll say on the subject. Discussion closed." She did not remove her hand. "My pushy American half finds you very attractive, Sam McFadden."

Recovering, he gambled. "What does your Filipino half say?"

Pausing for a moment, Regina propped a hand under her chin, her green eyes fluttering seductively. "For once they both agree on something."

CHAPTER 13

First week of May

Cebu Pacific's ten o'clock flight from Manila was full. On time. The muted roar of twin turboprops filled the cabin as the yellow-tailed commuter plane began its final approach. The seatbelt light flashed on. A few minutes later the ATR 72's landing gear lowered with a grinding noise. Flight attendants made a hurried last check of their seventy-eight charges.

From his window seat, Tom Wolf spotted the terminal's iconic pleated roof with its eighteen peaked gables. At nearby Edwin Andrews Air Base, adjacent to the civilian runway, a pair of toy-like UH-1 Hueys waited, their blades spinning. *Maybe a patrol just back from the bush*, he wondered. *Or they could already be loaded and outbound. For once I'm glad it's not me.* The commuter flight landed softly and taxied to the terminal apron. Wolf let the other passengers queue in the aisle and was the last one off the plane.

At baggage claim, he glanced up to see Sam McFadden heading his way. "Hey, Wolfman, good to see you. It's been a while, Big Dawg." The two embraced. "How's it feel to be back?" asked McFadden.

Scanning the crowded terminal, Wolf said, "Same heat and humidity, same sea of people. Same smells. Still 'The land of not quite right.' What's not to love?"

They both laughed. Shouldering Wolf's belongings, Mc-

Fadden led his friend outside. In minutes, he retrieved his truck, loaded luggage, and headed for town. Staring at the familiar crowded streets, Wolf mopped his brow, sighing. "Nothing's changed, Sam. Gone almost two years and not a damn thing has changed."

"Hey, we have more traffic. More chaos."

"Yeah, there is that. More crime?"

"Same-same. Comforting, huh?"

"Just lovely," groaned Wolf. He changed subjects. "When can I see the boat?"

"Tomorrow. Let's get you settled in the cottage first. You hungry?" Wolf nodded. McFadden drove two blocks and pulled over. A street vendor selling grilled chicken satay launched into a rapid-fire sales routine. McFadden waved him into silence and bought four skewers. Back in the truck, McFadden shared two skewers with Wolf and fished for beers in a cooler behind the driver's seat. The two ate while McFadden drove, reporting progress on the dive boat. "Name her yet?" asked Wolf.

McFadden shook his head. "Waiting for you, bro. Have something in mind?"

"Let me think about that one for a while."

"Gotta be catchy."

"I'm on it."

Glancing in the mirror, McFadden said, "Keep a sharp eye for motorcycles getting cozy."

"You kidding?" said Wolf. "They're always on your ass. You having a problem?"

"Maybe. I'll tell you all about it when we get to my casa."

Traffic was relatively light, no tailgating bikers in their wake. Nevertheless, McFadden altered routes, taking Pilar Street and then a left at the city's water district office. Dodging foraging dogs and feral kids, they bumped along a pitted alley wandering between houses.

"Eddie Delgado still on duty?" asked Wolf.

"He is. He'll be glad to see you. We have his nephew living with us now. His home was one of the casualties from that Moro National Liberation Front raid."

"Yeah, flying in I spotted a lot of burned-out homes and businesses in the Santa Catalina and Talon-Talon neighborhoods. What a waste, huh?"

"Amen. It was touch and go for a while. I hosted a squad of Filipino Army behind my walls for a couple days. Nice security. Our neighborhood lost two local homes to shellfire. Not bad, considering the scale of the fight."

"Moro jihadists, huh? Still crazy after all these years. That I don't miss."

"Anyway, Eddie will be glad to see you. He loves Navy SEALs, you know."

Wolf laughed. "So do the girls back home, Sam. Speaking of girls . . . you still hot for this general's daughter?"

Pulling up to the gate, McFadden said, "Hold that thought." Jumping from the jeep, he tugged on the bell pull. Back in the car, he looked Wolf in the eye. "Regina's a keeper, Tom. Did I tell you she's half-American?"

Wolf nodded. "Yeah. And you mentioned a sister. What's she like?"

The gate opened. McFadden pulled into the courtyard, killed the engine, and looked at Wolf. "She's a carbon copy. Twenty-four, single, and stunning."

"Outstanding! Did you tell her the navy has landed?"

"She knows. We're to meet them both on Saturday for lunch at the hotel. The general doesn't know about you yet. You'll get to meet him eventually."

"That'll be a first. I never got to meet the mysterious General Rosario and now here you are sneaking around with his daughter. I guess you army boys do need watching." The gate locked behind them, Eddie vigilant as usual.

"Funny how things turned out," said McFadden. "A drive-by shooting is a bizarre way to meet a girl's father. Next thing I know I'm dining with him, and then dating his daughter and being invited to play golf with him."

"Guns, golf, and a girl. Who woulda thought? You going all soft and cuddly on me?"

McFadden laughed. "Not a chance, Wolfman. Let's get you squared away. After that, we'll talk."

Eddie gave Wolf a welcoming hug and talked non-stop as he helped haul the new arrival's luggage to the cottage at the rear of the main house. That done, the gatekeeper kept up a stream of chatter until McFadden and Wolf excused themselves and retreated upstairs.

CHAPTER 14

Being an hour early wasn't going to help McFadden's golf game. A laborer gave him a lift in a cart from the clubhouse to the driving range. General Rosario was spraying errant shots left and right in the morning sun. A second cart with a watching shadow was parked under a tree. Between bad tee shots, Rosario hammered the ground with an oversized driver. Announcing himself with a loud cough, McFadden, bucket of balls in hand, joined his host.

"Morning, sir."

Rosario waved his club above his head like a sword. "Morning, Sam. I have spare clubs for you in my cart. Get your driver. Join me. I must punish myself before I play."

Spilling balls on the grass, McFadden, a wedge in his right hand, kicked a half-dozen to the general's tee. "I need the practice. I'm rusty. Haven't played a round for at least a year."

"You should get out more. Regina used to play before the hotel opened. Now she claims she has no time." He cracked a straight shot and whooped in delight. "You two have been seeing each other quite a bit, eh?"

"Lunch at the hotel mostly. More convenient given the demands on her time." McFadden switched to a three-wood and did some practice swings. Rosario kept banging away. "Regina's a wonderful lady. I appreciate your allowing me to see her."

"I am from another century, Sam. Regina does what she wants, even without my blessing. My permission was simply a formality. If she hadn't been interested I would have been given the sign to say 'no' had you asked."

"That's a morale booster, General." Keeping his head down, McFadden dribbled a few weak shots.

Shaking his head, Rosario clucked. "Don't embarrass me. I do that on my own. By the way, I arranged a foursome." Rosario sliced a wobbly shot high and followed the ball's flight with curses. "Sorry. Something I picked up at Fort Benning."

"The swearing or the slice?"

Grunting, Rosario barked, "Both."

For twenty minutes, the two whacked balls into the balding field. A cart pulled behind them and parked, the two riders content to watch. After another half-dozen balls, the cart's driver boomed, "Save some for the course, Pablo!"

Struck by the presumed intimacy, McFadden grounded his club to study the voice's owner.

Pausing in mid-swing, Rosario turned, a smile spreading across his flat brown face. "Burton, my friend. How do you know I don't hustle you with this display of poor driving?"

Heaving himself from the cart, a bulky, club-wielding golfer hiding behind mirrored sunglasses ambled to Rosario's tee, cigar held aloft. "Because we've played together too often for me to believe the man I see before me is not the same one from whom I will soon be extracting bets in the coin of the realm."

The two embraced. Turning to McFadden, Rosario introduced the loud arrival. "Burt Wickes, meet a fellow American, Sam McFadden." The two shook hands.

"McFadden. I know that name somehow. Help me out. Have we met before?"

"I don't think so," McFadden said. "Though I know you by reputation. Private security, isn't it? Ex-military, private contractors. That sort of thing, right?"

"Yeah, that's me. Geez, I didn't realize I had such a high profile."

"People talk," said McFadden.

Rosario put away his clubs. "Sam's former military. Special Forces."

Wickes blew a cloud of smoke, flashing a Cheshire grin. "Really? You know, security is a growth industry these days, McFadden. A guy with your skills could make good money in the business. We should talk."

"I don't think so. The whole military contractor thing is a bit sketchy for me. Too much testosterone flying around. Too much adrenaline pumping for my taste."

"Lot of ex-military making a good living at it."

"Well, I've got other priorities these days."

Rosario put a hand on McFadden's shoulder. "Sam's busy putting together a dive shop."

"Interesting," mused Wickes. "Commercial or a tourist kinda thing?"

Before McFadden could answer, the general interrupted,

shooing the men from the range. "Sort that out later, gentlemen. Let's go to the first tee. Sam, you ride with me. Who's your partner, Burt?"

Wickes waved the cigar at his cart. "My associate, Martin Storch." The man in the cart gave a limp wave. Grinning like a shark, Wickes said, "Marty's a killer with his short game, so-so off a tee. Likes to play lost-in-the-woods. But don't bet with him."

"Thanks for the warning," said McFadden, climbing into the general's cart, his rental clubs next to Rosario's bulging bag. The two-cart caravan, trailed discreetly by a third cart driven by one of the general's minders, headed to the first tee.

For the first five holes, McFadden held his own, though to his eye, Wickes was alternating shots, obviously playing below his capability. After a poor start, Rosario settled down, his touch on the greens making up for mediocre fairway play. On the eighth hole, McFadden and Wickes ended up far right, near a wall of spreading trees. The general drilled one left and dropped McFadden mid-fairway to walk. Taking a club with him, McFadden accepted a ride with a beaming Wickes.

"I knew it would come to me. You did a tour out here five years ago."

"Good memory."

Puffing on a cigar, Wickes smiled. "Told ya, I never forget a name. You serious about the diving thing? You'll have competition, you know."

Pointing to his ball, McFadden replied, "I am. I retired here to do just that."

"What about the other shops?"

"I plan to do a courtesy tour to smooth any ruffled feathers."

"Can't be cheap to start a business like that from scratch. Lot of equipment involved."

McFadden hopped from the cart and took a practice swing

in the rough. "I've done my homework to allow for that. Plus, out here my dollar goes a lot farther these days."

Brushing cigar ash from his knit shirt, Wickes said, "Yeah, I hear ya. Still, a guy like you can make some serious money if he's interested."

Punching a high shot through overhanging branches, Mc-Fadden put himself back in the middle of the fairway and turned to Wickes. "You're persistent, but I'm not interested . . . in security work, that is."

Shrugging, Wickes waddled to his ball. "That's not all we do," he said over his shoulder. "We travel throughout Asia with high-value business types. We do some advising."

"Still boils down to being a high-priced babysitter with a gun. Not for me. Your shot." Rebuffed, the big man shamelessly played a foot wedge, twice moving his ball closer to the fairway's fringe.

Wickes growled, "I shoulda been on the range with you and Pablo."

"I'm rusty myself."

"Hey, it's a nice day. And it's only a game." When his shot sailed into thick woods Wickes dropped a second ball and sent it toward the green. "Now that's more like it."

McFadden didn't stay to watch the fat man's recovery; he strode across open ground to Rosario's cart.

The back nine tested the foursome's patience. Narrow fairways crowded with trees, dry greens, and a brutal sun proved a contest. Rosario's game slowly came apart and he began shaving points when he tallied his strokes. Playing more mulligans on every hole, Wickes got into a noisy running argument with his playing partner, the two squabbling like an old married couple. The quartet's mediocre round ended behind schedule.

After thanking the general, McFadden excused himself from the nineteenth hole, waved goodbye to the other two golfers, and headed to his car. *Churchill was right*, he thought. *It WAS like hitting a quinine pill around a cow pasture.* Four hours in Zamboanga's sun had not improved his attitude. Four hours wasted. Four hours he could have spent working on his dream. Tomorrow would be different.

CHAPTER 15

Killing two birds with one stone takes cunning, patience, and timing. When the birds are the Clementes, father and son, the stone must be hurled with precision. To miss would be fatal to the thrower, anonymous or no.

Risking all, Gilberto "Sonny" Rosario had taken his time planning revenge against his former son-in-law, Davido Clemente. Still smarting over his public humiliation by Davido at a cockfight, Rosario was primed for payback. That his daughter Maria had once been shamed by this same wastrel boy only added fuel to his cause. To get to the son it was necessary to go through the father. Two birds, one stone. It began with a phone call.

Since his expulsion from the Blue Orchid, Rosario had taken to holding court in the Grand Astoria. Today, in the inn's Lotus Restaurant, a charming Sonny Rosario was devouring an excellent duck entrée with the help of two friends.

His cell phone danced across the linen tablecloth. Reading the number, Rosario excused himself to take the message in a nearby corridor. "Yes, what do you have for me?" The nervous caller raced through the details and rang off. Elated, Rosario returned to his luncheon companions wearing a poker face.

"Good news?" asked a moon-faced Chinese city hall bureaucrat.

"More pressing business as usual," offered Rosario. "I am buried in shipping requests these days. It never seems to end."

"In a day when so many of our countrymen are without work, to be busy is to be blessed," intoned a sallow-faced priest wearing an ill-fitting clerical collar.

"Then you must consider me blessed, my friends. My regrets. I cannot stay. A problem has arisen and I must be off to solve it. I beg your forgiveness for leaving early." Fighting to contain his rising excitement, Rosario palmed a wad of pesos with the clergyman.

Staring at the money, the priest smiled benignly at the Chinese diner beside him. "How unlike Sonny to pay the bill. His news must have been good indeed."

"Indeed," mumbled the city administrator, reaching for the duck leftovers.

Rosario's "good news" was a tip from an informant buried deep within Clemente's gang. The mole had learned of an important shipment of illegally harvested round timber bound for Zamboanga. With no time to lose, Rosario drove to Paseo del Mar and parked in the shadow of Fort Pila. Using a disposable cell phone and altering his voice, the former senator called a contact in the Philippine Navy. "A crew working for the Clementes is to take possession of one hundred trimmed hardwood trunks one week from tonight. On that night a fishing vessel towing a barge loaded with timbers from Tawi-Tawi will arrive in the Basilan Straits two hours before midnight. It will be met by Clemente's men and towed ashore. You must be prepared to act."

Immediately, the anonymous tip was routed to an officer serving with the Naval Special Operations Unit. At that point, all that was needed was an alert to a maritime patrol operating in the western approaches to Zamboanga. After a day of debating whether the call was genuine or a set-up for an ambush, headquarters ordered a two-boat patrol positioned for an intercept the following week.

CHAPTER 16

Halfway through a tour of the nearly completed dive boat, McFadden and Wolf emerged from the engine compartment to find Wickes's ferret-faced assistant, Martin Storch, roaming the pier.

"Hey, McFadden, good to see you." Without permission, Storch sauntered down the gangway as if an invitation to come aboard didn't matter. Studying the trawler, he let out a low whistle. "This rig had to set you back. How much you have in her?"

"Privileged information. What are you doing here?"

"Wickes sent me. He asked me to throw out a couple ideas for you." Without waiting for a response, Storch introduced himself to Wolf. "Martin Storch, Pan-Pacific Security."

Wolf looked to McFadden then back to Storch. "Tom Wolf." The two men shook hands.

"I played golf with your friend here," said Storch. "He hits a decent ball. Maybe he told you."

McFadden said rudely, "What do you want?"

Storch's narrow face broke into a salesman's ingratiating smile. "Wanted to see what your operation looked like. I'm impressed with what little I've seen. Mind if I do a tour?"

"Yeah, I do. Some other day. We've got things to take care of." Ducking into the main salon, McFadden called over his shoulder, "Stop by next month. Be sure to call ahead." Wolf stood by silently.

Storch leaned in the salon's opened door. "By the way, Wickes still thinks you'd make a terrific addition to the Pan-Pacific team. He'd like you to reconsider."

McFadden's face floated in the cabin's doorway. "Not interested. How many times do I have to say that?"

"Okay, so you're not interested. But think about this, McFadden, investments like the one you've got here are worth protecting. How about ten minutes of your time to explain what Pan-Pacific could do for your peace of mind?"

"Doesn't sound like he's interested," said Wolf.

Storch's inner salesman wasn't backing down. He changed tactics by appealing to Wolf. "If you've got money in this, friend, you might want to consider our services. Pan-Pacific Security can absolutely guarantee protection of your business assets AND provide you with personal round-the-clock peace of mind. Zamboanga's not Disneyland. Things can go haywire down here. Be smart. Think about it. We can show you a list of satisfied customers."

"I know all I need to know about Zamboanga," said Wolf.

Suddenly appearing on the bridge catwalk, McFadden gripped the handrail, his patience exhausted. "How can I put this politely, Storch? We don't need protection. We ARE the protection. For another thing, we can't afford you."

Interrupting, Storch said, "We can be very reasonable with our fee plan."

"We're not buying into your protection racket. Yeah, you heard me right—racket. Just so you know, Wolf and I have enough experience to cover all the bases. I also find it odd that you come here with a pitch about jobs in private security and when that doesn't work, you switch to a half-assed proposal to sell us protection. What part of 'NO' don't you understand?"

Wolf took another step toward Storch. Reading the ex-SEAL's body language, Wickes's envoy raised his hands. "You're a hard sell, guys. I pride myself in being able to close a deal but in your case I guess it's not going to work."

"Finally. The light bulb goes on," said McFadden from the bridge.

Storch backed up the gangplank. "I wish you well with your venture, gentlemen."

McFadden fired a parting shot. "Tell Wickes the next time we play golf . . . IF we ever play again . . . I'll be keeping the scorecard."

Watching Storch drive away, Wolf asked, "Sam, who the hell was that guy, and what was that about golf?"

"Long story. You ever hear of a guy named Burton Wickes?"

"Doesn't ring a bell."

"I'll fill you in about him and the golf thing, but you'll have to promise to buy the drinks."

CHAPTER 17

The next day, Wolf dropped McFadden at a local dive shop and waited as the counter man checked him out for another test run on one of the rental outriggers. The marina was the third one they had scouted in as many days. One of the shop's feral kids had volunteered to ride along as a last-minute addition and McFadden agreed. Opening up the throttle, he headed up the coast where his trawler was moored. Powered by a seventy-five horsepower Yamaha outboard instead of the usual converted car engine that similar craft used, the banca—commonly known as a pump-boat—was designed to cut through the water with ease. The boat's knife-shaped bow lifted from the surface, the long curving outriggers on both sides of the hull slicing the turquoise sea effortlessly. The narrow center shell, shaded with a wide white nylon cover, exceeded McFadden's expectations of comfort. The boats were everywhere in the Philippines. Built in differing sizes, some with planking overlaying the bowed outriggers, most used noisome automobile engines driving long metal rods welded to drive shafts. Two- or three-prop blades proved amazingly efficient. In coastal waters there were no faster boats. A favorite of smugglers, bancas were also extremely popular as snorkeling platforms or inter-island ferries. The boats were strictly calm water coastal craft, though, so in high winds and waves they were almost useless. Testing bancas as possible cheaper alternatives for coastal dive trips was McFadden's idea.

Following McFadden's progress from the road, Wolf raced in the pickup to the ferry terminal's dock. With the help of the city's infamous traffic, the banca won easily. Gliding to the moored trawler, McFadden tied alongside, told the kid to wait, and scrambled aboard. Below decks, Sal and Andy were supervising a six-man crew putting finishing touches of marine varnish on the berths.

Sal was happy, his usual mode. "Hey, Sam, you like what you see?"

McFadden was pleased. "This it? You already done with the forward compartments?" Saluting with a brush, Sal listed the completed tasks.

As he babbled cheerfully, Wolf came down the ladder. "Who's your passenger, Sam?"

"Just some kid from the dive shop. Probably came along to make sure I knew how to handle the boat."

"What's the agenda for the day?"

Leaving Sal and his crew behind, McFadden led Wolf up the ladder to the deck. "How do you feel about taking a run to Big Santa Cruz? We pack a lunch, do a little snorkeling, see how we feel about leasing one of these pump boats for day trips. Could save us a lot of diesel using outfits like this."

"What about our boat?"

"What about it? Sal and the guys will wrap it up today. We'll be back late afternoon. When we get back I'll drop you here and you can come pick me up at the dive shop. You game?"

Wolf rubbed his chin. "You think things are okay?"

"They have security patrols there on the beach. Shouldn't be a problem. But we could pack our pistols if you want. Out, have lunch, swim, come back. End of story."

"I'll pass. Tell you what. I'll run the boat back. You drive the truck."

"No problem. The kid will show you the ropes."

"I'm a sailor, remember? I know ropes."

Surveying the clutter-free deck, McFadden said, "It's looking good, Wolfman. We're going to make this thing work. We'll be ready for test runs early next week."

Wolf laughed. "We call it sea trials, army boy. And yeah, I'm looking forward to getting out on the water." Climbing over the side, he added, "See you back at the dive shop, Sam." Firing the big Yamaha, Wolf reversed, then goosed the throttle to turn the outrigger. Waving to McFadden, he threaded his way through a fleet of similar boats moored off the Lantaka Beach Hotel's shoreline.

Forty minutes later, McFadden pulled into a gravel lot next to the dive shop. Standing in the pickup's bed with binoculars raised, he spotted Wolf, one half-mile from shore, flying across the glassy sea with the kid at his side.

Cutting the engine, Wolf burrowed the banca's bow gently in the sand in front of the shop. He followed the youngster from the boat.

"Nice, huh?" said McFadden.

Nodding in agreement, Wolf pulled McFadden aside. "Tell him we like the boat. See if he's still agreeable to rent long term. I'll meet you in the truck."

"You're not coming in?"

"Nah, you go ahead. Looks like we wrapped it up just in time." They both looked seaward. A column of rain, gray and menacing, was marching its way across Big Santa Cruz. "Lot of snorkelers are gonna get wet."

"That's the general idea."

"I'll be waiting," said Wolf.

After returning the boat, McFadden got behind the wheel and drove without speaking. Wolf broke the silence. "I'm curious. Did the kid in the boat ask you a lot of questions?"

"Yeah. Like who I was, where I was from in America, what did I do, where did I live in Zamboanga. Was I married. Typical kid questions. Why do you ask?"

Staring at the blur of traffic and roadside shacks, Wolf said, "He asked me the same stuff. You find that odd? I mean, a kid his age asking all that?"

"Don't go all SEAL on me, Wolfman. What are you saying?"

"I'm saying the kid was fishing, Sam. Maybe I'm paranoid, huh? Whadaya think?"

Passing a pair of bicyclists, McFadden kept his eyes on the road. "I don't know. With all that's gone down . . . you have a feeling or something?"

"Sorta. What about the guy in the shop? What did he ask you?"

"Same kinda stuff. Just friendly banter. He was renting to strangers, after all." Silence in the cab again until they reached the turnoff toward the city's ferry terminal. McFadden said, "He probably knows we're in the scuba business but I'm not sure he knows what we're doing."

"He does now," said Wolf.

"How so?" A light went on as soon as the words were out of his mouth. "Of course. The kid. He saw our boat. Probably scoped it out. Came back to the shop for a show and tell."

"That's what I'm thinking."

McFadden said, "How would you feel about one of us staying with the boat? I mean, we'd rotate, of course, but we'd be running our own security detail to keep everything cool until things settle down. You game?"

He got a nod and three words from Wolf. "Let's do it."

CHAPTER 18

"So, are these Americans going to be a problem?" Disentangling himself from a young girl, Clemente wrapped a silk robe around himself and sent the naked whore sprawling with a well-aimed kick. She fell at the foot of his bed and lay there, glassy-eyed and unmoving. Ignoring her, Clemente, cell phone buried in his ear, reached for a half-full glass on a bedside table, downed its contents, and poured another four fingers of booze. Settling himself against a mountain of scented pillows, the big man listened to Davido report on two Americans who had stopped by a dive shop—one of two such fronts owned by Clemente.

"I don't know yet. Joseph swears these guys are military," said the son. "They told him they were divers and asked a lot of questions about prices, equipment, and trips."

"So they asked," growled Clemente. "Did you get names?"

"Yes, I have names. I have an address."

"Well, send your boys to check them out. Better yet, go yourself." He heard the expected whining and roared his displeasure. "A good leader always knows his enemy, never asks his men to do something he is afraid to do, and disciplines those who fail . . . even a son." Silence on the other end. Pleased that his scolding seemed to have worked, Clemente moved on, dealing with more "family" business, schooling his son about the week to come. There was the upcoming challenge of moving a small warehouse-sized shipment of smuggled cigarettes, whiskey, and rum. A long-time Chinese drug connection was due in Zamboanga in two days.

"Davido," his father told him, "you will be present to study how things are done with these people." Clemente's son was to remain silent and learn from watching his father manipulate the buyer.

Clemente's system of multiple warehouses, painstakingly disguised as deserted rooming houses, boarded-up factories, and vacant apartment buildings, served as a secure waypoint for the lucrative heroin trade. Illegal hardwood logging, often mixed with legitimate purchases and falsified receipts, poured more pesos into Clemente's pockets. He needed it. The cost of bribing law enforcement was rising, not yet outstripping his obscene profits but a worry nonetheless. Keeping payoffs to police and military officials compartmentalized was a constant headache for Clemente. Funding his army of sondolos—street soldiers—took cash, lots of it. Allowing them to dabble in kidnapping, petty thievery, drugs, whoring, and the occasional robbery kept the family's underlings happy.

One bright spot was that by providing a fleet of pump boats to take advantage of Zamboanga Peninsula's porous coastline, Clemente had another lucrative initiative: smuggling. It provided cash flow, aiding the Clemente crime syndicate in amassing power. Stolen weapons were easy to move by boat as well. Islamists in the south paid good money. It was a growth market. Of course, growing power caused jealousy, attracted attention.

Using scuba shops as cover for their fleet of pump boats had been Davido's brainchild. But now this American duo's questions and rental of a banca had Clemente's son worried. His father urged caution in how to deal with the situation. "If these two are government undercover, we unmask them and deal with them." Wearied by the call, Clemente ended the conversation with a warning. "We must never rest, Davido. We have enemies all around us. They are waiting for us to make mistakes. They do not sleep. Do not forget that, my boy. And do not forget, I'm going to Davao mid-week. In my absence I expect you to handle the lumber shipment. Understand?"

More of Davido's useless bleating filled his ear like an annoying mosquito. Clemente put away his phone. He would sleep. When he awoke in a few hours, he would drag the girl into his bed again and use her, conscious or not. She had not satisfied him, a failure he would not forgive. This pretty one, now passed out on his bedroom floor, had been much too slim, with small breasts and no enthusiasm for her assignment. That she was a farm girl from Zamboanga del Norte sold to settle a debt was no excuse. If she disappointed him again he would call for another whore, perhaps two, to take her place. As a lesson to others, he would punish Mama Selena, the madam who sent her.

Just another enterprise among his empire, Clemente's manoys—captains—oversaw multiple Zamboanga brothels run by a stable of worn-out prostitutes who had exhausted their talents and now served as the gang's madams. These women ultimately owed their escape from the streets, narrow stalls, and soiled mattresses to Clemente, the gang's Papa Manong—the top boss. That these madams lived just one slip away from a return to a curb meant Clemente expected unwavering loyalty. Mama Selena's mistake of sending a pretty but inexperienced

girl to his bed would have to be dealt with. Insults such as this
would not be tolerated.

CHAPTER 19

Wolf was doing pull-ups on an overhead bar McFadden had
rigged at the rear of his house. Dropping to the concrete deck, a
sweating Wolf knelt by the pool, waiting for McFadden to finish his quota of laps. "You have a name?" he asked. McFadden
surfaced at the far end and floated on his back. Wolf tried again.
"Did you come up with a name for the boat yet?"

Drifting toward the shallow end, McFadden was staring at
the sky. "Yeah, I picked one. How about you?"

"Got it. Asked you first, though. What's your pick?" McFadden dog-paddled to the side of the pool. "*Sampaguita*," he said,
arms resting on the tiled edge.

Wolf was shocked. "What?"

McFadden climbed from the pool and buried his face in a
towel. "*Sampaguita*. It's a flower."

Scowling, Wolf said, "I know what the hell it is. My question is why?"

"It's Zamboanga's official flower."

"I'm not going to sea on a boat named for a flower. No way."

"I thought it was pretty clever, actually."

Wolf snorted. "I'm sure you did. Damn, maybe you have
been out here too long. Or maybe little Miss Regina has turned
your brain to mush. You're a former Green Beret, Sam. You
can't go around on a boat with a name like that."

"You have a better idea?"

Grinning, Wolf leaned forward. "I do. It beats a flower
hands down."

Fishing in a cooler for a San Miguel, McFadden snagged one and opened it. "I'm all ears."

Gesturing with both hands, Wolf announced, "*Enterprise.* Whadaya think?"

"Where'd that come from?"

"*Star Trek!* It's the ship's name. You know, all that shit about 'Going boldly where . . .'"

Taking a long pull on the bottle, McFadden sat quietly, his expression showing he had no clue to his friend's logic. "Why the *Star Trek* connection?"

Brightening, Wolf made his case. "Okay, we're going boldly into . . . the Sulu Sea. Get it?"

"I never liked the show that much. It was kinda cheesy."

Wolf plucked a beer from the cooler. "Okay, but Sulu was cool. He was the helmsman for the *Enterprise.* Did you know his character was named after the Sulu Sea?"

Clueless, McFadden drank his beer, thought some more.

Wolf waved his bottle. "*Enterprise* is perfect, Sam. We're starting a new business. It's called an enterprise, get it? It's our dream . . . well, your dream mostly . . . but it's a new thing. *Enterprise.*"

"You don't like *Sampaguita*?"

Shaking his head, Wolf dismissed the word. "Not a chance. No self-respecting SEAL can sail aboard a flower. Sounds like a floating florist shop. Forget it."

McFadden tried again. "What about *Regina*? That's regal sounding."

"Apologies to your lovely lady, but I'm not putting to sea on a girly name either. Besides, six weeks after you pick a name like that you're gonna get in a fight with her and then what? Every time you take a group out you have to stare at her name all day. Bad idea, Sam. Trust me."

"I can't swallow *Enterprise*. It's too lame."

"Okay. I've got an alternative."

"I'm listening."

"Do you agree we need something snappy, something exotic, edgy?"

"I'm with you. What's your second choice?"

Beaming, Wolf announced, *"Laticauda."*

"Sounds pretty close to *Sampaguita*, Wolfman."

"Not a chance. Laticauda is a sea snake. Cool, huh? They're a local species in this part of the world. They do it all. Swim miles offshore, can stay submerged and yet have the ability to move on land. Like the SEALs, get it?"

"Sea Snake would be a turn-off to some people."

Wolf grinned. "I agree. So we go with *Laticauda*. Same thing, just sounds mysterious."

"You're incorrigible. Fine. *Laticauda* it is."

McFadden shrugged. Wolf gloated. The pair toasted the choice.

CHAPTER 20

Like commandos on a raid in enemy territory, three motorcycle riders broke from sluggish traffic clogging Veterans Avenue and shot into the mouth of a weedy alley. The little-used road ran alongside a block-long metal shed that was falling apart. The three-cycle team, two Kawasakis and a Honda CB, glided to a stop and idled. Davido, clad in the head-to-toe black jogging gear he favored, shed his helmet. His outriders preferred ball caps and wraparound, mirrored sunglasses. Flashing them a cell phone picture taken earlier in a dive shop, he outlined their task. "This is the American we want. He lives here, somewhere close."

Peeling back a glove, he recited the address written in marker on his left hand. "Look for this number. You got it?" Both soldanos nodded. "Good," said Davido. "If we need help looking for him, I ask the questions. Talking to these people is my job. You say nothing, understand?" The two nodded in unison.

"We supposed to kill this guy when we find him?" asked one rider.

"Not like that," answered Davido. "We just coming for a look."

The pair shrugged. Killing they understood, reconnaissance, not so much. Despite their disappointment, the pair were good soldiers and would do as told. "Okay, we going in. One quick look and done." Revving his engine, Davido replaced his helmet, drew down its dark glass, and glided along the back door track leading to the barrio.

Shaded by mature trees, an unbroken line of wooden houses with rusting tin roofs crowded the narrow alley leading into a community dating to the thirties. Burned out during the war, it had been rebuilt and fired twice, rising phoenix-like each time. Postage stamp–sized yards, cramped by overhanging palms and banana trees, created an unfamiliar labyrinth that challenged the bikers. Cinderblock and barbed wire–topped fences was the common style here, the houses hidden behind cobbled-together walls.

In the heart of the community, Davido confronted an alley that branched in three directions. He sent one rider left, one right. Keeping his Honda in first gear, he prowled the center route, his eyes hidden behind dark glass. Ahead of him, two weathered ten-foot-high walls met at a metal gate topped with spikes. Pausing, Davido shifted into neutral and planted a boot in the dirt. He checked the number on his wrist—McFadden's home. The residence was the only numbered dwelling in a sea of houses known by the name of the families who lived in them.

Behind the idling Honda, a child, unnoticed by Davido,

darted from under a torn wire fence and ran across the road to a square house of bleached wood. A barefooted woman padded across the home's tilting porch, cell phone to her ear, her eyes focused on the motorcycle ridden by a stranger. A pickup truck, its bed filled with sand topped by a cement mixer and tools, rumbled by. Two laborers in the cab studied the outsider with suspicion.

The second bike sent to do reconnaissance suddenly appeared, crawling in low gear along one wall of McFadden's house. The Kawasaki's rider spotted Davido and joined him. Above the pair, three teenagers shinnied up slender palms arching over the alley. Invisible in the hanging fronds, the watching boys were armed with their usual arsenal of slingshots and marbles.

Emerging from a beaten path between two hovels, the final member of the scouting party rode up. Davido studied McFadden's gate, then followed the wall to a secluded spot where a fruit tree's drooping branches gave cover from the curious. He ordered his men to investigate. The tallest biker stood on the motorcycle's seat and tossed a denim jacket over jagged glass embedded in the wall's rampart. Throwing an arm over the jacket, he clawed his way up to peer inside the property. He found himself staring at the business end of the .45 Colt held by Eddie Delgado.

"I drop you here, no?" The caretaker's cannon fired, grazing the intruder's scalp.

Throwing himself from the wall, the stunned biker tumbled backwards across his motorcycle, the bloodied dazed man and his machine both collapsing in a cloud of dust.

"Go!" yelled Davido. Leaving their hapless cohort behind, Davido and the other rider accelerated down a side alley only to find it blocked by a dump truck and five men advancing with clubs. Spinning in a circle, wheels spitting gravel and dirt at their pursuers, the two fled the trap. Bulling through a gauntlet of stick-wielding youth, Davido and his outrider were pelted with stinging marbles from above. A well-aimed shot shattered Davido's left wrist. A second missile cracked his helmet's eye shield. The Honda's tank and body, heavily dented in a dozen spots, took most of the punishment. In desperation, the Kawasaki's driver pulled a pistol from his waistband, firing wildly at their tormentors to no effect.

Finding the road they had taken sealed by an angry crowd waving picks and shovels over their heads, the two cyclists chose another route. Davido, his left hand useless, saw daylight to his right and opened up the Honda's throttle. Pilar Street and the safety of its streaming traffic beckoned. A Molotov cocktail flew past him, exploding against a concrete wall in a roaring ball of fire that engulfed the Kawasaki behind him.

CHAPTER 21

The scourging of Davido began the moment he returned to the waterfront compound. Alerted by his son's panicked cell phone call, Clemente waited with two of his toughest manoy. Propping his scarred bike in a company warehouse, Davido limped up the tower's stairs to face his father. Disheveled, dirty, his left arm useless, his clothing singed, a despondent Davido shuffled across the office.

"We found the . . ." he began.

"SILENCE!" exploded the patriarch.

Controlling himself with every ounce of control he could muster, Clemente sought an explanation for "how you lost two good men to a mob of women and children!" The two expressionless manoy stood like wooden statues during the de-briefing. Remarkably, Clemente asked few questions, instead letting his son explain a reconnaissance gone horribly wrong. When Davido finished, his father sent one of his tattooed guard dogs to fetch a doctor who had been waiting downstairs. While the nervous doctor cleaned Davido's minor wounds and fashioned a crude cast, Clemente took to the catwalk with his trusted subordinates to discuss punishment for the offending neighborhood.

"Such an affront must not pass without retribution," said Clemente. "It sends the wrong message to our enemies." His underlings agreed. "I have my suspicions about who betrayed us," Clemente snarled. "I give you the names, eh. I leave the timing to you. But I want this revenge to be swift and severe . . . and public." His senior aides endured Clemente's rant against his enemies. When they left, they took with them the doctor and the names of those marked for death.

Clemente then turned on his son. Two hours of volcanic browbeating followed. Only the fact that he was his father's last surviving son saved Davido from the fate of others who had failed Clemente—Papa Manong.

In the Basilan Strait one week later, a moonless midnight came and went without sign of the expected fishing vessel and its barge loaded with illegal timber. Circling in a motor launch at the rendezvous point, Davido's crew radioed for instructions. Pacing on the tower's catwalk, his left wrist in a cast, Davido instinctively knew something had gone awry. He made a quick cell phone call to his own informant in the city police. His suspicions were confirmed. Back on the radio, he ordered, "We've been set up. Leave area immediately! Do not return here! Avoid any patrol boats!"

His call reached the waiting men too late. From two directions, navy patrol craft closed on the hapless crew, bathing their idling launch in spotlights. From his perch in the tower miles away, Davido watched powerful shafts of light play on the horizon, saw a silent burst of red tracers float heavenward, and thought the worst.

Unbeknownst to Davido, his men had given up without a shot—though armed, they had not been expecting a fight. Resistance would have been futile given navy firepower. The textbook maritime interception was over in ten minutes. Marines boarded the fishing boat. The timber barge, having been captured earlier, arrived with its own prize crew. With patrol boats on either side, the convoy, including Davido's sullen, manacled crew, made its way to the navy dock in Zamboanga where more marines, police, and media waited.

In a quandary as to whether he should call his father in Davao or wait, Davido opted to remain silent for the moment. Nothing could be done anyway. His father was out of contact. Mistrustful of air travel, the senior Clemente was traveling by car and due back in two days. The eruption would come soon enough. Though it had been Davido's responsibility to see to the delivery, he had failed . . . again. As his father's heir apparent, Davido would have to break the news. He had no choice. *A leader takes responsibility for all that happens on his watch. There would be no club tonight or for the next few weeks.*

In two days, the morning would shatter like glass. When tempers cooled, if ever, a phalanx of lawyers would close ranks with Clemente for the inevitable courtroom assault by the government. Alibis would be rehearsed. Blame would be placed elsewhere. Act one of the legal charade would begin. It would cost Clemente heavily. Within the gang, knives would appear. Sharks would circle, drawn by the bloodletting to find another informant. War from within. Fratricide. Inevitable.

CHAPTER 22

Lunch at the Blue Orchid was becoming a welcome ritual for McFadden and Regina. As a gentleman, he picked up the tab more often than not. Her tales about her Uncle Sonny's freeloading stayed with McFadden. Yet to meet the politician, he had already developed distaste for the man, based solely on Regina's history with her father's younger brother. All that was put aside for the moment. He and Wolf claimed a table in a shaded corner of the hotel's open-air café. Out of earshot of other diners, the two sipped iced tea while replaying the biker's bloody neighborhood assault.

Wolf put down his glass, said, "Maybe it's time you thought seriously about moving to a more secure spot, Sam."

"You sound like you've been talking to Regina."

"Maybe you oughta listen to her."

Deflecting the comment, McFadden growled. "She should talk. You forget how we met? Two days after the shooting she was back at work. She turned down her father's offer to come back home and took just one day from work . . . and that was only for her friend's funeral mass."

"From what little I know about Regina," said Wolf, "I can't see her living under glass at the general's place. She's a free spirit. She'll keep her hotel apartment here. Can't run the place from a bunker."

A waitress approached, handed McFadden a note, and refilled their teas. After scanning it, McFadden chuckled, handed the slip of paper to Wolf, who read, "Sam, Held up. Will be down shortly. Hello to Tom. Order for me." McFadden sat back, laughing. Wolf returned the note. "I don't get it. What's so amusing?"

"It's Regina," said McFadden. "We have this thing. She's just like the general. Always wants to make a late entrance. Says she dislikes his habit of doing that, yet she's a pro at it."

"Women," sighed Wolf. "What can I say? Better get used to it, Sam. You look like a guy who's in for the long haul." They recalled the server to their table and ordered as instructed. Food arrived, along with Regina, stunning in a dark suit but subdued.

McFadden rose to meet her with a smile. They embraced. She shook Wolf's hand. "Getting settled in?"

Wolf shook out a napkin. "Yeah, but I must have said something wrong to somebody along the way. Did Sam tell you about our friendly little neighborhood riot?"

"Yes. Father called. He's going to ask friends in the police to offer you protection. Seems you two have stirred up something. Any clues?"

"Not a one," said McFadden. They began to eat. He lowered his voice. "But . . . speaking of the police . . . we talked to a detective before we came here. Two of the bad guys got left behind. Good thing the cops got there. My neighbors were going to lynch the guy Eddie wounded. The other one won't be doing any talking."

Wolf tore off a piece of bread. "Hard for a crispy critter to share his feelings." Regina blanched at his words and McFadden shot him a mild scolding look. "Sorry," he said. "Forgot the company I was with."

"You don't have to prove anything, Sam," she reasoned. "Won't you please consider moving someplace safer?"

"We've already been over that." Between mouthfuls of fish, McFadden defended his choice. "Besides, look what happened to these guys. They came looking for the ugly American and they got their asses handed to them in a sling."

Wolf backed him up. "He's right, Regina. If the neighbors and Eddie hadn't been there, these guys would have been over the wall and trashing Sam's living room. It happened to me back home. One brave soul came through my patio screen in Coronado while I was making dinner. Guys like this are the same everywhere. Hell, in Afghanistan we had village idiots following us door-to-door looking for televisions and rugs to steal right in the middle of operations we ran. Honest."

McFadden grinned. "You tell her, Wolfman."

"Tom, you're as bad as Sam. I seriously doubt these were typical thieves."

McFadden dropped the cheery facade. "You're right. The detective told us they ID'd the biker who got left behind. Said he's part of a barkada, a criminal family, a gang run by a major bad guy named Eugenio Clemente. Heard of him?"

Regina paled, put down her fork, and reached for water. "Yes. Father didn't mention him, but it's bad news, Sam. Why would he be looking at you?"

Wolf stared at her. "Sam's cop said these guys do break-ins, smash-and-grab stuff all the time. They probably figured he was a rich American with lots of shiny stuff to steal."

Finding her voice, Regina continued, her eyes playing between the two men. "It's not that simple. Clemente is pure evil. He controls Kuratong Baleleng. He rules a lot of sondalos, soldiers, men who do whatever he wants. Didn't the detective tell you any of this?"

"No. He's probably seen it all," said McFadden. "Didn't seem terribly upset. He didn't mention the connection with the Kuratong Baleleng. I've heard about them. We both came across signs of them when we served out here but what I don't get is why they'd target us. Maybe it has something to do with the Aussie ex-pat I leased the house from. Maybe there's some bad blood between the gang and him. He did leave in a hurry, after all."

Wolf interrupted McFadden. "She's worried, Sam." To Regina, he said, "What's going on?"

"Maybe I should ask my father to send one of his men to stay with you."

"You didn't answer my question," said Wolf. "Do you know something we don't?"

McFadden looked at him. "C'mon, what would she know?"

Backing off, Wolf said, "Sorry, Regina. It's just that your eyes are saying there's more to this than a couple guys doing a home invasion. For the record, I agree with Sam. We can handle this. The whole neighborhood's up in arms about what happened, but I don't think we'll see those guys again. At least not those two."

"There were three," McFadden reminded him. "Witnesses said the one who got away was the guy giving orders. Rode a different bike than the others. Dressed differently."

Her eyes downcast, Regina said softly, "They'll be back."

"How do you know?"

"Because if Clemente's involved it's unfinished business. It's his style."

McFadden said, "You're full of surprises. You seem to know a lot about this, Regina. I've lived here three years and I've never had a problem until yesterday. Is this some kind of 'get the Americans' vendetta? Are we looking at a jihad thing? Talk to me."

"I don't think so. Clemente may be many things but he's not Muslim. Not Catholic. He's a devil, a law unto himself. Judge, jury, and executioner in his world." Tossing down her napkin, she pleaded with McFadden. "Let me talk to Father, please. He can shed some light on this. He knows what goes on in the city. He has friends everywhere."

"I know," he said sarcastically. "I played golf with two of them."

She bristled. "What do you mean?"

Brushing away her question, McFadden said, "Nothing. Forget it. It's a topic for another day. Right now I'm mystified about this Clemente character. You're right about talking to your father. Will you call him? We need his take on this."

She rose, the men with her. "I'll phone him as soon as I get back to my office." Putting a hand on McFadden's arm, she said, "Watch yourselves, both of you. Don't take any chances until you speak with Father. He'll come to you, Sam." She kissed him on the cheek, did the same to Wolf. "Take care of Sam. I don't want to lose him."

"Neither do I, lady."

She turned away, her eyes teary, and hurried into the lobby.

CHAPTER 23

Vigilant, not panicked, McFadden and Wolf went about their business, but not as usual. Eddie began wearing the .45 Colt every waking hour. His nephew, taciturn, single, and unemployed, covered the nights with a sawed-off Remington twelve-gauge McFadden had in his arsenal. For the next two days, McFadden and Wolf left for the harbor at odd hours and varied their routes. Riding his motorcycle, SIG Sauer hidden in his waistband, McFadden shadowed Wolf when he drove the pickup, and vice versa. Trips to work on the boat followed no predictable pattern. Some days started in the pre-dawn hours, others in the afternoon. Market days when Rose Delgado foraged for food became irregular, her nephew steps behind her as she shopped. While the two were gone, Eddie sat cradling the shotgun on McFadden's screened balcony like a hawk studying its territory.

For a handful of pesos, two neighbors took turns patrolling the alley behind McFadden's rear walls. Two days passed without incident. On the third day, General Rosario arrived in a black armored SUV like a presidential candidate courting votes. It had been years since a dignitary had descended on the neighborhood. A small crowd gathered in the dusty street to gossip about McFadden's mysterious visitor. Stationing an unsmiling bodyguard outside the steel gate, Rosario greeted old soldier Eddie, then hurried with McFadden upstairs where Wolf waited with questions and fresh coffee. Following introductions, the three sat at the polished teak table as Rosario delivered good news and bad.

The general sipped his coffee. "This city is on edge. There are things happening, some I know of, some I do not. What I can tell you is this. You have run afoul of Eugenio Clemente, a difficult and dangerous situation for all concerned. Sam, you and my Regina are at risk because you two have become close."

"I regret that she is in danger, General, but I don't regret befriending her."

"Nor should you. Her happiness is mine as well."

Wolf asked, "Is this connected with the earlier attempt on her life, sir?"

"That was aimed at me." Brow furrowed, Rosario paused. "Let me give you a history lesson, gentlemen." Rising from the table, the general, hands clasped behind his back, paced as he talked. "Clemente is Papa Manong—father to a large family of criminals. His is a hierarchy made up of some of Zamboanga's worst lawbreakers, a vicious stew of ex-convicts, thieves, murderers, gamblers, drug dealers, whores and pimps. Loan sharks as well. We are sworn enemies."

"Is this connected to the Kuratong Baleleng?" asked McFadden.

Rosario returned to his chair. "Yes. A widespread scourge of our nation. One of just many such gangs."

It was Wolf's turn. "As I understand it, sir, the Philippine military formed this group as a vigilante force against communist guerillas."

Visibly sagging, Rosario nodded his head. "You are correct. I am ashamed to admit it. We thought it a good idea in 1986. Mind you, it was not my decision. I was a new lieutenant, having just graduated from West Point the year before. The idea appalled me when I heard about it. It was an admission that we, the army, had not the will nor the manpower to perform our own duties."

"Initially it was a success, was it not?" McFadden asked.

"Of course. They did exactly what was asked of them. It worked. But how does one dismount a tiger once it can no longer be controlled?"

McFadden excused himself from the table to flip a switch for the overhead fan. The air began to stir, cooling them. The general continued. "We ordered the disbandment of this monster we had created. But what do people like this do when they suddenly find themselves without work? What do they know?" He answered his own question. "They continue as they were taught to do. They kill, they rob, they turn to kidnapping. They spread themselves like a cancer throughout our country."

Wolf cast his eyes downward. "Hard to put the genie back in the bottle."

McFadden asked, "Where does Clemente fit in this picture?"

"He is a creation of the army," sniffed Rosario with disdain. "His father was one of the original and most infamous of these creatures. Eugenio Clemente is a second-generation devil incarnate."

"That's how your daughter described him," interjected Wolf.

"She's right. Old Clemente had three sons and one daughter by several women. When his father died ten years ago, Eugenio

Clemente eliminated his three brothers one by one, like a first-born shark in the womb. As his father before him, he fathered three sons and one daughter."

Whistling softly, Wolf added, "Sounds like the original dysfunctional family from hell."

"When I took over Western Mindanao Command, we were dealing with Islamist threats. We suspected Clemente of selling arms to them but were unable to prove it. During a fight with the Kuratong Baleleng in Zamboanga del Norte we killed two of his sons. Things quieted down for a bit, but Clemente was simply biding his time like a serpent in tall grass."

"So years later he goes for payback by trying to kill Regina?" asked McFadden.

Rubbing his temples and grimacing, Rosario nodded. "Yes, I believe he was behind it. By killing her he would have killed part of me."

"You're saying Regina was the target after all," said Wolf. "But then . . . what's our part? Is it because Sam intervened?"

"Precisely because of that. Clemente thought he could get to me through her. I believe this, yes. She survived, but her heart was broken by the death of her friend, Margarita, and my chauffeur."

McFadden didn't like what he was hearing. He sat back, hands jammed in his pockets. "This is insanity, General. You're telling me Regina has to live every day as if it might be her last. Then she should leave. Never come back."

"As must you, Sam. You saved her life. You stepped in, altered the moment. Clemente will never forget what you did."

"And I would do it again in a heartbeat. But I can't just pack up and leave," he groaned. "I've put my life's savings in my scuba operation and the boat. Tom and I are partners in this venture. It's been my dream. His too."

"Clemente will keep trying," declared Wolf, "until he succeeds."

A prolonged sigh escaped from Rosario. "No doubt. Unless he is killed."

Seizing on the comment, the SEAL brightened. "There's your answer. You hit him first."

"I cannot simply go about murdering my enemies, sir. I am a retired general officer. We do not employ the same tactics that scum like Clemente does."

Incredulous, McFadden asked, "So you plan to sit behind your walls and wait for him to strike?"

"I will not act until I am sure that he and his organization can be destroyed."

It was Wolf's turn to pace, his mind racing. "No good. To destroy a snake you've got to cut off its head. 'One must be audacious and cunning in one's plans.'"

"My Navy friend is oddly fond of quoting Von Clausewitz," said McFadden dryly.

"I'm impressed, Commander Wolf. True, one must be cunning. Well, I've done my part. Regina asked me to share this with you and so I have. You have become involved in this fight whether you wanted to be or not. You have been warned."

"I won't leave without her," insisted McFadden. "I'll tell her that."

"I appreciate that, Sam. But weigh the risks. Now I must go. Word of my whereabouts will have reached Clemente's ears by now. It's not safe for me to linger in any one place. Especially with what's happened here."

"Helluva way to live," said Wolf, "even for a general."

"Ah, but as soldiers we are trained to live with those conditions, are we not?"

"True," answered Wolf. "But that makes it even more imperative to strike one's enemy first. Timing is everything, sir."

"So it is. Goodbye, gentlemen. I will be in touch."

CHAPTER 24

For Sonny Rosario, waking in a strange bed was no cause for alarm. Sunlight poured in through tall, varnished shutters. Birds sang outside the flat's open windows. Propping himself on his elbows, Rosario, his heavy lids at half-mast, his mind fogged, surveyed his surroundings. Different apartment, different bed, and different woman tangled in silk sheets beside him. Staggering to his feet, a naked Rosario stretched, yawned and scratched himself, every joint in his body protesting. Shuffling stiffly across the tiled floor to the bathroom, he shot a furtive look at the sleeping woman. A beefy upper arm, disheveled mass of black hair and a hint of fleshy thigh offered no clues to her identity.

Closing the bathroom door behind him, he climbed into an ancient claw-foot tub and ducked under an antiquated shower. The frigid water shocked his memory into life. The previous night came back in fragments. A dinner party at a local television executive's home. Loud, late, and liquor-filled, a soiree lasting into the wee hours. Hours before, he'd shared a limo to the party with four others: two male Brits, boring and drunk, and two Filipinas. After the bacchanal ended, he recalled dropping the men at their hotel. In the hired car, both women, he was sure, had come on to him. An incorrigible lothario, Sonny had encouraged the playful flirting. The limo's final stop ended with an invitation for a nightcap from one of the ladies. *Which one? He had already forgotten their names. Surely this one in the bed had done the inviting.* More drinking, his fumbling attempt at se-duction, laughter, more liquor and then a naked, drunken romp ending in frenetic coupling. *Who was the seducer here?*

Rosario stumbled from the shower, his head in a vise of his own making. Heavy snoring echoed from the bedroom. Towel-ing himself quickly, Rosario peeked into the room and imme-diately regretted it. His partner, an aging voluptuary—her face a puffy-eyed mask with gaping scarlet mouth—had thrown off the sheet and lay beached in the morning sun. Collecting his clothes, Rosario dressed hurriedly, afraid the cow would awaken. He tiptoed past the woman's gilded bed, found the flat's entry hall, and let himself out, shirttails flapping, shoes in hand.

Blinking in the light, Rosario signaled a loitering cyclo driver and gave the man his address. He would stop at home, phone a lie to the office to cover his absence, and then arrange a late lunch. Rosario put his throbbing head in his hands.

Halfway up the block from the woman's apartment building, a motorcycle was parked in morning's purple shadows. Speaking rapidly into his cell phone, Moises Castro's eyes followed the cab carrying Rosario. He rang off, pocketed the phone and took off after the cyclo. Wearing a ball cap and windbreaker, Castro looked like a thousand other Zamboanga motorcycle riders. He closed with the cyclo.

Traffic slowed abruptly. The three-wheeled cab jerked to a stop in a sea of vehicles. Rosario raised his head and snapped at the driver's handling of the taxi.

Castro's trailing bike suddenly cut to the right, gliding along-side the canopied cab, trapping its passenger. Fishing a hand-gun from his jacket, the motorcyclist pointed the weapon at a stunned Rosario and pumped three shots into the politician's chest. Calmly pocketing the smoking automatic, Castro broke from the knot of snarled traffic. His Suzuki took to the sidewalk, scattering shocked pedestrians. Reaching an alley, he abandoned pavement for a dirt path glutted with garbage and disappeared.

CHAPTER 25

A Trojan horse, disguised as a silver moped scooter, pulled into the Blue Orchid's car lot. The hired off-duty cop watching the entrance had no reason to be suspicious of the well-dressed man. Later, surveillance video would show a helmeted rider arriving wearing a typical businessman's uniform—gray suit, white shirt, silk tie, and polished loafers. After parking in the lot's southeast corner, the rider fiddled with something in the scooter's small mounted trunk, propped his helmet on the handlebars, and strolled casually to the hotel's canopied entrance. Like so many before him, he carried a briefcase. Witnesses later remembered him as young, perhaps in his early twenties, with thick black hair. An observant concierge recalled a placid face with the beginnings of a moustache and oversized glasses that gave him an owlish appearance. Lobby cameras recorded the visitor setting his briefcase beside a potted plant and entering the men's bathroom just off the lobby.

Minutes later, another gentleman, possibly the same person, emerged sans suit coat and tie. In place of the spectacles, this individual wore mirrored sunglasses. Another camera recorded him exiting the main doors. In yet another frame, the hotel's liveried doorman hailed a queued taxi and held the car's door. The gentleman tipped him and slipped into the backseat. The taxi disappeared off-screen right. Ten minutes later, a bright flash filled the parking lot, followed by a dark billowing cloud of dust and debris. Security cameras caught everything but the explosion's sound.

Panicked hotel guests fled the lobby, stampeding to the outdoor restaurant. Sirens wailed. Fire trucks, chased by an ambulance and police vans, arrived to hose down what was left of
the scooter. A nearby hotel courtesy van, its right side crushed
and charred, had taken most of the blast. While firemen sprayed
foam on both sets of smoldering wreckage, a police bomb squad
ordered the hotel evacuated. They searched for a second or possibly third explosive device. None was found. The abandoned
briefcase, an apparent ruse to complicate the police response,
was isolated. Cautiously opened, it proved empty and was con-
fiscated as evidence. Firemen worked quickly while police in-
terviewed witnesses before their memories faded. Gathering
herself, Regina Rosario worked the crowd, calming guests, reassuring staff, and answering policemen's questions. A television
truck arrived. The local station's manager would later turn over
phone tapes of a call warning of the bomb exactly one moment
before the device detonated. No group claimed responsibility.

Miraculously, no one was killed. Injuries to those nearby, including the doorman who had ushered the suspected bomber
into a waiting taxi, were superficial and quickly treated. Aside
from shattered glass in doors and windows, damage to the lobby
and facade was light.

Making two calls, Regina assured her father and sister she
was unhurt. Her close call, on the heels of her uncle's assassination, had unnerved them. Her father in particular was enraged,
laying responsibility at Clemente's feet and vowing revenge.
Listening to his ranting for ten uninterrupted minutes, she rang
off and called McFadden. Unbowed, she told him not to worry,
to disregard news reports, and to wait for her next call. "I'm
okay," she said hurriedly. "I'll first take care of my people here.
I've got to get them back into line. We have a business to run.
I'll be fine. Promise not to worry."

Not convinced by her calm, McFadden insisted on driving to the hotel. "I should be with you. You'll feel it later, trust me. I know how this plays out."

"Your being there is enough . . . for now," she said. "I have to go."

Hours later, she called. McFadden, relieved to hear her voice, probed again, "How are you, really?" Admitting she was feeling some effects, Regina broke. McFadden let her sob until he sensed she was drained, then said, "I'm coming to get you."

"I can't leave, Sam. I'm needed here. The staff must know I'm staying."

"The people who did this might be the same ones who murdered your uncle. Have you considered that?"

"Father said the same thing. He blames Clemente. There were no fatalities. I think it was someone trying to frighten me . . . or cripple Father's investment."

"Or maybe you dodged a bullet again. Not like these people to miss . . . or care about collateral damage. Here's the deal. I'm coming over there. I'm going to stay with you until you come down from this. It's like combat, Regina. You're in the midst of a fight and then, suddenly, it's done, finished. Listen to me. You've been running on pure adrenaline. Now comes the 'after' of a traumatic event. You listening to me?"

"I am. Sam . . ." Softly, she said, "I think I need you."

"I'm on my way."

"What about the boat, your house?"

"You're more important," he declared, a hint of rage in his voice. "Wolf's with the boat. Eddie and his nephew will watch the house. I want to be with you. I'll be there shortly."

Her muffled sobs and whispered, "Yes, please come," was all he needed to hear.

CHAPTER 26

The hotel had been baptized with fire. For three days, McFadden, armed and vigilant, stayed with Regina in her hotel apartment, reassuring her with his presence. The two ate in the Blue Orchid's restaurant, took lunch on the outdoor patio and had dinner in a corner booth in the bar. While Regina supervised repairs to the entry's windows and doors, McFadden paced the car lot, his eyes constantly scanning his surroundings. In the evening, he lingered in the lobby, just outside Regina's office. At night he sat beside her in the dark until she fell asleep. Padding stealthily across her darkened living room, he kept watch until dawn showed in the banyans and palms. On the fourth day, McFadden surrendered his role to two of the general's men who took up their posts—one shadowing the hotel's doorman from a valet stand, the other roaming the grounds. Both men were discreetly armed. Wearing new coats of stucco and fresh paint, the restored walls showed no signs of damage, the bombing's scars erased. The flow of guests resumed. Business returned to normal.

On the fifth day, Zamboanga, the City of Flowers, showed both its floral side and a somber face. Sonny Rosario's funeral mass at the Metropolitan Cathedral of Immaculate Conception drew hundreds. Political allies, old school friends, and business associates showed. Out of duty, his former wife and their daughter arrived from Manila. General Rosario, flanked by security, sat in the front with his daughters, Frances Yadao in the pew behind them. Clemente sent an assassin and a large wreath. His mere presence a message about vulnerability, the gunman was discreetly arrested without a shot and the gaudy, over-sized floral arrangement was turned away at Rosario's command. Army and police stalked church grounds, checking cars and keeping order. Remembered by the general in a sanitized eulogy, former senator Sonny Rosario was given a lavish burial. The loyal feasted at Rosario's estate following the ceremony. McFadden and Wolf stayed away at Regina's request. They watched the funeral on local television, as did a pleased Clemente in another part of the city.

The next day, McFadden checked in with Wolf at the boat. Days from sea trials, the former SEAL was impatient to get into action. The two spent a day at the harbor double-checking electronics, communications gear, plumbing, and the trawler's mechanics. A subdued christening party was planned for the morning of the shakedown cruise.

Neighborhood watch committee members reported no signs of trouble since the botched scouting mission. With McFadden's blessing, Eddie hired his nephew as full-time guard for the house. A status quo of sorts reigned.

On the morning of the seventh day, things changed.

The day started well. Dropping Wolf at the boat, McFadden drove to the Blue Orchid for breakfast with Regina. A construction crew was pouring cement for a reinforced steel gate. Two gun-toting guards wearing Pan-Pacific Security uniforms had replaced the general's men. McFadden was waved through and parked. As he entered the lobby, a porcine figure in rumpled seersucker rushed past him. Burton Wickes. Halting, the jubilant private security firm's owner reversed course, stuck out a hand. "Hey, McFadden. What a coincidence."

Declining the outstretched hand, McFadden grumbled, "Still peddling your rent-a-cop protection scam?"

Wickes's grin dissolved into a knowing smirk. "See my boys out there, McFadden? They're on duty now, twenty-four seven." Waving a sheaf of papers, he crowed triumphantly, "I got myself a contract here to ensure the safety of this fine hotel and its guests. I told you, the private security business is good."

"If that's true I'm sure you had to kiss General Rosario's ass to get it."

"You'd like to believe that, wouldn't you? Just so happens your lovely lady, the good general's daughter, signed it not more than five minutes ago."

"I don't believe it."

Brushing past McFadden, Wickes tossed an insult over his shoulder. "Ask her. And while you're at it, think about a contract for yourself. From what I hear, you might need one of our home protection specials." A laugh and he was gone. A car drove under the hotel canopy, a gloating Martin Storch at the wheel. He gave McFadden a knowing wink as his boss settled into the passenger seat.

McFadden asked the desk clerk to page Regina and tell her he would meet her in the restaurant. She arrived within minutes, wary but alert. She kissed him on the cheek and took a seat opposite. They ordered breakfast. McFadden, his eyes averted from hers, poured coffee for both. "What is Wickes doing here?"

"He's providing security for the hotel."

Sipping his coffee, McFadden eyed her over the cup's rim. "He practically rubbed my nose in a contract he claims you signed."

"I had no choice, Sam."

"No choice? Do you know who Wickes is? He's a hustler, Regina."

"What could I do? The bombing interrupted our routine. People were cancelling reservations and taking their business elsewhere."

"What happened to your father's men?"

"He pulled them back to the estate. He strongly suggested I hire Pan-Pacific. It was his idea, Sam. I had to do something. Coming so soon after Uncle Sonny's death, the bombing made both of us nervous. He thinks whoever planted it might try again."

Rolls and fruit arrived and they began to eat. Cooling, Mc-Fadden took another tack. "Of course you had to do something. I just wish it had been anyone but Wickes. The guy's a fraud, a thief."

Arching an eyebrow, she said, "Sam, the man's a friend of Father's."

"Remember when we had lunch here with Tom Wolf. You were telling us about Clemente and you said you would talk to your father and set up a meeting?"

"Yes, I said Father could shed some light on what goes on in the city."

"That's right. You said he had friends everywhere."

"He does."

Waving away her comment, McFadden continued. "I know. I was being a jerk that day. I said I had met some of your father's friends, had played golf with them. You asked me who they were and I didn't answer."

She nodded. "You WERE being a jerk that day."

Smiling sheepishly, McFadden conceded the point. "You're right. I apologize. Point is, Wickes and his dim-witted assistant, Storch, were the guys we golfed with that day."

"Is there a point to this conversation, Sam?"

"Give me a few more minutes. Wickes used to work for DynCorp, a big private military contractor. Couple of years ago they did a lot of construction work on the base, Camp Navarro. They had a contract to build a base-within-a-base for the American garrison. I was serving here at the time. It was a hush-hush deal. Lot of money involved. Wickes got caught with his hand in the till. Padding the payroll and kickbacks for materials. It must have been sweet while it lasted for him to risk that. When someone blew the whistle the company fired him. We're talking a lot of cash, Regina. It was a messy situation. They settled out of the spotlight. Wickes walked. He had guardian angels in high places. He stayed on here. Opened up his little security company. Farmed out guards to businesses and wealthy folks. Even did some sub-contracting for his old company through a shell corporation. Who knows what else he does? He's what cops back home call 'dirty.'"

"So what am I to do, Sam? I have a hotel to run. My father insisted we hire him. It's his money. He has an investment at stake. I'm just his hired innkeeper, after all."

"Sure. I get it. I just want you to know the kind of guy you're dealing with."

She pushed away her plate and stood. "If his people make the Blue Orchid more secure, what does it matter? I don't want to argue over this." Leaning over him, she kissed McFadden, caressed his cheek. "I miss having you around, Plain Old Sam."

He bussed the back of her hand. "My pleasure, lady. You have my number. Call anytime you have trouble getting to sleep." He rose beside her. "Go to work. I'm going to sit here and finish my coffee. I want to see if I approve of the way these Pan-Pacific wannabes are protecting you."

"And the Blue Orchid," she added.

"Of course," he said, sending her on her way. At the restaurant's door Regina pirouetted and blew McFadden a sultry kiss.

CHAPTER 27

With Wolf's blessing, McFadden reluctantly agreed to another round of golf with the general with one condition: that they play as a twosome. To his surprise, Rosario agreed. At nine o'clock, three days later, McFadden arrived at the Zamboanga Country Club to find the general sinking putts on the practice green.

Two golf carts were parked nearby—one loaded with two sets of clubs, the other with Rosario's ever-present shadow.

"I want to offer my condolences in the wake of your brother's death."

"Thank you, Sam. Those responsible will pay. I will see to that."

"Regina said you think Clemente's involved."

"It's his way of operating. He strikes out at anyone in his path. You've already felt his anger. He murdered my brother and bombed the Blue Orchid to get at me."

"My friend Wolf thinks you should strike back, sir."

Rosario swung his driver to loosen up. "If only it was that simple." Pointing his club at McFadden, he said, "Let's do the back nine first, Sam."

Filling his pocket with tees, McFadden raised an eyebrow. "That's because you have it wired, sir."

"Oh, how I wish that was true."

They rode to the tenth tee and parked, a foursome ahead of them. "Did you know General John Pershing founded this golf course, Sam?"

"I was unaware of that."

"1910. He was governor of what was then called Moro Province. I cannot imagine what this place must have been like. I do know who they pressed into service to clear the grounds, though."

McFadden kept his eyes on the foursome's second man who was taking his time to hit. "It was a different era, sir. Lot of misguided policies in place."

Rosario's face darkened. "It was a colonial mindset, Sam. Our people chafed under two different yokes: Spain, then America."

McFadden shifted uncomfortably, unsure where the conversation was going. "It took World War Two to break that cycle, General."

The last of the foursome hit and the party's two-cart caravan rumbled down the fairway. Climbing from the golf cart, Rosario fished a driver from his bag. McFadden joined him at the back of the vehicle. "You know why I like to play this course?" Before McFadden could answer the general said, "One, it's close to my house. Two, because Filipinos were banned from playing here . . . on our own soil. Did you know that?"

"I did not. I'm sorry to hear that, sir. A shameful legacy."

"All part of the so-called gentleman's game, Sam. Every round I play is one round for those long-dead souls who were denied the right to walk these fairways in their own land. It's a point of pride for me."

"I appreciate your sharing that, sir."

Mounting the tee, Rosario shot McFadden a caustic look. "Don't patronize me, Sam. These are just the musings of an old man. Colonial past be damned, I don't expect you to cut me any slack out of guilt."

McFadden took a practice swing. "I'm not sure Black Jack Pershing's ghost would want me to."

Rosario cracked his ball in the middle, 170 yards from the tee. "He'd be rolling in his grave just to see us riding together."

McFadden matched the general's drive and joined him in the cart. "How come you didn't mention this when Storch and Wickes played with us?"

Rosario pushed the accelerator to the floor and the cart leaped ahead. "It would have gone right over Burt's head. I've known the man for years and he hasn't a clue about our history or culture. Burt doesn't care about those things."

"I admit I was surprised to find out you knew him socially, sir."

Braking just short of the two balls, Rosario grabbed a three wood and nudged his ball. "We go back a number of years. It's complicated."

The subject of the general's relationship with Wickes didn't come up again. McFadden tried, was rebuffed, and backed off. The general's second shot sailed to the left but stayed in the short grass. "Your turn," a pleased Rosario said.

McFadden aimed left to compensate for his swing and connected. His ball arced, bounced once, and kept rolling. "I planned that," he said.

The general chuckled. "I'm sure you did. Nice shot in spite of your swing."

They drove ahead, the second cart discreetly trailing them. McFadden glanced back. "You ever go anywhere without your man?"

Rosario rolled to a stop near his ball, scrambled from the cart, plucked an iron from his bag. "Wouldn't think of it. Out here I'm relatively free. That's why I like to play. I don't follow a regular schedule and I don't play the same nine each time. I vary my playing partners and never golf with someone I don't know. Can't take chances, Sam."

"Like Wolf said, helluva way to live, sir."

"That's a price I don't mind paying. My brother thought me too suspicious. He was wrong." He lofted his ball short of the green. "Damn!" McFadden caught him on the hole, went one up. On the next tee, Rosario brought up the boat. "How soon do you put to sea?"

"In the next few days. Wolf's been handling the bulk of the work."

"I'd like to help," said Rosario. "How are your finances holding out?"

"We're pushing the envelope but money is not a problem. Thanks for your interest." McFadden drove into the woods, was offered a mulligan and took it.

Rosario fired a "worm burner" and pounded the tee in frustration. "You might take this hole. I can feel it."

As they drove to their balls, he turned to McFadden. "I'm serious about helping fund your dive boat, Sam. I always look for places to park some money. I think your idea is good for the local economy. You'll face tough competition for tourist pesos."

Uneasy, McFadden turned diplomatic. "Again, I appreciate your thoughts on our scuba business, but at present Tom and I have our plans pretty well set."

"With my involvement you would be in a stronger position politically."

Puzzled, McFadden asked, "You think there might be a problem we don't know about?"

"You can never tell with these things, Sam. I want you to think about it. With my backing you could shore up your position in local tourism markets. Same time you'll have clout you might need. Could even get you the rights to visit Tubbataha Reef." The hint caught McFadden's attention. A license to take divers to one of the Philippines's jewels was a dream. "Situations change quickly. Sleep on it. Call me."

"I'll do that. Thanks." They played the remaining holes without mentioning Wickes or the dive boat again. Rosario chatted about his daughters, Manila politics, and local elections. Catching McFadden on the last hole with his short game and putting, Rosario promised a rematch in the next few weeks. Cordial but wary, McFadden agreed and excused himself to get back to the city.

Rosario's man returned the cart and checked the bags while the general paced outside the clubhouse, cell phone to his ear, repeating his conversation with McFadden, word for word.

CHAPTER 28

On a calm day, when the Basilan Strait was like glass and the sun directly overhead, a hired thirty-foot banca flew across the ocean's surface like a graceful egret. The slender outriggers became wings, giving the craft remarkable stability. Standing on a stern seat for visibility, the boat's pilot steered with a long bamboo rod equipped with a small metal rudder. Trailing blue plumes in the wake, a converted truck engine roared with ear-pounding power, pushing the V-shaped hull effortlessly. Shaded by a rippling, white nylon tarp stretched over a frame of poles, Wolf, Ivy, McFadden, and Regina curled together, each couple facing the other on narrow cushioned benches. Snorkeling gear sat at their feet.

"Great for speed in perfect conditions," yelled Wolf. "Not so good if we hit waves on the way back." The men had chartered the banca and guide from a local dive shop. A trip to Big Santa Cruz was the only agenda for the day, the island's famous pink sand beach, snorkeling and a picnic on shore the draw. The charter—one of several they arranged—was actually another chance for Wolf and McFadden to scout their competition. They studied the other shop's fleets of available boats, scuba equipment, knowledgeable guides, and pricing. With the overhaul of their dive boat close to completion, the pair was busy doing homework on what the tourist traffic would bear. Ignorant of ulterior motives for the excursions, Regina and Ivy had accepted the invitation. A day away from claustrophobic city traffic and demanding jobs made the day trip a welcome diversion.

They arrived to find six outriggers of varying sizes drawn up on the pink sand. One boat, hosting a jam session with four guitarists, attracted a younger crowd. Strollers waded in the shallows searching for shells and coral scraps or played in deeper water offshore. McFadden directed their helmsman to a vacant stretch of sand with a backdrop of trees. The pilot cut his speed and dropped a stern anchor. With a practiced eye, he played out forty feet of line. As the boat glided ashore, the line tightened and held. Clapping his hands, Wolf stood and saluted the man's judgment. "Well done. Couldn't have done better myself."

Wading in knee-deep water, the guide muscled a wide wooden plank from the platform spanning the outrigger supports. He let it down in the sand. The foursome came down the ramp—McFadden with a cooler on his shoulders, Wolf with canvas bags stuffed with towels, dry clothes, and snorkel equipment. As his party disembarked, the pilot dragged a tethered anchor to the beach, burying its flukes in the rosy sand. With nothing to do for the next three hours, he went back on board and promptly stretched out for a nap under the boat's awning.

McFadden's party headed to the trees, spread towels in available shade, and shared drinks and snacks.

When they finished, McFadden took Regina's hand. "Let's walk for a while." Out of earshot, he asked about her uncle. "Tell me about Sonny. What was your history with him? Why did you get so riled up whenever his name came up?"

Regina shrugged. "Sonny was a disappointment to my father for as long as I can remember. Perhaps it was the age-old rivalry of brothers."

"Like Cain and Abel?"

"Oh, no. Not like that. My father never hated his younger brother. It just happened that Father was groomed for the military, went to West Point, and became a rising star in the officer corps. He led the fight against Marcos, then the Moro guerillas. As one of our nation's youngest generals he seemed destined for great things. Then, for some unknown reasons, his world fell apart. Mother left and . . . well, I've told you most of it."

"And your uncle?"

Regina looked down at the sand as they walked. "There was a time when my uncle was also a man with promise. He was popular with the people, easily won election to the senate, and was riding a wave of reform in the years after Marcos. He was thought to be presidential material. All his friends wanted him to run for the highest office."

"I was vaguely aware of the Rosario name when I was stationed here. So what happened?"

"It all went to his head. He fell in with the wrong crowd. You need lots of money to run for president. The men with money . . ."

Interrupting, McFadden said, "It's always men with money, isn't it?"

"Yes, at least with Uncle Sonny." She waded into the shallows and he followed. "He was so naive about the people he was dealing with. Some of them showered him with drug profits he knew nothing about. There was also plenty of financial support from those doing illegal logging, smuggling, building contracts, and such. But the crowning blow was the selling of army weapons to the Moros."

"Was it all true?"

"Some of it. Maybe most of it. Someone leaked the story to the tabloids just before his last election. Charges were brought against him but that's as far as it went. Of course, the news ended his career." She and McFadden retraced their steps. "With politics no longer an option he needed a way to make a living. He went into partnership with some of those same men with money. I'd like to believe my uncle didn't know one of those hidden partners was Clemente."

"The Kuratong Baleleng godfather? The one who sent his goons after Wolf and me?"

"The very one."

"How did that happen?"

"When my uncle was still in favor, Clemente's son Davido married Sonny's daughter, Maria, my cousin. I think it was a ruse on Davido's part to gain some legitimacy for his father. It didn't last. Davido was so cruel to Maria, unfaithful from the start. They divorced after one year. My poor cousin was so ashamed she moved to Manila to live with her mother."

"Was your uncle still involved with this gangster when he was killed?"

"No. There was bad blood after Father pressured Sonny to break off the connection. Clemente has always been a dangerous man. News of the relationship reflected badly on our family. I'm sure Clemente blamed Father for making my uncle break off the relationship."

"Why would your uncle need a partnership with Clemente in the first place? I thought he headed one of Zamboanga's biggest importers." They reached the spot where Wolf and Ivy were swimming.

"He did run the company. My father and some of his wealthy friends put together the business and funded it. Uncle Sonny was given a title and an office but staff actually ran day-to-day operations. He may have been the face of the company but everyone knew he didn't call the shots. Uncle Sonny always preferred to gamble, run up bills, and sleep around instead of putting in an honest day's work."

"And your father tolerated that kind of behavior?"

"Sonny was . . . family. That trumped everything for Father."

Wading into deeper water to join Wolf and Ivy, McFadden pulled Regina to him and asked a last question. "This makes your father sound like Cesare Borgia."

"I love my father, Sam, but his hand seems to be everywhere.

I don't want your dream to become something other than what you want it to be. Am I making any sense?"

"What I'm hearing is a daughter walking a fine line between loyalty to her father and telling someone she cares about not to get too close to the fire . . . the fire being her father."

"Even I don't know how many things he's involved with. He has a secretive side that no one knows about. I think he prefers it that way. The mystery of it."

"How about you? Do you prefer not knowing?"

"He's my father, Sam."

Their toes barely touched the sandy bottom. With arms around each other, their faces inches apart, McFadden said, "Your answer speaks volumes. If it makes you feel any better, he's not involved in our dive boat business."

Regina kissed him. "Good. But be careful, he'll probably find a way."

"Unless you're part of the deal," he whispered, "he doesn't stand a chance."

CHAPTER 29

Pouring over navigation charts, McFadden glanced up as Wolf came through the pilothouse door. "I'd say you had a good time yesterday, Wolfman. What do you think of Ivy?"

"Beautiful girl. Lively. Smart. Knockout body. Why you asking?"

"Regina's curious about your intentions. She likes the fact that the two of us are dating the sisters. But I know you sailor types."

"We get a bad rap, Green Beanie Man. Seriously, Ivy's fun. I enjoy her company but she's a kid, Sam. Hell, I've got a good fifteen-plus years on her. We don't have the same taste in music. I'm guessing now, but I'd bet that's probably true for movies, too. Look, she's a typical kid sister. Hanging around her older sister's boyfriends, watching how she handles things. I mean, don't get me wrong, I'm happy to have met her. I know she likes me. But if you're asking me if she's someone I could get serious about, forget it. That's my take."

Rolling up the chart, McFadden agreed. "I figured as much. I don't want you breaking her heart, Wolfman. Like you say, she's young and I don't think the general would appreciate having both daughters involved with Americans."

"Does that mean you're dropping Regina?" Wolf laughed. "Just a thought."

"Promise me you won't sandbag me with this girl."

"You'd better have 'The Talk' with her then. Better yet, get Regina to sit her down and have one of those heart-to-heart lectures big sisters are supposed to give. I'll do my best to keep her on the straight and narrow. Just make sure she gets the message that Regina's going to keep an eye on her. By the way, Rosario wouldn't be the first irate father I've had a run-in with. It comes with the territory, Sam. You cover your own ass when it comes to Rosario. I can handle mine. He's got that mean 'father's eye' when he sees you cavorting with his princess."

"You don't really know the guy."

Wolf shrugged. "Yeah, well, I'm familiar with the look. If I had a daughter I'd feel the same way. Ivy's old enough to make her own decisions. Like I said, I enjoy her company. How about we leave it at that."

"Fine with me. Mission accomplished. End of discussion."

"Okay, let's tackle something worth talking about. Like how we're going to get this boat in the water and make some money."

CHAPTER 30

Two o'clock in the morning—an hour when dogs slept under porches and contented hens are nestled safe in wire pens, an hour when the neighborhood is dark and quiet. Behind the walls of McFadden's house, Eddie's nephew, Remington shotgun across his lap, sat invisible in the shadows. He dozed, awoke, and drifted off again. Hearing faint engine noises, trucks not motorcycles, he snapped awake. Distant voices. His first thought was night shift workers or drunks arriving home. Coming from the barrio's outskirts, maybe the northeast, the sounds grew louder, clearer. Trucks! Trucks being driven hard by men on a mission.

He ran upstairs to awaken McFadden.

A dozen sondalos in two pickups, their lights dark, pulled in front of a house on the outskirts of the community. While drivers stayed with the idling vehicles, two hooded men armed with AK47s crouched by the trucks' hoods to cover their comrades. Eight masked men with M16s stormed the Romulo family's bungalow, pulling adults and children alike from their beds and scattering furniture. Bewildered, the six Romulos were herded into the dirt street and forced to kneel in their nightclothes, facing their home. Barking dogs raised the alarm. The men worked quickly.

Gasoline was splashed throughout the dwelling's interior and across the porch. As the black-clad assailants fled the wooden house, the last man tossed a lighted rag through the smashed front door. WHOOSH! The resulting ball of fire turned night into day. Sobbing, certain they were to be shot, the Romulos huddled together, wailing and praying. When ravenous flames began licking walls and roof, the hooded men fired shots in the air and jumped aboard the trucks. Yelling and shooting as they roared away, the attackers disappeared as quickly as they had come.

McFadden stood in his open gate, the scent of burning wood drifting across the densely packed roofs. Light from flickering flames washed his walls in yellow. Spotting Wolf on the balcony above, he yelled, "That's no accident!"

"You think it's a diversion?"

"No. My guess would be a message from Clemente."

Within minutes, firefighters arrived to battle the blaze. Too late to save the Romulos' home, the crews hosed down adjacent buildings to keep the flames from spreading. What had once been a family home for a half-century became a mound of glowing embers amidst a collapsing shell of blazing timbers. The reprisal had been swift, brutal, and complete. From start to finish, the terrifying attack had taken exactly eleven minutes.

On the heels of the fire crews came police. Adding to the chaos, the entire neighborhood poured into the streets. The Romulos were the only witnesses, but even they could give only sketchy descriptions of the hooded men and their trucks.

"There must be one hundred thousand pickups in this city," fumed a frustrated senior officer.

"Likely more than that," added another ranking cop.

On the barangay perimeter, police cars blocked access to neighborhood streets. Dawn arrived along with crime scene technicians whose only duties were shooting photos and collecting spent shell casings. Police tape marked off a rectangle of ash that had once been a home. Another family took in the Romulos. McFadden and Wolf worked through the crowd in the company of barrio elders. Knowing the fire raid had been in retaliation for the stout defense his neighbors had mounted on his behalf, McFadden suffered pangs of survivor's guilt.

Before the ashes had cooled, volunteers began clearing the site for a new house on the same ground. "Look at these folks," marveled Wolf. "They're living in poverty and yet they get right back in the fight. They're tough. There must be something we can do, Sam."

McFadden had a faraway look in his eyes. "I've got a bad feeling about this."

"It's payback, pure and simple," Wolf said. "Clemente's hand at work."

McFadden didn't disagree, but prophesied something darker. "First we have Sonny Rosario's assassination, then the bomb at the Blue Orchid. Now this. My gut tells me it's just the beginning. A small taste."

"Well, they sure as hell got my attention," said Wolf. "We need to be proactive. Organize fire watch committees. Get the cops to do more patrols. Set up some kind of early warning system for the entire neighborhood."

"How long do you think that would last? These people have been doing that since the botched raid on our place. We got complacent. Clemente will wait us out."

"Gotta do something, Sam."

Tapping his boot against a charred timber, McFadden lowered his voice. "We could talk to the general again. He predicted something like this. He knows how Clemente operates. We need a plan in place, Wolfman."

"Okay, go home. Tell Eddie what happened so he can get up to speed. Then, make the call to Rosario. I'll stay here to help."

"You're right. I'll be back for you later. I still feel like this was my fault."

Wolf's eyes bored into McFadden. "Okay. This is round one, Sam. Let's hear what Rosario has to say." He asked for a shovel and began sifting warm ashes in the ruins alongside other volunteers.

CHAPTER 31

"Just how many nephews does Eddie have?" Wolf chuckled at the thought. He and McFadden sat on the screened balcony. An overhead fan stirred muggy air.

"I've lost count," said McFadden. "I swear, everyone in the Philippines is related to him one way or another."

"Ain't that the truth." Turning to McFadden's silhouette in the gathering dusk, Wolf asked, "What made you decide to put off asking Rosario for advice and ask Eddie instead?"

"Gut instinct. If anyone knows this city it's Eddie. I told him what we were thinking and he said it was time to talk to his nephew instead of Rosario. Eddie respects the general but he says this kid is a cop who works the streets and knows all the bad guys."

"So you think this relative has something we need?"

"Maybe. Eddie claims he's with the intelligence section."

"Could be the guy's got an ax to grind, Sam."

Leaning forward to survey the courtyard below, McFadden whispered, "Guess we'll find out. He's here."

Eddie cracked open the steel gate, allowing a man pushing a bicycle to slip through the narrow opening. Once the visitor was behind the walls, Eddie shut and locked the gate.

Wolf peered at the two Filipinos in the shadows. "Let's go meet our guest."

Eddie introduced his nephew, giving a first name only. "Major Sam, Commander Wolf, this my nephew, Nathaniel." The silent man shook the Americans' hands.

Like Eddie, the guest was small statured, muscular, and clean shaven. Younger, but possessing the same hardened look as his uncle, the visitor shifted his obsidian eyes from McFadden to Wolf and back again.

"Shall we talk upstairs?" asked McFadden, gesturing to his entry.

"Is okay here," the visitor said nervously.

"Here it is then," agreed McFadden. "Your uncle seems to think you have information that may be helpful to my friend and me. Is he right?" An affirming nod, no words. "We're all ears, Nathaniel. Will this news perhaps cost us something as a sign of our good faith?" A sour look crossed the man's face as if he had been insulted.

McFadden read the expression and quickly apologized. "No offense, but you must realize people sometimes sell information to others."

"Not like that. I only tell you this because my uncle says you are good people. You saved General Rosario's daughter, yes?" McFadden nodded. "The woman, the killer you shot died that night. Did you know that?"

"I didn't miss. I assumed she had been badly wounded, yes."

"The man she rode with was Moises Castro, Clemente's top assassin." He passed a mug shot to the Americans. "Castro is manoy. Big man. Right-hand man to Clemente. Do you know Clemente is big boss, Papa Manong for Kuratong Baleleng?"

"We were told that, yes."

"Did you know the woman you killed was Clemente's child?" Bad news. McFadden was speechless. Keeping his eyes on Nathaniel, he didn't answer. "His only daughter. You understand? Clemente knows who you are. You are dead man, Major."

Shaken, McFadden said, "I had no idea who she was."

"You could not have known. Spare any thoughts of pity. She was a killer, born and bred for that by her own father. She was dead before they turned the corner. Her death and burial were never acknowledged."

"Clemente will kill you," added the cop. "You should consider leaving."

The news darkened McFadden's mood. "But I can't go. My life is here. I have friends. I have a future."

"Future?" The little man shook his head. "Major McFadden, I am policeman, okay? When I become policeman I am half-dead already, you know? I am part in the grave already. That is my choice. But you . . . you save a lady's life and put yourself in the grave without knowing. Only your head is above ground now, you see? Only a matter of time before Clemente comes for you."

Steeling himself, McFadden looked to Wolf for encouragement but the SEAL's eyes were fixed on the policeman. "Can the police help me?"

Nathaniel shook his head. "No. Only when Clemente is dead are you free . . . maybe."

"And he is a hard man to kill," added Eddie. "Many have tried."

"My uncle is right. Many have tried and failed. We know what Clemente is but we lack the will to bring him to justice. He has many friends in high places."

Wolf finally spoke up. "So you bring us this news. What are we to do? My friend cannot run away from a fight. He is not that kind of man. And I must stand by my friend."

"Ah, you too, are a marked man, Commander Wolf. Two years ago you killed Abu Bakr, yes?"

It was Wolf's turn to be surprised. "How the hell do you know that?"

"It was a brave thing you did. You are remembered by many, sir. The news at the time was big story. Abu Bakr was not so important a man but he had many friends in Abu Sayyaf. They don't forget. Now you both are here. If a man kills either of you he will have respect. If he kills both of you he will have a big name."

"It's ancient history," scoffed Wolf.

"Welcome to the club," said McFadden.

"What can we do? How can we get to Clemente?" asked Wolf.

"There is a way," suggested the cop. "Clemente has big weakness: women. When he wants to be with women he has many places to hide. Some in the city, some in Zamboanga del Norte. Sometimes he goes to Davao City."

"We call those 'safe houses' in America," said Wolf.

"Yes, this is the same."

"Then why don't the police arrest him if they know where he is?" asked McFadden. "Certainly you have many charges you can use to put him behind bars."

"We have done so before. But he would be out so fast and we would look like fools."

His frustration showing, McFadden asked, "Doesn't your department know how to bring him to justice?"

Smiling ruefully, the nephew said, "Before we leave the building to arrest him, he knows we are coming. When we arrive he is gone. There are too many birds listening. We have tried. His lawyers are well paid . . . as are some of the judges. For now he is safe. Untouchable."

"Do you know where Clemente is now?"

"Tonight?"

"Yes, tonight. Do you track him?"

"We have ways. He is not invisible."

Wolf stepped in. "Bottom line, Nathaniel. How much advance warning could you provide someone if they were trying to find Clemente?"

"It can be done."

"Say a person came to you and asked where this man could be found on a particular day or night. Could you supply that information to such a person?"

"It can be done."

"Would your department know how many bodyguards Clemente had with him on any given day or night? It would be important to someone who wanted to find Clemente, yes?"

"Of course. Why do you ask?"

Wolf's face was a grim mask. "I think we understand each other. Much is better left unsaid."

"I see. I did not come here to arrange such a thing, of course. Clemente's death would be a great service to the people of this city but I have only come to warn you."

McFadden put an end to the meeting. "Of course. And we appreciate your warning. I hope we can stay in touch. If your uncle is willing my friend and I would very much like to know what such a formidable adversary as Clemente is planning . . . or his whereabouts on a particular night."

"I understand what you are asking and I understand why you ask. I will do my best."

Handshakes were exchanged again. "Thank you for risking this visit."

Eddie scanned the deserted street and motioned for the cyclist to leave. Once through the steel gate his nephew kept to the shadows.

CHAPTER 32

Back on the balcony, in the dark with their thoughts, McFadden and Wolf sat a long time without talking. Wolf finally broke the silence. "We're in some really deep shit with this Clemente thing. You, my friend, are a HVT, like it or not."

"High value target. Not by choice. You've got a target on your back as well. Look, this is not your fight, Wolfman. I stepped into this without knowing the players. All I know is that I saw a woman in trouble. I acted. I took out a killer without thinking much about it. You would have done the same thing."

Sinking in his chair, Wolf mused. "Amen . . . and amen. You did the right thing, Sam. You are correct. I woulda done the same without blinking an eye. Damsel in distress. Evil sorceress. Gun in hand. What's there to think about?"

"We're boxed in, Wolfman. How can we put our business plan into motion when we have Clemente gunning for us? Don't know his M.O. but I'd guess he's not one for subtlety."

"None of these gangster low-lifes are," said Wolf. "Just like being back in South Central L.A. It's all strutting macho bullshit. 'My territory, my homies.' Gangbanger rules and street strategy. They're all Neanderthals, every one of em. Manila, Chicago, Medellin, L.A., Miami, or Zamboanga . . . all the same." McFadden went into the kitchen, grabbed two San Miguels, and returned to the dark balcony.

Wolf took one, ran it across his forehead, asked, "How's the boat tonight?"

"We're good. Sal and Andy are on top of it."

"Nice guys," mused Wolf, "but kinda numb-nuts, don't you think?"

"They're not warriors but they're teachable. They'll be fine."

"So, what are we going to do? Now that we know why Clemente's all hot and bothered about you, and I'm on some towel-head's list, what are we going to do? What's our plan?"

"You tell me," McFadden said hoarsely. "I've half a mind to pack up for Cebu or Leyte."

"Run from a fight? Not the Sam McFadden I know. Besides, say you move north. What's to prevent a guy like Clemente from using the coconut telegraph to put a price on your head with scumbags up there?"

"Or let the local jihadists know you're back in town," said McFadden.

"Yeah. There is that to consider."

"We could sell out while we still have a chance," said McFadden. "Maybe the general would see fit to take over the business. He said he's always looking for places to park his money. He likes me. I could feel him out. See whether he's interested. We might get back most of our money."

It was Wolf's turn to pace, bottle in hand. "I don't see that happening. He doesn't want to run a dive shop. He just wants to make his money work for him. Besides, without you there is no 'me.' And without both of us there is no *Laticauda* dive operation."

"Your money's at stake here, too, Wolfman. You have a vote, you know."

Flopping in his chair, Wolf brooded. McFadden stared at the sweating bottle in his hand and downed the contents. "Let's sleep on it. Maybe something will come to us in the morning."

Wolf wasn't listening. "What if . . ." he began. "What if we called some of the old team? Told them what we're facing, asked them to give us a hand to get us through this crisis. Call in some chits. Whadaya think they'd say?"

"I don't want their money in this, considering what we're facing here."

"I'm not talking about money, Sam."

"Then what are you saying?"

Sitting upright, Wolf slammed down his bottle. "I'm saying . . . focus on Clemente for starters. What if we got some of the boys to come down here for a visit? Just a looksee, nothing more. We tell them the risks up front. No shame if they wanted no part of this. We study the situation, put together a plan, and take out Clemente."

"Are you serious?" Incredulous at what his friend was proposing, McFadden stared at Wolf. "You ARE serious, aren't you?"

"Why not?"

"Because you're talking about doing something illegal in a foreign country . . . with weapons we don't have."

"You kidding? We could buy whatever we need on the open market."

"Are you listening? Didn't you hear Eddie's nephew? Even the cops and courts haven't been able to corral Clemente . . . let alone convict him. And if I know you, you're not talking about arresting this guy."

Wolf grinned. "Guilty as charged. But who knows better than us how to pull off something like this?"

"The Filipino cops are some of the toughest in the world, Wolfman. They know how to deal with dirt like Clemente. Out here, they have a target on their backs from day one. Out here, battling crime is like trying to shovel shit upstream at the lower end of a downstream sewer. Look what these guys put up with day in, day out. Think of how many of their fellow cops they bury each year. If they can't do it . . ."

Undeterred, Wolf thought out loud. "We have a situation on our hands and it's not going to get better. I know it sounds crazy. But if we put together a team we could do this. Just keep an open mind. That's all I'm asking."

McFadden was not convinced. "You're thinking as though we're still in Special Ops. We're civilians, believe it or not. We're guests, not citizens. Clemente is this government's problem, not ours." Retreating to the living room, he sank into an armchair.

Wolf followed him. "You're wrong on this one. Clemente IS

our problem. If the locals aren't going to do anything about him, it's up to us. We do it or we pack it in. It's a no-brainer for me."

"I'm gonna hit the rack. I can't think straight," said McFadden. "I'm not talking about this anymore. We never had this conversation." Pushing himself from the chair, he walked past Wolf and shut the bedroom door.

Wandering back to the balcony, Wolf plucked his bottle from an end table and replaced it with a fresh one. He wasn't done with McFadden, not yet. Not by a long shot. *You'll come around, Sam. I agree—it's crazy. But it could work. We could pull this off and realize the dream. Tomorrow is another chance to lay out what I have in mind. I know you. You'll listen. When you hear what I have in mind you might even sign on.*

CHAPTER 33

While Wolf and McFadden slept, Sal and Andy finished the final game in their late-night dominoes tournament. Slapping down the last ivory piece in triumph, Sal whooped in victory as his befuddled playing partner sat with head in hands. It had been no contest. Sal's ten fast-paced wins against Andy's two was a repeat of the night before. Solicitous in his tournament sweep, Sal tossed a morsel of encouragement at his friend. "Hey, mebbe you do bettah next time, eh?"

Andy waved away the words. "Just like always. You win. You nevah lose."

"Hey, you get me two times tonight. Be happy, eh. Go check the lines."

"I did already."

Busy stacking ivory tiles, Sal ordered, "Check 'em again."

Grumbling, Andy pushed from the salon table and went out on deck. He started with the stern and worked his way forward, checking the tension on each of the heavy hemp lines securing *Laticauda* to the wharf. There was enough slack to handle the tide. Finished with his assignment, he returned to the lighted main cabin where Sal was building himself a comfortable nest. Using cushions lining the salon's starboard-side couch, Sal settled in for the night with a final reminder. "One more coat of paint on the dive lockers tomorrow and we done."

Nodding wearily, Andy climbed the spiral staircase leading to his preferred niche, a sea-cabin tucked behind the bridge. One light was left burning in the passageway to the galley.

An hour later, neither of the two heard the distant droning of a motorcycle crossing the deserted ferry terminal pier. Only when the bike covered the last fifty meters of concrete did Sal rouse himself. By the time his feet hit the deck, the motorcycle had filled the main cabin with its roar, then idled dockside.

In the sea cabin, Andy launched himself from his narrow bunk in time to see a melon-shaped object arc in a trail of sparks toward the boat's bow. A wobbly gasoline-filled balloon hit the forward deck with a blinding explosion of flame. Scattering across the deck, droplets of gas ignited like hungry tongues of fire. Even behind the bridge's thick glass windows, Andy felt intense heat. On the pier, the bike rider and his passenger stood out, bathed in the yellow-white light. Just in time, Andy fell to the deck as the man on the backseat began firing a sawed-off shotgun at every window on the boat's port side. He kept pumping, firing as fast as his hands could jack shells into the gun's chamber. All told, he fired a half-dozen shots, though Sal and Andy would later swear it sounded like one hundred rounds. As quickly as they came, the hit team raced from the scene, the bike's tires spitting rock in their wake.

Crouching with a fire extinguisher in his arms, Sal fought his way forward, snuffing every spreading finger of flame he found. Andy had come down the ladder and was throwing buckets of seawater drawn from the mooring slip's dark waters. Sal went through four extinguishers before the fire was quenched. Choking smoke billowed in the night air. Embers floated across the harbor like fireflies. A distant siren sounded, heralding a fire truck's arrival.

Within twenty minutes, police raced to the scene. Officers cordoned off the pier and began a preliminary investigation. Damage to *Laticauda* was more than superficial. Ugly charred wood, a soot-smudged bridge, and a main salon reeking of gasoline and wet ash meant months of labor lost.

Disconsolate at the damage, ever more evident in dawn's raw light, Sal and Andy wandered the deck in grimy clothes, trying to salvage what they could. Fire investigators and detectives had completed a third round of questions by the time McFadden and Wolf arrived to survey the damage to their dream. Stunned by the destruction, they shuffled to the edge of the pier like sleepwalkers.

They took quick inventory of the damage to *Laticauda*. Mostly confined to the bow and forward deck, the fire had destroyed storage lockers, torched the pilothouse's skin, and filled the bridge with soot. Every window on the port side needed replacing. Blistered bulkheads in the main cabin and galley would need to be scraped and repainted. Every light fixture and piece of upholstered furniture was water damaged and beyond salvage. The salon's golden paneling—waterlogged and painted with soot like tear-streaked mascara—would have to be torn out. Almost every square foot of *Laticauda* had suffered—either at the hands of the arsonists or the well-meaning efforts of the fire crews.

Wandering through an inch of standing water below decks,

McFadden and Wolf kept their emotions in check. Wolf read
the bottled rage in McFadden's eyes but didn't speak to his
friend. The heart of the trawler was intact. The big Cummins
diesel had come through unscathed.

"Thank God for small favors," murmured McFadden, exam-
ining the machinery. "We need to get Sal and Andy busy with
pumps. Get this standing water out of the passageways and staterooms." Running on autopilot, McFadden grasped at straws to
keep himself in the fight. Pausing on the threshold of one of the
ruined cabins, he spoke to Wolf without looking. "How much
time do you think we'll need to get *Laticauda* shipshape?"

"Two, maybe three weeks tops to clean this up," replied Wolf.
"Won't be cheap."

"Don't I know," rued McFadden. "I'm . . . going to have to
talk to the general."

"Why? He may not be interested when he finds out how
much damage there is. Besides, you turned him down once
before."

Glaring, McFadden shot back. "That was business. This is
personal. My guess is he won't let this stand. He'll want to help."

"Question is . . . do we really need him, Sam?"

"Are you kidding? Look around. It's not like we have a choice.
There's no way I can get our original investor, Felix Cataldo, to
put up more money. He'd end up owning us. He's a dead end
for more investment. You and I have poured a lot of our own
money into this. I'm responsible. I talked you into this. I don't
know where else to go. Rosario has the kind of cash we need
to . . . fix this." McFadden kicked at a charred doorframe. "This
is all my fault."

"Stow it, Sam. This was Clemente's show. I'd like to pin his
sorry ass to the wall for this."

Gesturing at the smoke-smudged passageway and dirty water bleeding from the overhead, McFadden answered, "Get your mind off Clemente for now. We've got other priorities. We're nearly out of cash. Hell, we haven't even outfitted the galley. The electronics may be fried for all we know. The paneling in the passageway and cabins will have to be trashed. We paid an arm and a leg for all this stuff. On top of that, the prime dive season is one month away. Yeah, we need Rosario. You think we have a choice, Wolfman? You think I like the idea of going to him?" Staring at the damage, Wolf avoided eye contact with McFadden. "Yeah, we're gonna need him," McFadden said to himself.

"I should go with you," suggested Wolf.

"No. Better for you to stay here and get the cleanup started. Toss most of this. Get Sal to round up a cleaning crew. Andy can start stripping stuff we can't use. You can cover my six by staying here and running things. I'll be back as soon as I can."

"I got your back."

With a last disgusted look at the ruined surroundings, McFadden climbed topside. Twenty minutes later, after a hurried phone call, he was on his way to Rosario, heart in hand.

CHAPTER 34

Wolf's repair timetable was right on the money—Rosario's money. Three weeks later, under a flawless blue Mindanao sky and noonday sun, a bottle of champagne wrapped in white silk and tied to a nylon rope sailed through the air, exploding against the bow of a transformed fishing trawler. "I christen thee, *Laticauda*!" squealed Regina Rosario.

Beneath a white dockside awning, a small knot of onlookers broke into applause and a mariachi band launched into song. McFadden and Wolf, grinning like new parents, mingled with

Zamboanga's mayor, city hall officials, and police commanders. Local politicians, along with the commanding officer of the American garrison from nearby Camp Navarro, had been invited to the christening.

Shepherding a handful of McFadden's neighbors, Eddie and his wife made their way to the refreshment table. Later, the one-armed veteran left his Rose behind to join the curious on a tour of the *Laticauda* led by Wolf. Causing a stir of his own, General Rosario arrived fashionably late and pressed the flesh. He sought out McFadden on the vessel's bridge where he was demonstrating the boat's Furuno radar and depth finder to a baffled but polite couple. When Rosario showed, the guests excused themselves.

The two greeted each other warmly. McFadden took Rosario aside. "If it hadn't been for your help there would be no celebration today, sir." Hand on McFadden's shoulders, an expansive Rosario smiled paternally. "I did not foresee our partnership evolving the way it did, Sam. I'm just glad this old soldier could be part of your dream. I wish you and Wolf success in this adventure of yours. I know Regina feels the same. I've never seen her happier."

"We won't forget your help. Now, no more talk of business. Shall we join the others?"

"Go ahead, Sam. This is your party, your day, not mine."

McFadden moved through the crowd, greeting visitors and making small talk with the city's mayor and staff. In contrast with the fanfare of his arrival, Rosario slipped away without notice.

After three hours, the music, food, and tours ended. The crowd thinned. Leaving what little socializing remained to his partner, Wolf took his leave to begin preparations for sea. The plan was to use the rest of the day making a circuit of the Santa Cruz chain. *Laticauda* would do a coastal run long enough to test the Cummins diesel and navigation systems, yet short enough to call for help if serious bugs showed.

On shore, the band packed and drove away. The hotel caterers loaded tables, chairs, and tent into a truck. Sal and Andy were deputized to bag trash, a task they thought beneath them but which they finished with McFadden's help. Ivy and Regina changed into jeans for the test run.

While the engine warmed, Sal and Wolf stowed the gangplank. Andy tossed mooring lines on board and leaped to the stern. The Rosario sisters, wearing wide-brimmed straw hats and long gloves against the sun, came topside and took up station on the catwalk in front of McFadden. Easing the sixty-foot *Laticauda* from the terminal dock, he nervously threaded his way through harbor flotsam—a fleet of moored bancas and ugly hulks. Clear of the jetty, McFadden goosed the throttle.

On the stern, an exultant Wolf felt familiar engine vibrations beneath his feet. "Now we're going to see how she handles, boys!" Sal and Andy, his novice deckhands, exchanged wary looks. Wolf went forward, yelling to McFadden, "You need an experienced sailor, army boy? At this rate it'll take all week to circle the Santa Cruz Islands. Want me to show you how it's done?"

"Come on up, Wolfman. I'll give you the wheel while I look over the charts." Saluting, Wolf shot up the ladder to plant himself behind the wheel. "You ladies ready for some real cruising?" Ivy and Regina laughed at some private joke and came inside the pilothouse. After clearing the harbor, Wolf pushed for more speed and adjusted his course. McFadden came in from the catwalk, binoculars draped around his neck. He slapped Wolf's back. "Can you actually believe it? We're finally at sea. We're in business, m'boy."

"All you need are some tourists," squealed Ivy.

"Who have money and know how to spend it," added Regina.

"Who are crazy about living aboard for three grand per week," said McFadden. "Five dives a day, two dive-masters on board, great food and maid service."

Wolf boomed out, "If you launch it, they will come."

The sea trial was perfect. No glitches. No gremlins in any of the systems. Running at different speeds, Wolf put the *Laticauda* through her paces. With the sun starting its descent, he took the dive boat along the coast. In early evening's cooling air, McFadden and Regina went out on deck. The wind sent her long black hair billowing behind her. McFadden couldn't keep his eyes off the beautiful woman in his arms. With her head on his shoulder, he felt more alive than he had in months, wanting to prolong the moment. The spell was broken by a clownish Sal dragging a long-handled boat hook and rubber bumpers across the deck. Unaware of the couple, the deckhand headed to the bow.

Sighing, McFadden kissed Regina and rose, pulling her with him. "All good things must come to an end. We'll be docking soon. How was your day, lady?"

Throwing her arms around his neck, she whispered, "Wonderful. To tell you the truth, I like this better than the hotel business."

"I take that as a hopeful sign," said McFadden. She climbed the ladder to the bridge, leaving McFadden to supervise the arrival. Gently kissing the concrete pilings, Wolf babied *Laticauda* alongside the terminal pier without mishap. McFadden jumped to the quay and secured the lines. Sal and Andy ran out the gangway and tied it down. Wolf cut the engine as the sun sank into a glowing copper harbor.

"How'd she handle?" asked McFadden from the dock.

"Perfectly. Responded to the slightest touch. Couldn't ask for a better outcome."

"Glad to hear it."

"The boat did well, too." Wearing a wide grin, Wolf hooted at his double entendre. "Hey, what can I say? I was multi-tasking." He went into the pilothouse and began shutting down systems. Ivy Rosario sauntered onto the catwalk and came down the ladder, a dreamy smile on her face. Regina stared at her sister without saying a word. The two went up the gangplank hand-in-hand, McFadden walking behind the women to his pickup.

He kissed Regina. "Tom will drive you and Ivy home. It's my night with the boat, remember?"

Her disappointment showed. "I forgot. Call me tomorrow. Promise?"

"Wouldn't miss it for the world."

Wolf strolled by McFadden, whistling the theme from the ancient TV show *The Love Boat*.

"I never cared much for that one either," yelled McFadden after him.

"Different strokes for different folks, man. *Star Trek* was better," retorted Wolf over his shoulder. The truck rattled away, leaving McFadden in the dark with Sal and Andy for company.

CHAPTER 35

Two days passed before disaster struck McFadden's neighbors again. This time a single pickup loaded with six masked men attacked just before dawn. The results were the same. Forcibly evicted from their home, a terrorized family watched helplessly as fire devoured the vacated house in minutes. Police and fire units arrived in time to keep the flames from spreading but too late to trap the perpetrators. The firemen were efficient. The police sympathetic but impotent. Seeded with sparks, a pall of acrid smoke drifted over the gathered crowd. Mounds of glowing embers and charred stumps were arson's mute reminder of the price being exacted by Clemente for defending the American in their midst.

At the scene to console neighbors, McFadden heard sotto voce murmurs of dissatisfaction about his presence in the neighborhood. The unsettling comments were the first crack in what until then had been a wall of solidarity. Bottling his emotions, McFadden returned to his house where he found Wolf cleaning the shotgun.

"How'd it go out there?" Wolf asked. "More of the same?"

"Another fire-bombing. The natives are restless. They're starting to grumble."

"You're not surprised, are you? I expected as much. How would you feel if it was your home? Unless you pack up it's only going to get worse. There will be a third house, then a fourth . . . ."

Sighing, McFadden said, heavy-laden, "Yeah, I know." He paused, his brow narrowing. "Okay, enough is enough, call your boys."

"I already did. They're on their way."

Puzzled, McFadden said, "What? When did you make that call?"

Wolf rammed a freshly oiled patch through the Remington's barrel. "The day after Eddie's nephew the cop came to see us."

McFadden hissed, "Without telling me?"

"Knew you'd come around eventually, Sam. Thought I'd save us some time."

"Damned risky if you ask me. What if I had said no?'"

Threading a new patch in the cleaning rod, Wolf laid the gun across his knees. "There is no 'what if.' It's a done deal."

With new energy, McFadden took to the stairs. "How many? When?"

Pushing the clean patch through the barrel, Wolf glanced at

his friend. "Three. They should be here in eight or nine days. Standup guys. Served with all of them."

"Guess we'd better do some homework before they show. The least we can do is to have an op plan in hand for them to look at."

Wolf called after him. "Outstanding. First thing tomorrow. And Sam . . ."

His foot on the top step, McFadden turned. "What?"

"About calling my guys. Trust me, you wouldn't have said no."

CHAPTER 36

Wolf's three-man team of retired SEALs arrived in Zamboanga eight days later. They came separately and from three different directions. The less attention paid, the better. Milford "Shorty" Severson, a wiry veteran sniper with perfect vision and twelve years in the teams, arrived on a midday flight from Honolulu, via Manila. He took a taxi to the Blue Orchid Hotel and went to a room where Wolf waited.

From San Diego, "Tiny" Tim O'Neill flew to Manila, stayed one night, and caught a ferry the next morning. On his arm, the six-foot-four, long-haired, bearded man sported an eager-to-please Zamboanga-bound Filipina he had met in the hotel's bar. On arrival, he shed the woman and took a taxi to the Blue Orchid. He had a short reunion with Shorty Severson and Wolf, then waited until dark to drive to McFadden's house.

One day behind Tiny, former special operations chief Denny "Preacher" Hackett boarded the next day's ferry but kept his distance from fellow tourists. Traveling the farthest, the bearded Minnesotan had taken Wolf's call while remodeling a log home overlooking Lake Superior. Like his fellow SEALs, a call for help from Wolf was not one Preacher would have turned down.

That pull of loyalty, plus the promise of a fight, had settled it for him. Met at the ferry terminal by Sal, Preacher was driven to McFadden's home.

Despite the reason for the gathering, the reunion was loud and joyous. Even McFadden was caught up in the SEALs' celebratory mood. After numerous toasts with sweating bottles of San Miguel and a sumptuous meal served poolside by Rose Delgado, the five men went upstairs to McFadden's dining room. The big table was covered with photographs and maps of the city and its coastline.

"Thanks for interrupting whatever you were doing," said McFadden. "We're in a tough spot here. I appreciate your coming on such short notice. Wolfman will brief you. We've worked up an op plan. Can't lie to you. This is gonna be very dicey, gentlemen."

"Sam's right," Wolf began. "Let me add my thanks as well. The two of us have our backs to the wall. One thing we have going for us is that we're dealing with sloppy people who only operate in one style: whacking folks to get their way. Not much sophistication in the way they conduct business, though they are good at what they do. On the down side that means they don't care about collateral damage. They're also used to challenging police on their own turf. That said, let me lay out what we know for sure and then you can pick out the flaws."

For the next hour, Wolf ran through a profile of Clemente and a chronology of events, beginning with McFadden's intervention in the attempt on Regina Rosario's life. Following that, he sketched an op order he and McFadden had put together to eliminate Clemente, then asked for questions.

"Let me get this straight," drawled Tiny, beer in hand. "This guy runs his own little army, parks his sorry ass in a waterfront fortress, and is set on taking out you and our friend McFadden here."

"That's it in a nutshell, Tiny."

"There are five of us. How many of them?"

"Could be twenty-to-one odds. We'll get good numbers from our cop source."

Tiny continued. "None of us came in-country packing. We have no armory, no communications gear, and no way to get around. How do we fix that?"

Wolf held up his hands. "We'll have access to all those things. We're at the planning stage, Tiny."

Preacher, the group's lone teetotaler, followed Tiny's questions with two of his own. "What's the timetable? What's our exit strategy? Do we have an ex-fil plan?"

Stepping in for Wolf, McFadden said, "Good questions. We need to get the logistics taken care of to your satisfaction. As far as hauling ass when we're done . . . we think we've got a workable ex-fil plan. We have just one week to get set up."

An audible groan escaped from the trio. "Yeah, I know," McFadden said, "it's extremely tight but we may have no choice given the way things are moving. As for the gear . . . I'm responsible for lining up whatever we'll need. Wolfman will fine-tune the ex-fil plan. We'll spend this week doing covert surveillance in Clemente's backyard. When we're satisfied with what we know and I've got the weapons, commo, and transportation lined up, we'll go in. Not before."

Rubbing his hand together, Preacher liked what he heard. "We get to snoop, shoot, and scoot just like the old days. It's great to be down range again."

"I'm with Preacher," said Shorty. "It's all good. Get in, get the hit, get out."

"We're going to need your demo skills, Shorty. Getting inside Clemente's crib won't be easy. Once we're done, we may need some fireworks for diversion."

"I can handle that."

Preacher let out a low whistle. "Any remote chance we'll have more than one week to do this?"

McFadden was apologetic. "We don't have time on our side. Clemente likes to drop out of sight every so often. We think he's due for one of his disappearing acts soon. Gotta go with the intel we've got on this bad boy."

Uncapping another bottle, Shorty raised it to his lips, paused, and asked, "What about cops? Any help there or are they gonna be a problem?"

Wolf took the question. "That's our one source, a good one, inside their shop. We'll know where Clemente is at all times. We marry that with our own intel and we'll get a good shot at this guy. But this is strictly an off-the-reservation operation, Shorty. As a department, they're not going to be an asset for us."

"Might be trouble if we step in it," added Wolf.

"That's not helpful," said Shorty. "They could hang us out to dry if we fail."

"We don't have that option," boomed Tiny.

"That's why you're here," replied Wolf. "If we had more guys, Clemente's eyes would make us before we had a chance for our house call." The room fell silent. "Okay, that's it for now. You guys need to acclimate and get some serious rack time. Preacher and Shorty bunk here with Sam. Tiny stays with me out back in the guesthouse. We'll share security duties with Eddie and his nephew. Sam's got some of his own hardware on site. And we have a schedule made up."

He gestured to McFadden, who explained. "Stay in the compound, out of sight, unless you're doing recon on Clemente. We'll do that around the clock in pairs, starting tomorrow. Once we're satisfied we know this asshole's schedule better than he does we'll hit him, and not before."

"I'll take the first watch, midnight to two," volunteered Wolf. "Sam after me, Shorty after him, then Preacher and Tiny. Let's get you guys settled in your quarters. The fridge in both houses is always open. Get plenty of liquids. We've stocked water, beer, juice, and more beer. Help yourself. Remember, keep a low profile even if you're not on recon. You guys look like you've taken care of yourselves but feel free to use the pool and weights if you need it."

Rising and stretching, Preacher yawned. "Well, if you'll excuse me, gentlemen, I am going to head for the rack. I need my beauty sleep."

"In that case," drawled Tiny, "you'd best stay in bed for a month."

"Same old Tiny, always full of compliments. Just like the old days."

"Welcome to Zambo, boys," said Wolf. "Save your pillow talk for Clemente."

CHAPTER 37

In four days' time the SEALs had what they wanted. Their surveillance skills were still sharp. Added to daily reports about Clemente's whereabouts from Eddie's policeman nephew, McFadden's crew soon had a working profile about the gang leader's routine. However secretive Clemente may have been in his dealings with others, or mercurial in temper, he was a creature of habit. It was a failure due to the man's arrogance but a godsend to Wolf and his fellow SEALs.

Tiny first noted the weakness. He plotted the routine on a wall chart after comparing notes with the others. "He's a night owl, guys. Sleeps till noon. Gets up, has a late breakfast meeting with his cronies in a little café steps from his marina gate. They always sit at the same table in the back. He keeps one pair of eyes on the street, another at the doorway. He stays an hour or so, talks business, and then goes back to his ivory tower in the yard. His son, Davido, usually stays there with him all day unless the old man has a mission for him. Otherwise, they're both up there in the tower. Top floor of three. He's got layers of security on the first two floors. Hard to take him out there."

Wolf said, "There's a catwalk, Tiny. We thought about a long shot. Two, three hundred yards depending on your hide. Piece of cake. We could reach out and touch him and be miles away before it hits the fan."

Tiny thought for a moment and dismissed the idea. "If—and it's a big if—this asshole were to cooperate and stand our there in plain sight, yeah. Too risky waiting all day for a shot that may never come. Plus, we don't have gear for that."

In a sleeveless T-shirt and shorts, Preacher got up from the couch and walked to the wall. Laying his hand on O'Neill's chart, he traced their target's rhythms. "Once he's inside the yard, Clemente's cocooned pretty much all day. Hard to get to him. Too many witnesses. Too much foot traffic. Unless he's off to a whorehouse he's untouchable except for—"

Shorty jumped to his feet, joining Preacher at the chart. "The breakfast club."

"That's what Wolfman and I thought," announced McFadden. "We hit him first thing in the morning before he gets back inside the yard. Once he's there, he's behind walls and out of reach. It has to be the café. Otherwise we'd be sitting there all night waiting for him to visit one of his girls. Which one would that be on any given night? And what if he's got a headache?" Chuckles broke out among the men. "Anyone disagree?" Letting his comments sink in, McFadden raided the refrigerator for chilled bottles of beer. He tossed them to Wolf, Tiny and Shorty.

"I hate the idea of giving up cover of darkness," said Wolf, "but we can't predict where he's going to be at night. Even our cop friend won't know for sure. We only get a fix on the target once he reaches his destination. Too iffy."

"I agree," said Shorty. "The café is the only sure thing. He's in a routine with that spot. I vote for 'Clemente's House of Pancakes.'"

All eyes shifted to Wolf. "That's what we originally thought. Looks like it's the café. That works for me. Clemente feels comfortable there. Question: besides the two goons Tiny talked about, how many of his guys are with him on any given day and what are they packing? Let's iron out the details. I'll finalize the ex-fil route. Shorty, tell me if you need frags, flash bangs, or smoke for a diversion. Tiny, you and Preacher figure out the hit. Sam and I will line up gear, commo, and wheels. We good with this?"

Silence.

"Okay, let's get to work. We'll break for lunch at twelve-thirty hours and go over the plan. Meantime, if you see flaws, something we've missed, bring it up."

Despite their planning it was not to be. As he was known to do, Clemente dropped from sight. Surveillance turned up nothing. Until they heard from their police contact, Clemente was a ghost.

To keep the team intact and in shape, McFadden and Wolf put together a dive trip. Regina had introduced Australian guests at the Blue Orchid to McFadden. On a Pacific jaunt, the four experienced divers, tanned and blond—a married couple and a pair of lovers—were quickly enamored by the idea of a four-day, live-aboard expedition. Arrangements were made with a handshake over rum dessert. Wolf warned his team to be on their best behavior. Clemente would be given an unearned reprieve in exchange for four days in the sun. Diving seemed preferable to stalking.

CHAPTER 38

A sleek black outrigger with a hull shaped like a saber came ashore at General Rosario's estate during a brief squall that drowned out its engine's throaty roar. Using a slender cell phone tower's blinking red eyes as a landmark, the helmsman aimed the long hull at the beach and cut his engine. Piercing a curtain of rain, the outrigger grounded on gritty sand. Eleven men wearing black, military-style uniforms and web gear filed from the boat with practiced precision and took up positions in waist-high brush. Each hooded man carried a loaded AK47, four thirty-round magazines in chest harnesses, and grenades. They broke into two teams of five, four in each group carrying two sections of twelve-foot bamboo ladders. Two raiders stayed behind, kneeling by the outrigger, weapons ready.

The group's point man sprinted ahead to the base of the estate's concrete wall and crouched, listening. With a wave, he sent both teams forward. Two men on each team propped their ladder against the wall and held it as a second pair scaled it, carrying their own section. At the top of the wall, they slid their ladder section forward until it hit the ground, the sound muffled by the rain. Crabbing up the ladders, the marauders came down inside the walls and lay prone, rifles tucked into their shoulders. In teams of two, the masked men dashed forward. Just as they were about to reach the big house, the rain lifted.

At the far end of the house a door opened. An armed guard emerged with a dog. Sniffing the moist air, the canine suddenly barked in alarm. Tugging at its leash, the big dog led its handler toward a towering banyan where a pair of raiders pressed against folds in the wrinkled trunk. Suspicious, the sentinel called over his shoulder. A second armed man emerged from the house. Releasing his dog, the first guard drew a pistol and flashlight, pointing both at the barking dog circling the banyan. One shot felled the guard, another the dog. From the house, automatic fire slammed into the tree's thick trunk. The second sentry was firing from the shadows. The attackers stormed the house. One of them went down in a burst of bullets.

A shadow fired from an open window on the darkened second level, hitting two raiders. When the guard on the ground floor changed magazines, an attacker rushed him, spraying shots from the hip. The sentry went down. Firing erupted from another side of the house. The raid's leader sent two of his men in that direction. They killed a third watchman along with another dog. Stepping over a fallen guard, two hooded raiders entered the house's first floor and moved from room to room, Kalashnikovs at the ready. At the bottom of the stairs, one of them went down in a burst of bullets fired from the landing at the top. Sheltered behind a wall, the team leader hurled a grenade at the upstairs hallway. The blast showered glass from a chandelier, filling the stairway with glass shards, dust, and plaster. Ordering two men up the stairs, the group's commander crept behind them as they cleared each room. At the back of the house, in the master bedroom, they discovered an open window, a knotted rope tied to a bed frame. The room's occupant—Rosario—gone.

Time was running out. Having missed the man they had come to kill, they backtracked down the stairs and barged into the living room. Two who survived the upstairs assault tallied their losses with three who swept in from the garden. "What have we so far?" rasped their leader.

"Sapdula and Jammar are dead. . . ."

"Fool! No names! Give me numbers."

"Two killed, two wounded."

"What of the others? Have they searched those outlying houses?"

"They haven't reported in. The general's out there. He's armed."

"He wouldn't be foolish enough to try us."

"Should we burn the house?"

"It doesn't matter now." Glancing at his watch, the headman gave an order. "Tell the others we must leave."

"What about . . ."

"Carry them. No bodies left behind. Go, check on the others. Move!"

Rain began to fall again, lighter this time. The men went through the house and grounds, shouldering the fallen, helping the wounded to the beach. Shouts from one of the estate's cottages caught the leader's ear.

"Jefe, over here!" Two raiders dragged a disheveled, barefooted woman between them, her nightgown torn and muddy.

"Who have we here?" The chief roughly grabbed the woman's chin in gloved hand. "Ah, Frances Yadao, yes?" Defiant, she remained silent. He struck her. The woman sank to her knees in the grass, distraught.

"Ah, Senora Yadao, despite you say nothing we know you are the general's whore." She kept her eyes on the ground.

"Two more, Jefe!" Four of the hooded team arrived with a tiny older woman— Rosario's housekeeper, Amihan—and a companion in tow. Arm in arm with a younger, glowering female, the general's servant and Ivy Rosario were thrust into the circle of men alongside Frances Yadao.

Pointing at the dark-haired scowling captive, the man in

charge crowed, "Rosario's youngest daughter." Pleased with the take of hostages, he said, "Excellent. Bring them!"

"What about the general?" The men tied the women's hands behind their backs with plastic flex cuffs.

"No time. We have the daughter and Rosario's woman. Is enough for now. Quick! To the boat."

As quickly as they had come, the raiding party left with their prizes. Having missed their chance at Rosario, holding his daughter and mistress was the next best thing they could have hoped for. The housekeeper would serve another purpose.

Aboard the boat, their heads covered with filthy sacks, the bound women were rolled in blankets to be hidden. Heading north, the outrigger hugged the coast.

Wedged between two stiffening corpses, Ivy Rosario wept silently. An hour passed. She slept and awoke to groans of the wounded filling her ears. *Father will come*, she told herself. *He will come and take me home. These fools will fall on their knees and plead for mercy when he finds them. He will come and he will kill them.*

CHAPTER 39

On the morning of October 23, 1944, the *Yogaku*, a Myoko-class heavy cruiser launched in March 1928, went to the bottom of the Sulu Sea in eighty feet of water off a small uncharted island 100 miles southeast of Palawan.

The doomed *Yogaku*, part of Vice Admiral Shoji Nishimura's Southern Force, lies half-buried on its port side, shrouded in soft corals, a reef home to myriad sea life. The 662-foot cruiser's trio of forward turrets is the haunt of eels, sharks, and gliding rays. Fifty feet below the surface, silenced eight-inch guns aim at vast schools of rainbow-colored fish. In long-abandoned open turrets, small crustaceans and angelfish share their home with anti-aircraft guns muzzled by soft corals. Visibility on *Yogaku* is forty feet at noon on good days, one-quarter that after a storm. The rare dive boat anchors between the wreck and an unnamed island two hundred yards away. Awed snorkelers drift the length of the huge Japanese vessel, taking in the unforgettable sight of one of the Imperial Navy's warships. Venturesome divers can gain access to the *Yogaku's* interior through its massive slanted funnels or the gaping hole aft that was once turret number four. Porcelain dishes, bowls, and sake sets can be found scattered in the officer's mess—now a dim underwater cavern. Exploring the *Yogaku* is not for the timid. The more daring among the dive party can work their way to the lower decks through claustrophobic corridors overgrown with tumorous coral and filled with two feet of silt. They do so at their own risk.

Seventy years after the *Yogaku's* sinking, *Laticauda* raced a dying sun to the remote, crescent-shaped reef where the 11,633-ton ship lay in its underwater grave. On board were McFadden and his team. Serving as deckhands, Sal and Andy had signed on in exchange for full-time employment, three squares, and onboard quarters. With Regina's help, McFadden had hired a cook, Sylvia, and her divemaster husband, Roberto. Escorted by a dozen spinner dolphins, the dive boat anchored between the wreck and the deserted, forested ten-acre island ringed in pristine white sand. Leaping alongside the converted trawler until bored, the gray-bodied cetaceans rocketed away as darkness fell.

On the bow, McFadden checked Sal's handling of the twin anchor lines. Satisfied, he climbed to the bridge where Wolf paced behind the wheel. "We're good, Wolfman. Two anchors set. Plenty of line played out. We're okay for the night."

Wolf relaxed. "Just in time. We have about ten minutes of light left."

"I'm going below," said McFadden. "Chow should be ready soon."

"Gonna check weather reports one more time," said Wolf.

In the galley, Sylvia and Roberto put finishing touches on the evening meal. Small white lights shimmered in the awning above a dinner table set on the stern. What wind there was had died, leaving a gentle breeze cooling the night. Preacher and Shorty claimed seats at the table and traded war stories from their time in the teams. Tiny showed, adding his tales. With the exception of Preacher, alcohol fueled the evening's camaraderie. The two Aussie couples, the boat's inaugural customers, sat mesmerized by the trio's tall tales, the women in particular—much to their male partners' envy.

McFadden took a chair and talked about the next day's dive. Halfway through his description of diving on the *Yogaku*, a smiling Wolf joined the party. "Everything okay with the weather?" asked McFadden.

"We're good to go," Wolf answered. "We might get a bit of rain late afternoon. There's a low working its way in our direction but nothing to worry about for our morning dive. If the rain stirs up the bottom we'll try another spot." Turning to team members and the Aussies, he added a caution. "Keep in mind the *Yogaku* is a bit challenging. Stick with basics. Plan our dive and dive our plan. It's a team thing, folks."

Sylvia and Roberto came bearing dish after dish and the group dug into the stir-fry and rice enthusiastically. Preacher rose from the table, slipped in a DVD of previous dives on the *Yogaku*, and hit the play button. As they ate, wartime newsreels, spliced with ghostly images of divers exploring the sunken ship, flickered across the screen. By the time dessert and coffee arrived, the rapt audience felt as if they had actually been aboard the warship. After lingering over cigars on the upper decks, the men, including the Aussie husband and friend, traded small talk about previous diving trips until one in the morning. McFadden and the boat's crew stood watch through the night. Running lights and a small white strobe at the top of the mast marked their anchorage until dawn.

CHAPTER 40

Though the image was grainy and at times unfocused, the work of amateurs, the threatening message was clear enough. A pair of masked men forced a grim-faced Amihan to her knees. Pacing behind the diminutive servant, a bolo-wielding figure in military fatigues waved his weapon menacingly. A ragged off-stage voice threatened all three captives with a gruesome fate if a ransom was not forthcoming. To underscore his point, the voice ordered Amihan beheaded. The blade rose and fell in a blurred arc. The housekeeper's head thudded to a dirt floor, her frail body toppling forward in a fountain of blood. A cacophony of panicked shrieks flooded the scratchy soundtrack—Ivy and Frances Yadao.

Refusing to break, despite the image of his faithful housekeeper's headless corpse in blood-soaked dirt, General Rosario replayed the DVD for the fifth time. He grimaced at the sound of Frances Yadao's halting voice. "Pablo, listen carefully to what these men ask of you. We are being well treated. Amihan did not have to die. Until now, they had not harmed us. You will be contacted. Please, for our sake, Pablo, do whatever they ask." Sentinels in masks remained silent, threatening. Behind Rosario's kneeling mistress the general saw his daughter, arms bound behind her, a masked gunman hovering over her, bloodied bolo at his side. Ivy did not voice an appeal but the terror in her eyes spoke volumes.

"Turn it off," barked Rosario.

Nodding at a policeman, Burton Wickes ordered the portable player shut down. "How did you get this DVD?" he asked.

"One copy went to the newspapers," said the cop, "others to the local television affiliates, and one to our headquarters."

With a visibly distraught Rosario sagging in the leather chair behind his desk, Wickes spoke for the general. "What plans do the media have for this video? Will they hold it back until the kidnappers contact the general?"

The cop shrugged. "Perhaps if the general made a personal appeal . . . ."

"No!" bellowed Rosario. "I will not give them satisfaction."

"But sir, your daughter . . ."

Smashing his fist on his desktop, Rosario bristled in defiance. "I cannot appeal to these animals! You understand? Your department must find my daughter and Senora Yadao and bring them back unharmed! What are you doing to accomplish that end, Lieutenant?"

Shaken by the outburst, the officer retreated. "We are doing everything we can, sir. I must return to headquarters and initiate new search measures immediately."

"Has the army been notified?" asked Wickes. "The general has many friends there."

"We have not been in touch with the defense forces, sir."

Glowering at the junior officer, Rosario growled, "I am going to call Colonel Santos and bring him into the search. Inform your superiors when you return to headquarters. This affront must not stand. Do you understand?"

"Of course, sir. We will do everything we can. Every resource we have will be thrown into the search for the members of your household, I assure you."

"See that it's done," sighed Rosario. "I want you to monitor my phones in case these scum call me with demands."

"It will be done, sir."

"See to it yourself, Lieutenant. I hold you responsible."

The man paled under pressure. "Of course, sir. I understand. I'll have my men here within the hour."

A solicitous Wickes ushered the flustered policeman from Rosario's study. At the driveway, the porcine American cautioned the visitor. "Use what influence your office has to keep the video from being broadcast until we can see what we're up against. Also, see that your communication technicians return here immediately. The general will also require extra security, perhaps a squad of officers to keep the curious away until we can conclude this matter."

Retreating to the safety of his car, the policeman assured Wickes he would follow up on all the suggestions. "Please assure the general I will do my best."

"He'll expect nothing less, Lieutenant." Wickes's voice turned silky. "I have confidence in your skill to do just that." The jeep roared away.

A pair of Pan-Pacific Security men in khaki uniforms strolled past, M16s slung over their shoulders, radios clipped to their belts. With Rosario's guards dead or in the hospital, the general's security was in Wickes's hands and the American was determined to keep it there.

CHAPTER 41

In the morning after a light breakfast, the ship's dive master, Roberto, readied the party's buoyancy vests with tanks and regulators. Wolf and Shorty, each guiding one couple, would lead the Australians in a preliminary dive on the sunken warship. Sal and Andy wrestled an inflatable into the sea, mounted an engine on the plywood transom, and tied it alongside. As Andy started the small outboard and let it idle, McFadden lowered a two-gallon can of gasoline, then a soft-sided cooler packed with bottles of water and snack bars. Exchanging places with Sal, Shorty knelt on the rigid gunwales. Wolf handed him six weight belts. Dressed in identical black short-sleeved wet suits, the Aussie men handed off their women to Shorty and joined them in the rubber boat. Last in, Wolf scrambled aboard, worked his way to the stern next to Shorty. The dive party pushed away from *Laticauda*.

Accelerating across the glassy sea, its blunt bow raised above the turquoise water, the rigid inflatable reached the *Yogaku* in minutes. With the sun two hours from its noon peak, the ghostly outline of the ship hovered below their starboard bow. In mask, snorkel, and fins, Wolf, with ninety feet of tethered nylon line in his hand, slipped over the side. Stroking forward, he pulled the rubber boat behind him. Spotting one of the warship's coral-encrusted guns, he gulped a mouthful of air and dove beneath the surface. Behind him, one of the Aussie men played two-thirds of the line. Long minutes passed before Wolf surfaced behind them. "We're good!" he shouted. He swam to the boat, wriggled aboard, and rested in the bow to catch his breath.

Pushed by a cooling breeze, the little boat drifted until the line held, taut against what little current there was. "We're tied off to one of the big guns. Water clarity is outstanding. Check your partner's gear one last time. We'll start down when you folks are ready." Crabbing to the stern to fasten a weight belt around his waist, Wolf said, "Remember, Shorty leads the Harpers. I lead Valarie and James. Stick together. Don't make us come after you." Nervous laughter. "We'll have plenty of time to make a second dive after lunch so don't get anxious. We're not going below sixty feet on this dive. Questions?" His grinning charges shook their heads. Wolf slipped into his dive vest with a tank and tested his regulator's airflow. He threw his legs over the side and finned a short distance from the boat.

The four Aussies and Shorty tumbled backwards from the inflatable, surfaced and adjusted masks and snorkels. Herding the Aussie foursome over the cruiser, the SEALs bit down on their mouthpieces and gave a thumbs-up, which was returned. Releasing trapped air from their vests, the six divers sank slowly, the dead ship rising to meet them. They swam past shaggy silhouettes of eight-inch barrels, through a canyon guarded by muted anti-aircraft guns spiked with coral, and around an eyeless bridge.

Hovering in neutral buoyancy, the two teams gazed into the gaping hole of turret number four. The Aussie men shot pictures as they followed Wolf the length of the huge cruiser. As he led them along the buried port side, rays fled at their approach. Two patrolling reef sharks, drawn by the divers' large shapes and towers of bubbles, lazily crossed their path. Watching warily, Shorty played attentive rearguard, though he expected no problem with the curious fish. Curtains of rainbow fish parted for Wolf and his trailing divers. After a prolonged flurry of picture taking, he led them back across amidships and then to the bow where he pointed to a coral-encrusted imperial chrysanthemum, the emperor's symbol of a capital ship.

At Wolf's signal, the Australians joined hands and used the remaining air in their tanks to inflate their vests and slowly float to the surface. Exuberant but fatigued, the couples babbled excitedly about what they had seen.

Before climbing aboard the rubber boat, Wolf tied off a small buoy to the anchored line and handed off his vest and tank to Shorty. "That'll hold for our next dive." Removing flippers and mask, he flopped over the gunwales. "Want to snorkel a while or head back to the ship for lunch and a nap?"

The Aussies voted to linger at the dive site. For an hour, the quartet swam over the ship. When they climbed back aboard, Shorty fired the engine, aiming for *Laticauda*. The plan was to return in early afternoon's good light for a deeper dive. If the weather held, even a night dive was a possibility.

CHAPTER 42

Finished with lunch, the Aussies opted for two-person hammocks temporarily rigged in the shade of the stern's nylon awning. Sprawling on the forward deck, Sal and Andy sought refuge from the sun and whatever duties McFadden had in mind for them. He and Wolf worked with Roberto and Shorty, filling tanks, hosing down dive vests, and rinsing regulators with fresh water. Manning the bridge, Tiny was regaling Preacher with stories of his stay in Manila. He stopped, stared out to sea, and announced, "We got visitors."

Preacher followed his friend's gaze. Two motorized outriggers had appeared out of nowhere, fast approaching *Laticauda* astern. Fifty yards out, the vessels split in two directions—each drawing close to the dive boat on opposite sides. Dropping to the main deck, Preacher and Tiny found McFadden and Wolf handing out shotguns from a hidden closet behind the galley.

McFadden, pump Remington in his hand, was pocketing

shells. He tossed a box to Preacher. "We have two outriggers on our tail. They're trying to distract us by coming alongside both port and starboard. Get yourself a scattergun, Preacher. Go topside and cover me!"

Pointing to the hidden armory, Wolf yelled at Tiny. "Take one and get your ass topside with Preacher! You watch starboard. Do not let these people on board!" Wolf raced for the starboard hatch.

McFadden yelled at Shorty, "Get the Aussies below. Make sure Roberto and Sylvia go with them. Pull security until this is over!" Jacking a shell in the M10's chamber, McFadden took up station as the outriggers circled the dive boat.

On *Laticauda*'s starboard side, a diminutive man, barechested, wearing shorts, stood at the bow of his wooden boat, balancing a frail child in one arm.

Waving, he kept repeating, "Maayong hapon! Maayong hapon!"

In the middle of the stranger's boat was a long, arched, tentlike bamboo shelter. Aside from the man and infant and a silent woman manning the tiller, the outrigger appeared empty. Suspicious, McFadden leveled his shotgun, peering at the makeshift cabin, sure he detected others, shadows. Uneasy, he bellowed, "Close enough! Stand off!"

Ignoring the warning, the man raised the child. "Wala ko kasabot. Palihug hinay-hinaya pag istorya." A confused minute passed. "Tabang! Tabang!" the man repeated. The distance between *Laticauda* and the native boat narrowed.

McFadden called to Preacher on the pilothouse roof. "Let him know you're there."

"He's seen me, Sam. I've got you covered but I got a funny feeling."

"See anything in that shelter?" yelled McFadden.

"Couple of people. Not sure how many. They ain't moving."
Pacing, his shotgun at port arms, McFadden kept his eyes
on the wooden boat. "Get Roberto up here. Maybe he can talk
to this guy. My Visayan dialect is just so-so."

"This guy on the boat might be playing dumb, Sam."
Preacher backed into the pilothouse, yelled down the spiral
staircase for the boat's Filipino dive master.

Meanwhile, on the other side of *Laticauda*, Wolf had traded
the Remington for a twelve-foot boat hook which he wielded
to keep the second boat's visitors at arm's length. Balanced on
the knife-edged bow, two sullen boatmen stared at Wolf. Their
helmsman parroted what McFadden was hearing. Amidships,
shadows in the outrigger's flimsy shelter stirred. Tiny—shirt-
less, his eyes hidden behind wraparound sunglasses—leveled his
shotgun menacingly.

The dive master came on deck behind McFadden, who said,
"Ask him what they want, Roberto."

Wary, Roberto edged to the rail, hailed the man cradling
the child, "Taga-diin ka?" Unleashing a string of Visayan that
sounded to McFadden like pleas, cursing, or a mixture of both,
the wooden boat's spokesman gestured wildly, sounding off for
five uninterrupted minutes. Roberto let the man rail, translating
as fast as able.

"They want help. They need fuel, water, food, whatever you
can spare. They have been without these things for several days.
He says they are poor fishermen from Zamboanga."

"Zambo my ass," boomed Tiny, eavesdropping from the top
of the pilothouse. "Pirates from Basilan is more like it. I caught
a glimpse of a barrel, Sam! It's going down!"

"Hold on," said McFadden. "We don't need a fight if we can
avoid it." Calling Roberto to his side, he said, "Say we have no
fuel to spare but we'll share what we have of their other needs.

Tell them to back off astern. When that's done we'll pass supplies to one boat. They'll have to share."

Relaying McFadden's decision, Roberto dismissed whatever complaints he heard about the paucity of the Americans' charity. When finished, he crossed to starboard, repeated the offer and heard the same ungrateful response.

Unmoved, McFadden said, "That's the deal. They have to back off." Eventually, both boats fired their engines and retreated the required distance astern *Laticauda*. Tiny and Preacher kept vigil on the pilothouse roof as a precaution. Wolf sauntered next to McFadden and Shorty at a post on the stern. Creeping to the main deck, the curious Aussies caught the unfolding drama on their cell phones from the safety of the rear hatch. McFadden ordered them to stay inside the main salon. Using boat hooks at Wolf's direction, Sal and Andy were drafted to pass four one-gallon jugs of water and a pair of plastic bags stuffed with rice and canned goods to one of the wooden boats. Facing five shotguns and men obviously willing to use them, the lone outrigger approached, took the donations, and motored away, its skulking crew's original purpose seemingly thwarted.

Praise for McFadden's diplomacy erupted from the Australians and the crew. "Good work, Sam," said Wolf. "That was close. The pucker factor was high."

The Australians high-fived McFadden. "Fantastic job, mate," exulted one of the men. "You stared 'em down. With you doing the talking we knew she'd come out all right."

Dinner was a welcomed respite. The former SEALs knew it had been a close-run affair. Without knowing what firepower they faced, McFadden had gambled on his bluff. "I don't understand why these idiots split their forces," a relieved Shorty crowed.

Echoing his friend, Wolf said, "Probably thought we were a bunch of soft westerners playing in their backyard."

"Bet they were surprised to see a crew with shotguns," gushed one of the admiring Aussie women. McFadden's stock with Sal and Andy had also risen with the encounter. He and Wolf could now do no wrong in their eyes.

Tiny and Preacher remained aloft, shotguns cradled in their arms. Suspicious, the two sat facing the tiny emerald isle one mile distant. There, motoring in tandem, the outriggers had retreated to a lagoon to share the fruits of their extortion.

Binoculars glued to his eyes, Preacher said grimly, "They'll be back." He focused on armed men from the outriggers wading to the beach where a fire blossomed. "Huh, looks like they're having dinner on us tonight. There sure are a lot of them." He passed the glasses to Tiny.

"I hope the little brown bastards choke on it," fumed the big man, watching the tribal circle clustering at the flames. "Little buggers. I think we oughta pay 'em a visit tonight and tuck 'em in . . . permanently." Chuckling, the glasses to his eyes, Tiny sent Preacher below. "Better tell Sam and Wolfman our friends didn't go far."

Taking the ladder to the catwalk, Preacher paused, sarcasm in his voice. "Where's your charity, brother? The Bible says we'll always have the poor with us."

His eyes trained on the island, Tiny shot back, "Ten bucks says the Bible doesn't have anything to say about the poor carrying AK47s and RPGs. Tell Sam your hunch is right. These guys are gonna pay us another visit."

CHAPTER 43

After an uneventful night, McFadden awoke to the aroma of coffee and the echo of gunfire. Scrambling from his berth, he met a wide-eyed Aussie crouching at the foot of the ladder leading topside. "Hell of a fight going on, mate!"

"Keep your friends below," McFadden yelled. Bounding up the ladder two rungs at a time, McFadden found Wolf and Shorty on the main deck, both men glassing the horizon. "Are we taking fire?"

Pumping a fist, Shorty let out a rebel yell. "Negative. It's coming from the island!" The familiar hammering sound of a .50 caliber boomed across a placid morning sea.

On the pilothouse catwalk, Tiny and Preacher focused on a column of black smoke rising from the island's lagoon. One of the two outriggers, abandoned and burning fiercely, was down at the stern in four feet of water. Its crew had leapt into the turquoise shallows, weapons held high.

"That'll teach 'em," sang Tiny. Expecting a nighttime assault from the previous day's visitors, he and Preacher had slept on deck all night, shotguns at their side. Their vigilance had been rewarded at dawn. Lowering his binoculars, a grinning Preacher pointed south. Standing one quarter-mile offshore, a Philippine Navy cutter fired another long burst of .50 caliber.

A large, rigid black inflatable loaded with marines raced to the island's fringe of sand. Armed with a pair of M60s on the bow, the assault boat skimmed the sea, aiming for the beach to cut off outrigger survivors before they reached a jungle refuge. Sal, Andy, Roberto, and Sylvia, plus the awed Australians, crept on deck despite McFadden's warning. The morning show was going full tilt. Opening up with a 20mm deck cannon, the cutter was after larger game. The second outrigger, leaving its twin to a fiery fate, cut a rooster tail wake in a hopeless attempt to reach the island's windward side. It was a futile game. The overloaded craft was doomed. Despite being bracketed fore and aft by warning shots, the wooden boat defied the odds and lost. A third shell found the range, severing the narrow hull in a geyser of flame and spray. It was the end of a deadly short-lived nautical game. Preacher raised his shotgun in salute to the cutter's gunners. The cutter lowered another boat of marines, too late to save anyone but a shocked elder and a bawling child clinging to scraps.

Tiny, impressed but not unsympathetic to the survivors, solemnly said, "Hell, everybody knows these people can't swim worth a lick. What were they thinking?" Despite having witnessed worse outcomes, he and his fellow SEALs might have secretly rooted for the underdog had the same not been poised to kill them just hours ago. Spectators aboard *Laticauda* lingered at the rail as the marines landed. Small arms popped in the jungle's margins. Grenades thumped in flashes and smoke. It was over in minutes. Through the glasses, Preacher and the others watched losers being corralled. The second inflatable of marines beached to lend a hand.

One by one, those aboard *Laticauda* deserted the rail for the main salon where Sylvia had busied herself setting a breakfast table. Sobered by the morning's theater, everyone but the SEALs ate quietly, the others only whispering, "Would you pass the jam, please?" or, "Might I have another roll."

Sal, on watch, hollered down to McFadden. "Small boat coming in, Skipper."

Arriving topside with Wolf at his side, McFadden welcomed a lieutenant from the cutter. "What was that all about?" he asked, extending a hand as the man boarded *Laticauda*.

"We've been tracking these two bancas, sir. They refused our order to stop this morning. We suspected them of piracy and wanted a look. They foolishly fired on us."

"They gambled and lost," said McFadden. "We're grateful to you, Lieutenant."

"My commander's compliments, sir." His politeness was followed by questions. "Are you and your crew unharmed? Anything to report about these pirates? What exactly is your business here?"

"Tell your captain we were gratified to see your ship arrive. These 'pirates' as you call them, encountered us yesterday just as we finished our dive. They asked for water, fuel, and food. We complied, but suspected they had something else in mind. We kept a watch on them all night because we expected trouble this morning. Please tell your captain we're impressed by his crew's marksmanship."

The young officer smiled. "Very well, sir. I'll pass your words along to Lieutenant Commander Guzman. He'll be pleased at your comments, sir."

Wolf brushed past McFadden to offer a hearty handshake and a "well done" to the Filipino lieutenant. "Excuse me, I overheard. You said your captain's name was Guzman. Would that by any chance be Lieutenant Commander Carlos Guzman?"

"Yes sir, that is correct."

"Lieutenant," said Wolf, "please tell your ship's commander that Tom Wolf requests permission to come aboard."

Plucking a VHF radio from his vest, the puzzled junior officer did as requested. A bark of static and an invitation followed. "He says that you are most welcome, sir."

Turning to McFadden, a beaming Wolf said, "Guzman and I used to run ops together when he was newly commissioned. You know, that Abu Bakr business. Sam, let me take Preacher with me. Shorty and Tiny can run the morning dive with the Aussies."

"You think it's safe to do the dive?"

"I don't think we're going to have any trouble on site."

"Okay. I'll tell them it's clear. If they still want to make the dive I'll get them moving. Make sure you pass along my thanks to your friend for his timing."

"Will do. Give a holler to Preacher down below. Tell him to launch the other inflatable. We're going to make a courtesy call."

CHAPTER 44

While the dive party readied for the final exploration, Preacher and Wolf fueled the second rubber dinghy and left *Laticauda* for the cutter idling nearby. Guzman, the ship's captain, was surprised but delighted. "I can't believe that our paths have crossed again. Good to see both of you again. Long time. How are you?"

Wolf put aside the morning's carnage. "Lieu . . . pardon me, Commander Guzman . . . I'm glad to see the admirals recognized your leadership and rewarded you accordingly."

Preacher chimed in. "Congratulations, Commander! It's good to see you, sir." Shielding his eyes from the sun, Guzman glanced at Preacher. "Chief Hackett, I thought you retired."

"Aye, aye, sir. We both did. But Wolfman . . . Commander Wolf . . . called me and my friends for a favor. Guess he couldn't get along without us. Glad to see you got your stripes. You deserved them."

"Our service together," remembered Guzman, "showed me many things. Taught me a lot about waging what you called asymmetrical warfare. There was no one better at it than you two."

After a rehashing of the morning's fight, Wolf and Preacher were given a tour of the Filipino warship. Retiring to the privacy of the cutter's wardroom, the three shared an hour's worth of coffee and war stories. During the reunion a radioman interrupted, passing a message to Guzman.

The officer's brow darkened. "Seems our reunion will have to be cut short. Our assistance is needed by one of our sister ships. Likely more of these troublemakers such as we dealt with this morning. What troubled times we live in, eh? I'll see you to your boat, gentlemen." Rising with them, Guzman escorted his visitors to the cutter's starboard side where their inflatable was tethered. "Given the gravity of these circumstances it's likely our paths may cross again."

"No one I'd rather have watching my back," said Wolf. He shook Guzman's hand and saluted. "It was a privilege to work with you in the past and it was a godsend to have you show this time. I'm proud to call you friend."

"As am I you," replied Guzman. "Chief Hackett, it was a pleasure."

"My feelings as well, sir," said Preacher saluting. The Americans clambered down the cutter's side to their boat and cast off for *Laticauda*.

Immediately upon reaching the dive boat, a grim-faced McFadden met them at the rope ladder with bad news.

"Ivy Rosario's been kidnapped. That sonofabitch Wickes sent a radio message. Unknown assailants hit the general's compound two days ago. They've taken Ivy, Frances Yadao, and Rosario's housekeeper. The old man's gone ballistic."

"Why didn't they radio earlier?" asked Wolf. "What about Regina?"

"Safe. She's hunkered down at the hotel for now."

"You think Clemente's doing more payback?"

McFadden gripped the railing, his knuckles white. "Possibly. No details yet. We gotta get the hell out of here as soon as possible and haul ass for Zambo."

Wolf said, "You think this little encounter we had yesterday was part of it?"

"Don't know. That whole thing seemed random to me. Those people were definitely up to no good but whoever they were, they were no match for Guzman's crew. Brave but stupid.

Nah, it would be a stretch to tie it in to the kidnapping. I don't sense a connection."

Preacher overheard. "You saying this might be Clemente?"

"Hard to tell at this stage," said McFadden. "If it's him, Regina's in danger. I should have been there for her. I'm no good to her out here."

Wolf said, "I hear you, Sam, but we've got divers down." He glanced at his watch. "They should be surfacing soon. Preacher, take the boat and tell them no snorkeling. Emergency. We've got to pull out. We'll move as soon as you get back."

"I'm on it," yelled Preacher. He went over the side to the rubber dinghy.

The next thirty minutes were agony for McFadden. He paced, checked his plotted waypoints to Zamboanga, checked them again. His patience eroding, he barked at Sal and Andy for minor things and stood at the rail, staring at the black inflatables returning from the *Yogaku*, willing them to hurry.

Matching McFadden's mood, a brief squall swept across the anchorage, driving him inside to brood until the sun reappeared. Once the divers were on board and the inflatables stowed, McFadden put everyone on notice about the reason for the need to make a quick return to the city. Oddly enough, talk of the kidnapping only heightened the Australian's sense of adventure. A difficult dive on a Japanese ghost ship, a standoff, a mini-war, and now a kidnapping. The two couples talked of nothing else for the next eight hours, teasing details from Wolf or coaxing war stories from Preacher, Shorty, and Tiny.

Bemoaning his sea-bound impotence, McFadden chased the clock, squeezing every ounce of power he could from the ship's diesels. Agitated at the progress, he fled to the pilothouse, leaving Wolf to play diplomat to his cranky ship's master. Only when they reached Zamboanga and offloaded the Aussie dive party did McFadden regain his usual composure. He needed it. Waiting on the pier for *Laticauda* was the unwelcome sight of Burton Wickes.

CHAPTER 45

Chief among Wickes's myriad noxious traits was gloating. Waiting impatiently for *Laticauda* to dock, the security company owner finally waddled down the gangplank, demanding a meeting. To keep their presence a secret, Wolf told his SEAL team to make themselves scarce in the staterooms belowdecks. Their absence didn't fool Wickes.

"Get off the boat or I'll call the police," yelled an irritated McFadden.

"A toothless threat. I seriously doubt you'll be calling anyone," bellowed Wickes. "We need to talk. I'm here on behalf of General Rosario. Did you get my radio message about the kidnappings?"

"Yeah. What have you done about it?" snarled McFadden. "Have you called the police? What about the army? What's the general say?"

Wickes, the picture of self-importance, stared at the suspicious pair. "Perhaps we might talk in the main salon. General Rosario sent me with details and a request you cannot refuse."

Reluctantly settling themselves on the salon's settee, Wolf and McFadden eyed their visitor with undisguised loathing. "No bullshit," said McFadden. "Say what you have to say and leave."

"General Rosario needs a favor from you."

Wary, McFadden planted his elbows on the teak table. "I don't believe you."

Holding his secret, Wickes plucked a cell phone from his

breast pocket, pushed it across the table. "Give him a call if you like."

Pausing, McFadden traded glances with Wolf. "I will . . . later. After I've seen Regina. We're wasting time here. Tell us what you want."

"When's the last time you talked with the general?"

"At the launch, why?"

"The assault on his compound. Do you want details?"

"Cut to the chase," said Wolf.

"A group of men attacked two nights ago. They killed two of his security and wounded a third. Ivy Rosario and Frances Yadao were kidnapped, as was the housekeeper. There were at least eight attackers. The general believes several of the assault party were severely wounded. The main floor of the house was badly damaged."

"Was the general hurt?"

"No. He escaped from his bedroom. He fought back. The raid was quick and efficient. He thinks it possible these men might be ex-military."

"So what does Rosario want?" asked Wolf.

"He wants you to find his daughter and Senora Yadao and bring them home." Wolf snorted in amazement. "What, the two of us? You can't be serious."

"I am. The general wants this done quickly and quietly."

"We wouldn't know where to start looking," pleaded McFadden. "We don't have the resources or intel to track these people. What he's asking is out of our league."

Shifting his bulk, Wickes, opened a notebook and poised a gold pen over a blank page. "I think not. You're too modest, Sam. Name your price, weapons, whatever you need. The general is also prepared to accompany you if you accept. You can't refuse him."

"We'd love to help," said Wolf. "But the numbers and mission don't add up."

Lowering the pen, Wickes said, "What's this? More bullshit? What about your crew of SEALs? We know you're gearing up for a raid on Clemente's headquarters. You want Clemente? Help the general. The clock's running. The kidnappers have already killed one of the hostages."

McFadden paled. "Which one?"

"The housekeeper. They've threatened to behead one of the others."

On his feet, McFadden yelled, "Then why the hell are we sitting here talking? What are you doing about this, Wickes? You've got this great security force. Why not use it? Do something!"

Seizing on McFadden's outburst, Wickes said, "It's not that kind of operation. Look, rescue his women and he'll see that you get whatever you need to take down Clemente. He can even guarantee your friends' safe exit from the Philippines afterwards. But you have to move fast."

Wearing a poker face, Wolf said, "Where did you get the idea we're thinking of Clemente? And who spread the rumor about our having people here to do that?"

Wolf looked at McFadden.

Arching an eyebrow, Wickes turned on Wolf. "Please, let's not play games. I'm in the security business, gentlemen. It's my duty to know these things. If I wanted to impress you I'd give you a list of your three colleagues on board, all of them former SEALs, friends of yours. I can name their hometowns and shoe size if need be. I sincerely hope that won't be necessary."

"You self-righteous sonofabitch," mumbled Wolf. "You're wasting our time."

Sighing, Wickes folded hands over his paunch. "Could we dispense with the petty resentments, Commander Wolf?"

Ignoring the testy exchange, McFadden pressed for details. "Any idea who these people are or where they are keeping the women? Have they sent a ransom note? What do they want?"

Brightening, Wickes said, "From your questions I take it you're willing to help."

McFadden didn't take the bait. "What exactly does the general know?"

"He's supposed to be contacted tonight or tomorrow. The way these things go there will undoubtedly be a ransom demand. We'll know more then. I'll contact you. What am I to tell General Rosario about his request?"

Knowing he was cornered McFadden said, "Get us whatever details you can. I'll have a list of weapons and commo gear we'll need."

"Good. I'm sure whatever the general provides will come in handy later for your run at Clemente." The meeting at an end, Wickes hustled up the gangplank and drove away.

Mystified, Wolf and McFadden went up on deck, their plans for Clemente on hold. "What now, Wolfman? I'm trying not to think about Regina and . . . Ivy . . . ."

Wolf tried gallows humor. "A fine mess you got us into, Ollie." The joke fell flat.

Lost in thought, McFadden massaged his temples. "Do we go ahead with our Clemente hit or do we help the general?"

"Can't see leaving Ivy with those scumbags," Wolf said tersely. "But I don't trust our friend Wickes. The guy talks out of both sides of his mouth, Sam. Either way we were bound to tap Rosario for gear, right?"

"Correct. But we have to decide to help or not. We have to ask our guys."

"Okay, but before we commit, tell Rosario we want a meeting. Let's at least hear what he has to say."

Nodding in agreement, McFadden said, "I was thinking along those lines. I'll call. If he won't meet, the deal's off."

McFadden made two calls. The first to Rosario to arrange a face-to-face. The second, to Regina. She finally answered. Despite pleas that her father had insisted on absolute secrecy, McFadden delivered a scolding for not calling that left her in tears. After Wickes's bombshell, he had little patience at being in the dark. He rang off with a vague promise to call again. Ten minutes later, McFadden and Wolf briefed the hiding SEALs and headed west from the city to Rosario's estate.

CHAPTER 46

Encountering a ring of new security men surrounding the general's home, Wolf and McFadden abandoned their truck at a checkpoint and were escorted to the main house. A team of plasterers, laborers, and painters was restoring the ground floor under the eyes of Pan-Pacific Security men who seemed to be everywhere. Seeking privacy, Rosario ushered them to his study. Sitting in the shattered retreat lined with plywood instead of leaded windows, the two learned where the women were likely being held.

"A small fishing village, fifty miles up the coast in Zamboanga del Norte," explained Rosario. "This is not the first time this place has been used for such a thing. One cannot blame the poor people who live there. They are at the mercy of a handful of criminals. These men depend on the cover of such villages to conduct their hit-and-run raids. There are no roads. We'll have to come by sea at night. I'm told they are being held in the rear of a large house at water's edge and guarded by two women."

Marveling at Rosario's intelligence sources, McFadden was

puzzled. "Excuse me, General, but it sounds as if you've already got this thing planned in some detail."

"Of course," bristled the retired officer. "This is no time to sit idly by. We must act. As you can see . . . I can do nothing here."

"Has there been a ransom demand? What do they want, if you don't mind my asking?"

"Ah, yes, the demand," sighed Rosario. "Another reason why time is so important. They demand five million dollars American, an extraordinary sum. Another complication: I find myself in a bidding war with my nemesis to save my daughter and Senora Yadao."

"Your nemesis?" asked McFadden.

"Yes. The kidnappers say they have also offered my loves to Clemente. The price has risen to reflect my personal conflict with him."

"Have you considered the possibility that the men who have your daughter and Senora Yadao are using Clemente as a straw man to jack up the price you're willing to pay?"

Rosario began to pace. "Is possible, yes. But I have made arrangements to buy time. I told these men I needed ten days to get that much money. They gave me one week. If need be I will send Wickes to deliver the money. In six days, we are to meet their man somewhere outside the city. We are to be instructed where to make the transfer. So you see, as of today we have only six days to save them."

"Pardon my prying, but do you actually have such a large sum, General?"

"Yes. I am prepared to give it to them if you cannot succeed. That is why the six days is critical. I trust you to return my family and I will get to keep my money."

"Wickes said you feel you cannot depend on the police or army to carry out this rescue."

Rosario shook his head. "My influence is not what I thought it was. There are excellent Special Forces units, but I have exhausted my powers of persuasion. I have urged those in authority to act but they are treating this as a routine kidnapping. It is anything but that." He slapped the table for emphasis. "I have to move quickly. I need men I can depend on. You and your friends have my full confidence, Sam."

Scooping up a handful of color aerial photos and maps, Wolf scanned each one quickly, dropping them into a growing pile one by one. "How current are these?"

"Taken twenty-four hours ago. Not all my army friends abandoned me."

"Outstanding. How certain are you that this is the very same village?"

"A source living in the village passed along the information to fishermen. They in turn gave it to a passing navy patrol. I've had it checked as thoroughly as possible."

"Then why won't the navy act?"

Rosario shrugged. "They will not act on rumors."

"Rumors or not, somebody's taking a big risk to let the authorities know about this. I hope this intelligence is good."

"I believe it to be genuine. There are still patriots among the people, gentlemen. So, what are your thoughts?"

McFadden was blunt. "Speaking of risks, sir, I think we'll have you sit this one out if you don't mind."

Rosario was surprisingly calm about being rebuffed. "If you think it right. I know you have my best interests in mind. What are your reasons, Sam?"

McFadden smiled. "It's just that my friends operate as a team. A new man would complicate things. As you say, we don't have the luxury of time."

"I understand. I agree." While Wolf stuffed maps and photos into an envelope, McFadden gave Rosario a list of weapons, munitions, and communications gear. "You'll have this by tomorrow, Sam," he said without looking.

"You're right. You haven't lost all of your friends, General."

"Though it seems I can count on no more than a handful of loyal men." Rosario walked them past a pair of Pan-Pacific guards to McFadden's truck. Scanning the list, he said, "I'll have these things delivered to your house."

"Not the house. Have your man bring them to *Laticauda* . . . after dark tomorrow."

Rosario was pleased. "As you wish. Godspeed."

CHAPTER 47

While driving to the city, Wolf pondered their conversation with Rosario. "He seemed a little too eager to accept your telling him he couldn't come along on this job."

"Yeah, I wondered about that. Whatever his reasons, I think he'd be a liability. He's past his prime for a job like this one."

Wolf stared out the window at Zamboanga's bustling streets racing past. Speaking of 'past his prime,' I'd like to think that doesn't include us."

McFadden sighed. "Don't I know it. The difference between the general and us is he acknowledges his limits. Guess the hardest thing to do next is convincing your guys to switch missions mid-stream. I don't think it's fair to do this to them but what choice do we have? It's not gonna be an easy sell, Wolfman."

"Don't sweat telling them the missions been changed. I'll do the heavy lifting on that. As far as limits go, I wouldn't worry. My guys don't believe in limits. That's why they're here."

"Everyone has limits," cautioned McFadden. "And everyone's mortal."

"Try telling them that."

As promised, the general saw to the delivery of four 9mm Berettas and magazines and ammo. "I'd prefer Sam's SIG Sauer or a Glock .45 cal," sniffed Tiny.

"Can't be too picky," said McFadden. "Gotta go with what we have."

Rosario's pilfered arms included five M4 Colt Commandos, complete with suppressors and ammo. He added two pair of night vision goggles—three sets less than McFadden wanted—a crate of mini-frags and smoke grenades plus a dozen flash bangs. A Remington M870 twelve-gauge shotgun with one hundred rounds of buckshot and slugs filled out the weaponry. For communications, Rosario provided five portable radios, headsets, and batteries. A duffle bag bulging with black clothing and web gear completed the haul. Though Rosario's choice of handguns had caused some minor grumbling, the small armory was enough to satisfy Wolf and his team.

Late afternoon, after refueling and with Sal at the wheel, they raced the clock, taking *Laticauda* north. In the salon, the five ex-military men studied surveillance photos until they had memorized the village's layout perfectly. Alone at sea, the team zeroed their weapons by firing at cardboard boxes drifting in their wake.

Wolf had broken the mission into two teams. McFadden, wearing one pair of night vision goggles, would secure the village entry point with Shorty. The two would provide cover for Wolf, Tiny, and Preacher, who would go for the hut where the women were being held. Wearing the second pair of night vision goggles, Wolf would lead his team in. Their goal was to be in and out in ten minutes, no more.

CHAPTER 48

At dusk, Wolf set a course of 115 degrees at ten knots and brought the blacked-out *Laticauda* five miles offshore. There was a faint breath of wind and no moon.

At midnight, they moved closer, anchoring in gentle swells one-half mile offshore in ten fathoms. *Laticauda* rode north of the village, her silhouette screened by a sandy point choked with trees. Unless the kidnappers had stationed a lookout on the beach, which Wolf gambled against, the boat would be invisible to anyone in the village.

Wolf ordered Sal to keep the screws barely turning to keep position. A blackout was in effect. Andy was to monitor the radio in case things went south. On deck, the five men saddled up, synchronized watches, and blackened their faces with grease. Preacher mumbled a prayer.

Andy and Sal helped the team lower the portside rigid inflatable. The small mounted outboard engine would only be used on return. The five men scrambled aboard. Paddling in unison, they slipped ashore unseen on the sandy point and dragged the rubber boat into ragged brush.

Wolf led the single file of men along the beach to the sleeping village two hundred meters south. The kidnappers' slipshod security was immediately evident. Lounging on a rickety leaning dock, a solitary sentry smoked a foul-smelling cheroot. Wolf sent Preacher and Tiny into the water. Submerging, the pair surfaced a minute later underneath the skeletal pier. Shorty disappeared into foliage lining the shore and reappeared on the rickety dock, walking casually toward the unsuspecting guard. He leveled his suppressed M4 and fired one round when the man finally turned at the sound of footsteps. Tumbling backwards, the kidnapper fell into Preacher and Tiny's waiting hands. Letting the dead man's AK47 settle to the murky bottom, the pair looped the guard's belt around a skinny piling to keep the body from drifting into view.

A quick scan of the lineup of boats gave Tiny an idea. Altering the rescue timetable slightly, he and Preacher worked their way along the shallows, unhitching outboard motors on three launches. They let the motors sink beneath the surface. Pointing to a huge Malaysian-style jungkung drawn up on the muddy shore, Tiny headed for the boat's massive Yamaha outboard mounted on the transom. He and Preacher struggled to unhitch the heavy motor. They dragged it into chest-high water and dumped it quietly. Any motorized pursuit by the kidnappers would now be out of the question. Outriggers pulled up on the narrow beach were obviously fishing boats so they left them alone. The two retraced their steps, wading ashore, their dripping gear and wet, squeaking boots sounding like an army on the move. Luckily, voices, laughter, and guitar chords drifting across a clearing in front of the huts helped cover the noise of their approach.

Lights the size of fireflies flickered in the huts. Wolf signaled the team forward. Alerted, a solitary dog ambled to its feet and barked a challenge. The team froze. Padding toward the dock, a low growl rising in its throat, the curious canine headed straight for Shorty, who dropped the dog with a muffled shot. Emerging from a hut on the right, a shadowy figure wearing a pistol belt, bottle in hand, relieved himself from the doorway. He bellowed something drunken, unintelligible, into the night air. A quick-thinking Shorty, playing the part of the guard he had killed, waved casually and turned his back, strolling to the end of the pier.

Evidently satisfied security was in place, the questioner shrugged, took a long swallow, and went back inside to a lantern's glow. Shorty quit his role and joined McFadden. The pair knelt, their weapons covering the shacks, backup for Wolf wearing the night vision goggles. He and the others went straight to the biggest hut.

Once in position, the three stormed in, moving quickly to their left across the threshold. Wolf picked out Ivy Rosario and Frances Yadao huddled in a blanket to his left. In the center of the hut a woman knelt, about to light a second oil lamp. Yelling an alarm, she reached for a Kalashnikov leaning against the wall. Preacher tapped her twice in the forehead. She went down in a fountain of blood, the rifle clattering on the hard-packed dirt floor.

There was supposed to be a second guard. She's out there somewhere, thought Preacher. *She might be waiting for us.*

"Can you walk?" Wolf asked the prisoners. They nodded as one.

Their cover likely gone, Preacher took the lead through the door. Aroused, angry voices shouted. Half-stumbling, half-running, the newly freed captives followed blindly behind Preacher, Wolf urging them to hurry. At the column's tail, Tiny swept his M4 back and forth, backpedaling to stay with them. In ten steps, they reached McFadden and Shorty.

A hornet's nest burst from the same hut where the drunken man had emerged earlier. Wolf grabbed Ivy's arm, pulling her with him along the shore. Limping across the muddy shore, Frances Yadao tripped on a half-buried stone, crying out in pain.

A wild crossfire pierced the night. Green tracers shot high and wide. Withdrawing, McFadden fired short, three-round bursts at the center mass of tumbling figures. Shorty tossed the first of three frags, igniting the night in thunderous, brilliant white flashes. Momentarily stunned by shrapnel, pursuers milled in confusion. Shorty threw two more frags, added a smoke, and turned to join McFadden. An errant round caught the back of his right thigh. Shorty went down.

McFadden turned back, spraying a full magazine at the grouped men, buying time. He yelled to Shorty, "Can you move?" Getting a painful nod in return, he slapped in a new magazine, got off several three-round bursts, and tossed a frag. He offered his arm to Shorty, the pair limping along the beach, passing Tiny covering their flight. Switching weapons, Tiny shattered the night with the shotgun, pumping seven rounds toward the village. He reloaded from a six-round sidesaddle pack.

Preacher was already dragging the inflatable into the water when Wolf reached the rubber boat. Tossing the captives over the gunwales, Wolf grabbed a paddle and pushed off from the beach. He and Preacher began stroking. McFadden and Shorty flopped in behind the women and took up paddles.

Tiny fired a few last rounds to discourage the chase, threw a pair of grenades for good measure and another smoke for cover. Holding the empty Remington overhead, Tiny high-stepped through the shallows to the rubber boat. Piling in, he picked up a paddle and got in rhythm. Shorty lay back and slit a trouser leg to apply a pressure bandage to his thigh.

"How bad?" asked Tiny.

Shorty grimaced. "Bad. Been worse. I'll manage." The stoic remark was nothing Tiny hadn't heard before—or said himself.

The men stroked, digging deep, sending the inflatable through gentle swells, gaining precious distance from the lethal shore. McFadden tipped the prop in the water and started the outboard, giving the paddlers a much-needed break. The sound would draw the kidnappers' attention but time gained would be worth it. Hornet's nest or not, given the success of the shoestring operation the gangsters might be having second thoughts about chasing a group they probably thought to be Filipino

Special Forces. The suddenness of the rescue would work in the Americans' favor. Past initial danger, their adrenaline began to fade. Fatigue nibbled at the edges. Muscles cramped.

In shock, Ivy Rosario and a bewildered Frances Yadao hugged each other for warmth in the crowded inflatable. Only vaguely aware of where they were, or what had happened, the two remained mute.

At the helm, McFadden, expecting pursuit, spotted *Laticauda*'s outline and aimed for it. Twisting the little motor's throttle to increase speed, he saw Shorty surrender his paddle and fall back, obviously in pain—not a good sign given the man's iron will.

On board *Laticauda*, Wolf wasted no time in getting the women and Shorty below. He sent Tiny and Preacher to look after them. Sal and Andy raised the anchor and McFadden took the helm, swinging due south. He gradually coaxed top speed from the diesel—all of twelve knots. Compared to the lighter jungkung's speed, *Laticauda* was a wallowing pig, nothing like its sleek namesake.

But Tiny and Preacher had made sure the kidnappers' knife-shaped hull was not going anywhere without its one-hundred-horse Yamaha—now submerged in five feet of water. Aside from Shorty's wound and Frances Yadao's twisted ankle, the recovery had gone like clockwork.

With the women given water and bedded in the largest cabin, and Sal at the wheel dutifully following plotted waypoints, Mc-Fadden convened a sit-down with the team in the main salon.

CHAPTER 49

Bandaged and pumped full of antibiotics, Shorty propped himself behind the mess table, trying to stay awake. McFadden demanded feedback. Wolf got the de-briefing rolling. "Points to Tiny and Preacher for dumping those motors in the drink. That wasn't part of the plan but it sure as hell came in handy. That was damn smart thinking, guys." The two high-fived each other.

"Outstanding job, all of you," said McFadden. "Wolfman and I owe you big time. The general is gonna be one happy dude to get his girls back. But one thing troubles me. These kidnappers were a sloppy bunch. Their security was shit. We walked right in and their response was pathetic."

"Lucky they couldn't shoot straight," barked Shorty, gently patting his wrapped thigh.

"Sorry about that," said McFadden. "What I meant was, their discipline from start to finish was piss-poor. Rosario described these guys as a well-trained team who hit his compound with precision. It's only been a week since the kidnapping and yet these guys acted like amateurs when it hit the fan. Anyone else struck by the apparent contradiction?"

Squeezing his bulk behind the galley's bar, Tiny helped himself to a bottle of whiskey, pouring generous shot glasses for everyone but Preacher. "I have a theory, Sam." He sipped, waiting for McFadden.

"The floor is yours, Chief."

Tiny leaned across the bar. "Given everything you just said, and given the general's description—"

Arching an eyebrow, Wolf interrupted. "And given enough time you might actually make your point."

Pointing with his half-filled glass of rye, Tiny smiled. "Aye, aye, sir. Okay, my point being . . . these guys are not the same crew. I peg them as caretakers. I agree with Sam. They were piss-poor excuses for security. They were dangerous, yeah, but they were not the original bad guys. These assholes were sitting on these ladies, waiting for the money to change hands or something."

"And then get their cut for babysitting," chimed in Shorty.

"I'd buy that." Toasting his wounded teammate, Tiny raised his glass. "That's two votes." Wolf agreed, signaling McFadden with a raised eyebrow and a nod.

"Preacher?" said McFadden, looking his way.

"Makes sense when you think about it. Tiny's right. Despite the risks, we were the only pros there tonight. Hard to believe these clowns were the same guys who could have pulled off a kidnapping at the general's place."

Shorty shifted to ease the throbbing in his thigh. "Where does that leave us?"

McFadden cautioned, "It means the genuine bad guys, whoever they turn out to be, are still out there somewhere. When they find out they lost their piggybank they are going to be mad as hell at whoever did the deed. Namely us."

"But they don't know that yet," said Wolf. "Right now we know it. Rosario will soon know it. And Wickes will know. Too many people to keep a secret, Sam. News travels fast."

McFadden tossed a suggestion at the men. "Except, as of now, no one has a clue we've been successful. We'll keep radio silence until we reach port. I'll get hold of the general and arrange for his ladies to be returned. I'll also get a doctor to treat Shorty's leg . . . onboard if possible. Next, we'll go to ground at my place until things quiet down. Once we sort this out we'll get you guys out of the islands."

"Wait a minute," objected Preacher. "What about unfinished business?"

"You mean Clemente?"

An indignant chorus of "Yeah, Clemente" filled the salon.

Turning to Wolf, McFadden gestured. "Are they serious?"

Signaling for silence, Wolf said, "Sam, why don't you go topside and check on Sal. Make sure he knows what he's doing. That would make me feel better. Give me a few minutes with my guys, okay?"

McFadden retreated up the spiral staircase to the darkened bridge, where he found his amateur pilot gripping the helm white-knuckled, his eyes like saucers. Andy, completely useless as a navigator, hovered by the radio for moral support.

"Sal, relax," soothed McFadden. "You're doing a good job. Take a break. I'll take over."

Only too happy to give up the wheel, the Filipino backed from the controls. McFadden sent both crewmen outside for fresh air.

Minutes passed before Wolf emerged from below. "Guess they're not ready to give up the Clemente contract just yet. The guys want a shot at him. Give them a week and they'll be good to go."

Pleased, McFadden smiled, asked, "What about Shorty?"

"He's in. We'll see what a doc says but Shorty doesn't have to be our shooter."

"Okay. Let's get some chow. I'm going to heave-to off Zambo and take her in at dusk. We can tie up in the dark. Once the general collects Ivy and his Frances, and we get a doc for Shorty, we'll secure for the night. Two of us will have to stay on board with Sal and Andy. I don't want them out of my sight until we wrap this up."

"You worried about them talking?"

"I'm worried about them going AWOL. We need all the bodies we can get."

"I'll make some coffee and get some chow started. Should I wake the ladies, Sam? They might be hungry."

"Nah, let 'em sleep. They probably need it. Get 'em up when we hit port. Check on Shorty while you're below."

"Aye, aye, Skipper." Wolf headed for the staircase. "By the way, did you actually say, 'I'm going to heave-to and take her in around dusk?'"

"Yeah, why?"

"Damn, we're gonna make a sailor out of you yet."

CHAPTER 50

Following McFadden's radio call, three armored SUVs met *Laticauda* at the dock. A much-relieved Pablo Rosario had brought along a doctor as requested. That night, after a brief tearful dockside reunion, Ivy and Frances Yadao were hustled into separate vehicles crowded with armed Pan-Pacific Security men. The two-car caravan left immediately for Rosario's compound. The doctor, a nervous retired general practitioner indebted to Rosario, scurried on board and went to work on Shorty in the main cabin. Judging that the errant shot had hit mostly muscle, leaving messy entry and exit wounds, the doctor expertly cleansed, stitched, and bandaged. Marveling at the former SEAL's ability to tolerate pain during the emergency surgery, the physician promised a house call in two days.

While the doctor worked, a nervous Rosario huddled with McFadden and Wolf on the forward deck where he delivered stunning news. Without Rosario knowing about the successful rescue, the kidnappers had turned the tables earlier that afternoon, demanding immediate payment for the return of the women.

"Up to that point I had no news from you," said Rosario. "I was tempted to make the delivery myself but Wickes persuaded me not to expose myself to a possible trap."

"Makes perfect sense," agreed Wolf. "I would have advised the same."

"Wickes deputized his man Storch to make the exchange. We stayed in touch with him by cell phone. He followed the gang's directions to the letter."

"What happened?"

"We lost contact." Rosario went on to explain the police theory of how things went awry. An undercover officer assigned to the case had been tracking Storch without the American's knowledge. Even Wickes, Rosario said, had been unaware of the surveillance. The cop later told superiors that Storch had met and then argued with two men, envoys of the kidnapping gang. Things went from bad to worse. Storch pulled a gun and was severely wounded—mortally, thought the cop—during the confrontation. His apparent refusal to hand over the money without the women being produced led to his shooting. According to this same witness, Storch had been shot and left for dead. Rosario's money was gone.

"Is this undercover officer credible?" asked a skeptical Wolf.

"Yes. He is a loyal man. A patriot I have known for years."

"What about Storch? Do we have a body to confirm this version of events?" Rosario shook his head. "In the confusion his body was not found. The undercover man followed the kidnappers. When other officers reached the scene, Storch's body was gone. Perhaps those sympathetic to the criminals took it away to hide the evidence."

McFadden shared Wolf's skepticism. "A nagging detail to say the least. Not that I'm doubting this witness's version of events, but it does seem odd. At least we have the women."

"Yes. But I am to be ruined by this turn of events," fumed Rosario. The two Americans exchanged puzzled looks. "I should never have offered the money," he moaned.

McFadden tried, but failed, to be tactful. "General, try to look at the bright side of this whole affair. Two lives have been saved because of Commander Wolf and his friends. They risked their lives to save your daughter and . . . your woman."

Letting the words sink in, Wolf added, "Yes, it's a shame about the money. But if had you gambled and ignored the new deadline, what then? What if our rescue attempt had failed? Either way, your loved ones may have met the same fate as your servant."

"I had no choice. They moved up the deadline. Perhaps these men suspected such a rescue attempt. Time was running out. If you had immediately radioed me of your success I would not have paid. What was I to do? We had not heard from you."

Rosario's subtle try at spreading the guilt rankled McFadden. "You insisted on radio silence, sir."

"Wickes thought it best. I shouldn't have listened to him."

One look at the general's furrowed brow told McFadden the retired officer was searching for a scapegoat for his mistake.

"The men who took my daughter must have connections within the military. That has to be it. Yes, these enemies of mine want to ruin me. They'll stop at nothing. Don't you see?"

McFadden's anger erupted. "Who are these enemies you keep mentioning? Do they exist? Forgive my bluntness, General, but what I'm hearing is the paranoia of an ungrateful, isolated man who, instead of rejoicing at his daughter's release, is so self-absorbed he can't think straight. My friends could have died trying to rescue Ivy and your . . . your mistress." He spat the last word. "One of our guys was wounded. Where is your gratitude, your perspective on all that's happened?"

Stunned at first, Rosario responded with righteous indignation. "How dare you talk to me in this way! You have been a guest at my table. You became like family. My daughter has fallen in love with you . . . and you say these things?"

"Because you're not thinking clearly," said McFadden, calmer. *Generals are not used to being talked to this way*, he knew.

Rosario was livid. "I promised you that I would see your friends safely from the islands when you finished with Clemente. I will honor my word. But you are no longer welcome in my home, Sam McFadden." Turning his back, Rosario stalked to his car, ordering his driver to take him home.

"Well, that went rather well," said Wolf.

Seething, McFadden took a call from Regina and warmed a bit to her attempt at peacemaking. It was a beginning. *No reason to burn all the bridges in our relationship. She'll hear from her father soon enough.* They promised to talk again. Pocketing his phone, he stomped down the gangplank behind Wolf. There was still the small matter of Clemente. McFadden's blood was up for all the wrong reasons. He was in the mood for war.

CHAPTER 51

Leaving Preacher on the boat with Sal and Andy for security, McFadden and Wolf returned to the city with Shorty and Tiny in tow. To add to McFadden's misery, another house in his neighborhood had been torched in his absence. The barangay's collective patience was at an end.

Next evening, at a testy parley with community elders, McFadden and Wolf sat quietly listening to a litany of complaints. "We have been punished enough," was a common refrain. "Whose home will be next?" was a close second.

Prodded by Wolf to speak, McFadden stood before the barangay's leaders and pledged that within a fortnight the fires would end or he would be gone. Asked how he would accomplish this, McFadden demurred, saying only that his word would be the guarantee. After much animated discussion, some of it bitter hearsay and accusatory, the meeting adjourned.

Back behind his walls McFadden reprised Wolf's previous jest. "I think that went rather well, don't you?"

Roaring with laughter, Wolf threw an arm around his friend. "You got my vote back there, Sam. But seriously, what the hell were you thinking when you made that promise about stopping these fires?"

"Because we're going after Clemente and putting an end to it."

"Now you're talking. Is Operation Fireball on again?" The tag was one Tiny had suggested.

"It is," answered McFadden. "Eddie says his nephew has news for us. Wants a sit down with us tomorrow night."

"Is that why you went out on a limb with your neighborhood committee?"

"That, and the fact I'm pissed off the way this thing with the general ended."

Wolf wore a sympathetic face. "The guy's a chameleon, Sam. A cloistered weasel. He still owes the guys a thank you in my book. Screw the man and his money. I just hope this doesn't end up costing you Regina in the end."

McFadden shrugged. "I figure things may cool with her over this. I hope it's temporary. Have to admit I love the girl, Wolfman. She just doesn't know what a sonofabitch she has for a father."

Chuckling, Wolf said, "Oh, I don't think you give her enough credit. I get the feeling she knows exactly what kind of man her father is. As the Aussies like to say, 'She'll be all right.' Trust me."

"Thanks for the analysis, Doctor Wolf. Care to divine how this thing with Clemente is going to turn out?"

"Operation Fireball is a go, Sam. Tomorrow night, if Eddie's nephew-cop tells us the bastard's in town, Clemente's toast."

"Agreed. But once we take him down I want your guys on their way out of town fast. You savvy?"

"I copy. But I'm staying to keep your ass out of trouble. I may not be able to fix your Regina problem but I'll have your back on everything else."

"Appreciate it, Wolfman. Let's get the guys fired up for what's coming."

"Not a problem. Even Shorty's cocked, locked, and ready to roll."

CHAPTER 52

Two days later

A nondescript white Mitsubishi van wearing a faint beard of rust on its bumpers pulled off a busy street and parked. It sat one block away from the shabby hole-in-the-wall café Clemente favored. The tin-roofed, dirt-floored, open-walled structure was where the crime boss held court with his top manoys, a shadowy CEO overseeing a criminal empire. McFadden's police source said Clemente would arrive and linger as usual over late-morning coffee.

Behind the van's tinted windows, Wolf panned the scene with small binoculars. The underbosses had assembled as expected. The six commanded the corner table, their silhouettes visible against a corrugated iron wall of a neighboring store. Clemente was due momentarily. He was keeping to his routine: arriving in an SUV, taking coffee for an hour, then entering his marina yard just steps from the café. The team's original plan to hit him before he had a chance to reach the gate of the boatyard was still good. Once inside his base, Clemente would be untouchable.

In the back of the van, Shorty, his leg heavily wrapped, held a loaded, suppressed M4, a round in the chamber, a thirty-round magazine locked in place. A second loaded magazine was taped to the first for quick reload. McFadden was in an eagle's nest—the fifth floor of an unfinished hotel framed with skeletal scaffolding. Abandoned rooms filled with construction trash overlooked the street and café.

"We're looking good," whispered Wolf. "In position. Waiting for our boy." Shifting his glasses down the street, he found his assigned target. One of Clemente's goons leaned against a splintered wooden fence opposite the café. A set of eyes on the street for the boss. Security. Shorty would take him out before he had a chance to disrupt the hit on Clemente.

Straddling a "borrowed" motorcycle one block away, Preacher and Tiny waited, their earbuds alive with McFadden's voice. Both carried fifteen-round Berettas hidden beneath voluminous flowered shirts. Each man carried two extra magazines tucked in their jeans.

"Tally ho," McFadden announced softly. "Big Boy approaching. Stand by." Clemente's hulking SUV bulled its way down the teeming street and stopped at the open-air café.

"Show time," McFadden said. "Go."

Swerving into traffic, Wolf aimed for Clemente's sentinel opposite the café. As they drew abreast, Shorty flung back the side door, blocking the man's view of the shop. His assignment disrupted, the bodyguard pounded a fist on the opened side door. His last view was the suppressor's muzzle. Shorty drilled one shot center forehead. The gangster crumpled next to the vehicle, out of sight to passing motorists. At the wheel, Wolf steadied his weapon in the crook of his arm and double-tapped a sondalo guarding the entry to the café fifteen feet away. He went down at the rear of Clemente's parked SUV.

Startled, the men at the corner table looked up to see Preacher and Tiny roar past Wolf's side mirror. The bike, Tiny barely in control, flew past Clemente's vehicle, plowed over the fallen guard, and flew through the doorway. The airborne motorcycle sent chairs and tables flying. Leaping from the out-of-control bike, both SEALs fired at the stunned sextet. Only one of the six had presence of mind to draw his pistol. He got off one wild round before he went down with a bullet to the head. Pandemonium reigned. The remaining five were shot where they sat. The bike bounced off the upended table, its rear wheel spinning, smoking, its damaged frame gyrating crazily.

"Where's Clemente?" yelled Tiny. "Shit! I don't see Clemente!"

Ducking two shots from the vehicle, Preacher shouted, "The SUV!"

"I'm going for it!" Leaping over the fallen gangsters, Tiny fired twice at a figure crouching in the driver's open door. Clemente's chauffeur tumbled headfirst in the dirt, a pistol in his lifeless hand.

Another burst of automatic fire from the SUV shattered a mirror behind the serving bar, barely missing Tiny. The enraged SEAL crabbed forward, firing at the unseen shooter. The gunman was Davido. He emptied his handgun and hurtled out the other door with Tiny in hot pursuit. Panicked, out of ammo, Davido scrambled down a garbage-choked alley with the SEAL on his heels. Cornered in a dead end of locked doors, he was reduced to throwing his empty pistol, then rocks. Closing on his prey, Tiny easily ducked the clumsy missiles. Backing against a hovel's wall, Davido fell to his knees, his trembling hands raised in a pleading gesture of surrender. Tiny took one step and shot him in the forehead. Davido fell face first into a mound of rotting scraps.

With Tiny gone, Preacher stepped among the fallen, firing a coup de grace at each man. Startled by a noise behind him, Preacher whirled, his Beretta held at arm's length. The café's shaken owner rose, both hands overhead, his bloodied scalp peppered with shards of mirror. He stared wide-eyed at the American. Waving his pistol, Preacher sent the man fleeing.

"WHERE'S TINY?" yelled Wolf from the van.

"Musta seen something," said Preacher, pointing his weapon in the direction he had last seen Tiny running.

"FIND HIM!"

Preacher took two steps. "The SUV! Clemente!"

The hulking vehicle began rolling toward the marina gate in low gear. Wolf shot out both rear tires. The machine wobbled but kept going. Sprinting after the hobbled SUV, Preacher emptied his Beretta at the driver's door and reloaded. Wolf slipped from behind the van's wheel and fired at four armed sandalos clustered at the marina's gate. Late to the gunfight, the men swung open the barrier only to scatter as Wolf's marksmanship took its toll. Two of the four fell. Firing another nine shots at the weaving SUV, Preacher fell back toward Wolf's van. Clemente's surviving hires ran to meet their boss's limping vehicle.

Suddenly, Tiny appeared, adding his firepower to Preacher's. He sprinted with him to the van. Tumbling into the cargo area, the two huddled next to Shorty.

"Where you been?" asked Preacher.

"Later!"

Wolf accelerated down an adjacent alley. After a series of turns in the slum's maze, they abandoned the vehicle, one man at a time, Wolf slowing only for the bandaged Shorty. McFadden followed in his Mercedes, collecting team members at prearranged pickup points. At a previously selected dead-end street, Wolf parked, got out, and splashed a plastic jug of gasoline throughout the interior. Lighting a gas-soaked rag, he tossed it inside and walked away.

CHAPTER 53

"The entire operation took eight minutes, from start to finish," said a subdued McFadden. "This morning we did something the police and courts could not, or would not, do. We've delivered a major blow to Clemente's organization. They have to be hurting right about now. We got one Clemente—Davido, the son. Our intel was good. Clemente was there."

Normally mellow, Preacher was upset. "We were two seconds early. I knew it when I took a close look at each of the guys we whacked. None matched Old Man Clemente. Good news is we got six big dawgs. Bad news is we shoulda waited."

McFadden calmed him. "Not your fault, Preacher. You guys went in hot. At that point you and Tiny were committed. No turning back. You both did the right thing. Took out some major bad guys."

"Nothing to be ashamed of," said Wolf. "'Fog of war,' as they say."

McFadden added, "Tiny kept his head and went after Davido. Got him right between the running lights. Good thinking. Had me worried, though. Thought we'd lost you for good. Problem is, we now have a very pissed off Clemente senior out there somewhere."

"He was in the SUV, Sam," said Preacher. "I'm sure of it. I'm thinking we hit him. Just a guess, but the way he was driving tells me he was hurt. Lucky the car wasn't armored. He was surprised all right. Pissed, yeah, but he's gotta be hurting."

"We need to focus on what happens next," said McFadden. "Cops might make a house call soon so here's what I'm thinking." Pointing at each team member, he said, "For starters, you guys are done. Time to get lost."

Murmurs of protest filled the room. Holding up his hands, Wolf signaled for silence. "Stow it. If we don't get you out now the likelihood of your being picked up grows greater every hour. The cops will figure this out soon enough. Bunch of white guys come in here shooting up the place. How long do you think that will take to solve? Besides, not all of them are going to be happy with what we did. Clemente knows you're here. Wickes knows. Sam and I will deal with Clemente somehow but you have to disappear ASAP."

"What if we found ourselves a hide outside of town and waited until things cooled down?" asked Tiny, on his feet. "The fight's here. None of us has anything back in the world that can't wait. Right, boys?" He got affirming nods from Preacher and Shorty. He sat down, pleased. "There you go. We're locked on."

McFadden echoed Wolf. "You're missing my point. Your disappearing is not a subject for discussion. Even the general said he'd make sure you got out."

"I don't trust the little bastard," snarled Tiny. "What's to prevent him from setting us up?"

Shorty and Preacher added, "Amen, brother."

Shrugging, McFadden announced, "I hear you. Wolfman and I actually agree, but we have an alternative. You sail east tonight to Cotabato City. Indian country. Muslim land. A full day at sea at the most. Wolfman at the wheel. Sal and Andy will play steward, seeing to your every need." The thought drew a round of laughter, defusing the room's tension. "Wolfman has a deep cover contact there from the old days. He's been in contact with him as backup. Anchor offshore for a couple of days until I see how things shake out here. If they put up wanted posters for you in the post office I'll radio you. Wolfman will then put you on the beach in the inflatable. His contact will take you by truck to Davao City. Six hours at the most. There's a safe house near the airport. Get some sleep and food. Next day, run your ex-fil. Take separate taxis to the airport. You'll have open tickets on SilkAir to Singapore. From there you fly to Narita and connect to an LA flight. We can do this on General Rosario's dime without his knowing the details."

A muffled impromptu conference broke out among the three SEALs.

"Tiny would rather have a Bangkok layover," said Shorty, drawing laughs from the men. "Seriously, Preacher and me are good with your long-range plan. But consider this . . . what if we stayed one more week to take another crack at Clemente?"

"Noble thought," said Wolf, "but it's too risky."

Silence. "Okay. Pack up. Dump weapons and gear if you have to go ashore at Cotabato City. Same drill if it looks like you're going to be stopped at sea coming or going. That's it. The ship's topped off and provisioned. Sal and Andy are waiting."

Filing out, each team member offered McFadden a quick hug and handshake. Eddie stood by the truck, shaking his head. "You crazy to do this alone, Major Sam. Your friends always best for when you got troubles like this."

"No choice, Eddie. They risked so much to come help. I couldn't ask them to stay until the end. But you're right about them being the best to have around when bad times come."

They parted, McFadden to narrow his options, Eddie to drive

the team to the harbor. Wolf would return in three days if things quieted. The next move would be Clemente's.

Thirty minutes later, the truck returned. There was a knock on McFadden's door. He opened it to find Shorty, Preacher, and Tiny standing alongside Wolf.

"What the hell? You guys crazy?"

"Wasn't my idea," said Wolf. "They outvoted me, Sam. Seriously."

"Okay. I get it. What can I say? Things are going to get ugly soon. Better get some rack time, guys. You're going to need it. And . . . thanks." Moved almost to tears, McFadden retreated to his bedroom, closing the door.

Wolf said, "OK, let's divide up the watch. Eddie and I take the first two hours. I'll let Sam sleep. He's had a hard day. Hell, we all have. The only easy day was yesterday. HOOYAH! From tomorrow on it's only going to get harder."

CHAPTER 54

Rising after dawn, Rose Delgado prepared breakfast for Eddie and their nephew. While they ate, she took a mug of strong coffee to Tiny, who sat behind the wall like a statue, shotgun in his lap, empty beer bottles at his side in a sagging carton. She returned with a plate of garlic-fried rice, Spam and two eggs over easy.

A puffy-eyed Tiny toasted her. "Rose, you're an angel. If you ever decide to leave Eddie, give me a call."

Still not used to the burly American's teasing, she blushed, refilled his coffee mug, and retreated to her kitchen to eat a spartan meal before dressing for church.

McFadden padded to the edge of the screened balcony overlooking the wall where Tiny sat devouring his breakfast. "Quiet night?" he asked.

"Nice change," said Tiny between bites. "Always quiet before a storm, eh?"

"Hope not. Rose and Eddie are making early mass. I'll spell you when they go."

Looking up, Tiny shoveled food at his face. "No hurry, I'm good, Sam."

"Still have that hollow leg, I see." He went to make coffee and wake Wolf.

Thirty minutes later, like clockwork, Eddie and his wife crossed the courtyard, nephew in tow. McFadden, mug of coffee in hand, was waiting at the bottom of the stairs. He tossed a set of keys to Eddie.

"Take the Mercedes."

"Truck is okay," said Eddie.

"Not today. Ride in style. Your missus deserves a treat once in a while."

Nodding at the couple, McFadden swung open the carport's iron grillwork. Grinning, Eddie got behind the wheel, his nephew in back. Easing the black car forward, he waited as McFadden held the door for Rose. Tiny pushed open the gate and winked at the stoic woman in the passenger seat. After the Mercedes passed, he shut the gate and laughed. "Bet you I'm gonna get a smile out of that old girl before I leave, Sam."

"That'd be a sucker's bet, Tiny, and I don't want to take your money."

A steady stream of the early faithful climbed two curving wings of stairs leading to the second level of the Metropolitan Cathedral of Immaculate Conception, where Sonny Rosario's funeral had been held. Bathed in sunlight, the church's stark white, soaring façade with its stained glass and towering cross stood out against a morning sky scrubbed of clouds. Intent on delivering Rose and his nephew to the cathedral's entrance, Eddie inched forward along La Purisima Street. The morning's second mass was scheduled to start in fifteen minutes. He pulled to the curb. Deep, solemn tones from the bell tower rang out across the city.

"Okay, you go inside. I will join you."

"You can park around the corner, Uncle. At this hour there is no problem."

"Yes, yes, I know. You two go. I'll be with you soon."

The nephew got out, offering his arm to Rose. They crossed in front of the idling Mercedes and joined a colorful flow of parishioners—those leaving and new arrivals. Eddie pulled around the corner and found a vacant spot in the paved lot adjacent to the church. He got out, locked the car, and turned. A smallish figure in a dark robe, clerical tab at his throat, approached.

"Excuse me, my son. Is this your vehicle?"

The young priest gestured to the Mercedes. Eddie briefly took his eyes off the man, glancing back, thinking perhaps he had taken a reserved spot.

"Yes, Padre. Is there a problem?"

"No, my son."

From under his robes, the young man drew a suppressed pistol and fired three shots. Clutching his chest, a stunned Eddie Delgado dropped to his knees, his one arm thrust out, keeping him from falling. Taking two steps closer, the assassin in clerical disguise kicked away Eddie's supporting arm, sending the amputee face-first into the pavement. He fired point-blank at the top of Eddie's head, finishing it.

A woman and her daughter who had seen it all screamed.

The phony priest waved his pistol in the witness's direction. She fell to the sidewalk, covering her child's body with her own. The killer fled across Campaner Street, his robe flapping in his wake like a raven's wings. He got into the backseat of a waiting car and was gone.

The Sunday faithful, their attempt at worshipping brutally disrupted, stood immobile at the top of the cathedral's graceful stairs, among them, Rose and nephew. Two policemen sprinted across the lot. One called in the killing; the other held back the curious.

A chorus of sirens wailed in competition with bells. Rose stumbled down the stairs, her shrill keening added to the shattered morning's call to worship.

CHAPTER 55

At midnight, in a rutted dirt alley crowded by walls of flimsy shacks, an armored SUV rolled to a stop. The driver of the hulking vehicle blinked the car's low beams twice, killed the lights and waited. In the backseat, the car's owner, a large sweating man wearing a blindfold, fidgeted, irritating the man behind the wheel. "Okay, now you take off blindfold," said the driver.

Wickes tore the rag from his eyes. Appalled by the slum surroundings, the owner of Pan-Pacific Security had serious doubts about the wisdom of his being there. Two hours earlier, a volcanic Clemente had summoned him. Two days ago the man's leadership had been decapitated in broad daylight, his son among the dead. Police informants hinted at American involvement. Wounded, unable to attend his son's funeral, Clemente was consumed with a raging need for revenge. The meeting's time and location had not been Wickes's choice but the crime boss would not be denied.

"We meet. You will come tonight. You listen carefully." Clemente's instructions included a stop to pick up Moises Castro, his second-in-command. With his heir apparent Davido dead, Clemente now relied on Castro, a battle-tested veteran of the street wars. Wickes would be his tool. The ex-pat had proved useful in the past and would do for the purpose Clemente had in mind.

Accompanied by a visibly nervous bodyguard, Clemente, his left shoulder heavily taped in grimy bandages, rapped on the car's hood, acknowledging Castro in the driver's seat. The two spoke in low whispers, adding to Wickes's foreboding.

"We go with the boss," ordered Castro.

Resigned, the American gave up the comfort of his car . . . along with fleeting thoughts of flight. With a teenaged triggerman close behind, he waddled behind Castro and Clemente to a hovel squatting on stilts in a pool of malodorous water.

How far the mighty have fallen, thought Wickes.

In the one-room hut, the three sat facing each other across a rickety table. A huge brass bed took up most of the house. A sputtering kerosene lamp cast their elongated shadows on the walls. Clemente held court, Castro silent. "You know who these Americans are? The ones who killed my son?"

"No," lied Wickes, "but give me time and I can find out."

"But you know of this McFadden, yes? He was there."

"I've heard of him. I believe he is the man who saved Regina Rosario's life."

"That one," snarled Clemente, gingerly rubbing his wrapped shoulder. "I will burn his entire barrio to the ground for what he's done. For that, you will help me."

"Why me? Your men have already been at work there. I don't want to get involved with this. Too many innocent people will die if you continue this."

The lamp's glow painted Clemente's face a ghoulish yellow. "You have no choice. You will draw this McFadden out from behind his walls. Moises will do the rest." He paused, his eyes narrowing, thinking. "Perhaps you will get this American to come to the Blue Orchid Hotel. He and his lover Regina Rosario can die together. I like this idea of mine."

Stalling, Wickes tried logic. "This plan of yours will bring you a lot of unwanted attention just when you don't need it."

As if he had not heard the suggestion, Clemente continued. "And then I will kill Pablo Rosario as I did his brother, Sonny. Everything started with these two. The general remains the source of my troubles. Once he is dead, things will be right for me. I know it."

Wickes bought time. "You must give me forty-eight hours to make this work."

"I am a reasonable man. I will give you this time. I will have this McFadden's head . . . or yours if you fail me." Clemente stood, dismissing Wickes, waving him to the door.

At the car, Castro bound the American's eyes with the cloth and pushed him into the rear seat. On the way back to the city Wickes played his first bold card.

"This plan is crazy. If the American is killed, police will turn the city upside down to find his killer. Everyone will know who is behind it. And to go after General Rosario is madness. Friends in the military will come to his aid. Your organization will have to battle police and the army." Pausing to let his words sink in, Wickes added, "I have a better idea. I can make the Americans leave without firing a shot."

"Shut up! You will do what the boss wants!"

Bumping along a rock-ribbed road and then smoother asphalt, Wickes sensed they were headed to Zamboanga. Relieved to know he was going back to the city, he risked another overture. "I have an offer, an idea for you."

"I tell you, shut up!"

Emboldened, Wickes kept on. "Clemente is finished. You know it. I know it. The people know it. This is your time. Be smart about this. Without you, he is nothing, running from the police, living in a slum, out of touch. Scared."

Despite taking a backhand across the face, Wickes sensed he was making headway. Tasting blood, he continued. "I can arrange for the Americans to leave. They will make no problems for you. If you want to kill McFadden, I can arrange that, too. But you have to move quickly while there is time. Think about this."

His answer was another blow to the face. The big car raced on. Recovering, Wickes swallowed blood from his split lip but kept talking. "Face it, Clemente is a dead man. Take control. Become Papa Manong while there is still time. I can also get you one hundred thousand American dollars. All for you."

The car slowed. "Where do you get this many dollars?"

Wickes set the hook. "I have the money. It can be yours. Interested?"

"You lie to make me turn on the boss."

"I'm not lying. I have the money. But we have to make an agreement, you and me. We must agree before my forty-eight hours are up."

The SUV stopped. Wickes was unsure where they were, uncertain whether Castro was about to shoot him. *No, he would have killed me when I first raised the issue of his replacing Clemente. He's interested, thinking it over. The man's greedy. Be careful. Don't blow it.*

"Maybe I think about this. Give me some money first before I trust you."

"Five thousand American to show my good faith."

A long pause. "Okay."

Treason is cheap. Raising the blindfold, Wickes found himself in shadows at the foot of Fort Pilar's ancient walls, a cocked .45 automatic held by Castro prodding his chest. Fighting panic, the American steeled himself despite sweat soaking his shirt. He stared Clemente's hit man in the eye. "So, do we have a deal?"

Easing the hammer, Castro nodded. "Now you tell me. What are you wanting from me for this money?"

"I want you to agree to tell your men to stop fire bombing the American's neighborhood. It brings the police. Bad for business, you understand?"

A shrug as if the two were discussing a broken window or torn screen that needed replacing. "No problem," promised Castro.

"Secondly, Clemente must be killed. I want to see his body for myself once this has been done."

Smiling malevolently, Castro said, "Ah, so you don't trust me, eh?"

"Not yet. But it's part of the deal."

"No problem. I don't trust you either. Okay, I call you." Withdrawing the pistol, he said, "You will bring me this McFadden, yes?"

Nodding, Wickes said, "I will arrange for you to meet with him. If he thinks I can actually get the fire bombings stopped he will trust me. Do you understand? Then he will agree to meet with us. At that time you may kill him if you wish."

"How will you do this? Does he know who I am?"

"Leave that to me. Just stop the fires. It's my part of the deal."

"Sure, I said already I do this. No problem. And the money?"

"Delivered by messenger to a place of your choosing when our business is concluded. Will that satisfy you?"

"Maybe you will be stupid and try to kill me to keep the money, eh?"

Sighing, Wickes scolded Castro. "My dear man, since we are getting what we want from each other why would I do something like that? We both have to live in this city, do we not? It would be bad for business. Bad for both of us."

Castro got out, the pistol tucked in his waistband.

Wiping his bloodied mouth with the back of his hand, Wickes traded places. Slipping behind the wheel, he started the car. "Can I give you a lift?" he asked.

Turning, he saw an empty street in dawn's faint light. Glancing at his swollen mouth in the rear-view mirror, Wickes touched his tender lip, conscious of how near he had come to death. Shaking with the closeness of it all, he eyed his wristwatch. He had forty-seven hours to pull off his plan or die trying.

CHAPTER 56

Peddling steadily, a ten-year-old boy, wearing shorts, sandals, and a too-large shirt falling below his knees, guided his bike through strange streets. Repeating the precise verbal instructions he had been given, he glided to a stop outside the home of the American he was told lived there.

He pulled on a dangling cord outside the metal gate.

From the other side, Eddie's nephew studied the skinny child from a peephole. "What you want?" he barked.

The boy pulled a wrinkled sheet of paper from his breast pocket and showed it. Opening the gate slightly, the nephew holstered his dead uncle's .45, waving the boy into the courtyard. Explaining he was to give the note only to the American, the youth refused to surrender the piece of paper.

Eddie's nephew called upstairs to McFadden. While the boy patiently waited, Shorty limped from the pool area, towel around his neck, Beretta behind his back. As a precaution, he stood to one side, eyeing the boy. Eddie's widow gave the youngster a mango, which he greedily devoured, the note clutched in one hand.

McFadden and Preacher, pistols hidden beneath their shirts, showed in the courtyard. Accepting the note, McFadden read it, his eyebrows rising. He quizzed the boy. "How long ago did you get this? Did the man who wrote this give it to you? Do you live close to where this man is staying?" After hearing the answers, McFadden read the letter aloud to the others, explaining its significance.

Eddie's nephew overheard. "Mebbe a trap, Major Sam. Somebody ambush you when you go there. I think it's better you wait for Commander Wolf."

"He may be right, Sam. Ought to call the others," said Preacher.

"I'm with Preacher," said Shorty. "Can't be too cautious now. We'd have Tiny with us as well. What's the rush?"

Satisfied the boy was telling the truth, McFadden said, "It won't keep. We don't have the luxury of time. This is too important. Shorty, you and Eddie's nephew watch the place. Tell Wolfman we'll call with updates on where we are. Preacher, come with me. Put the kid's bike in the back of the truck. We're going armed." McFadden got behind the pickup's wheel. The boy, his bike in the back, sat next to Preacher. McFadden drove from his sanctuary, hoping Shorty's warning would be proved wrong. The contents of the note in his pocket could potentially change everything.

In an unfamiliar part of the city bordering on Muslim neighborhoods still showing scars from the Moro National Liberation Front's aborted attack in 2013, McFadden carefully picked his way along claustrophobic alleys. Disinterested stray dogs sniffed in charred ruins passed by the slow-moving pickup.

Exposed and increasingly anxious, Preacher held his Beretta just below the open window. The tiny messenger sat stoically, directing McFadden with barely audible replies as the Americans followed a garbage-strewn track. The urban canyon was the perfect spot for an ambush.

Pointing to a tin-roofed, two-story cinderblock house with a set of rotting stairs clinging to one wall, the boy gripped Mc-Fadden's arm, nodding, his black eyes wide.

"Here?" The child's vigorous nodding was affirmation enough for McFadden. He drove past the house, reversed, and backed into a scruffy patch of dirt and weeds. Parking his pickup's tailgate snug against the back wall of the house, they got out. Preacher hoisted the kid's bike from the bed. McFadden gave the small messenger a twenty-peso note. Smiling, his job done, the boy disappeared. A wizened, white-haired elder in a ragged T-shirt and baggy shorts suddenly materialized, along with a tiny nun in a threadbare habit and linen coif. The odd couple stared quizzically at the Americans, a strange sight given the surroundings. McFadden spoke over his shoulder. "Preacher, might need some help here."

"There is no need," croaked the old man. "Sister Angelina and I speak good."

"This way, quickly, before the curious gather," ordered the nun, hiking the hem of her black habit. Ducking beneath a sagging doorway set in flaking yellow plaster, she pulled the others in her wake. Despite the entry's size, McFadden and Preacher emerged in a dank, high-ceilinged dormitory lined with beds and heavy dark wardrobes: a Catholic island refuge anchored in an Islamic sea. Wooden crucifixes hung from the walls. From the cots, dull-eyed emaciated men and women stared as if Mc-Fadden and Preacher were passing ghosts. Light streamed from smudged glass panels set high in the opposite wall. Humidity coated the walls. Dripping water echoed from a shower room somewhere down a dark passageway.

Taking McFadden's elbow, the little nun ushered him down the narrow hall, past a tiled water closet, to a smaller room. Under a bare bulb, a prone figure on a bunk in the corner stirred. A pained, gravelly voice croaked from the bedridden form. "Sam McFadden, of all the sonsofbitches I never expected to see . . . sorry, Sister." Clucking disapproval, the nun moved to the man's bedside.

Bandaged, unshaven and thinner than he remembered him, McFadden gaped at the sight of Wickes's wounded flunky, former Marine Martin Storch. "What the hell . . ."

Turning to the hovering nun, the wounded man managed a ragged chuckle. "My apologies, Sister. I am not the only one who does not bridle his tongue." Storch fell back on his pillow, as if the effort of talking had taxed him. "Who's your friend?"

"Name's Preacher." McFadden's eyes adjusted to the room's poor light.

"One of your SEALs?"

"Could be," said McFadden. "You can trust him." The nun busied herself, replacing oozing wrappings with fresh ones. A vile stench filled McFadden's nostrils.

"Gangrene," whispered Preacher.

At the nun's side, her white-haired helper collected bloodied strips and carried them away for washing.

"We heard . . . we thought you were dead," said McFadden.

"So did Wickes, the bastard."

Pausing in her task of changing the dressings, the diminutive nun scolded her patient. "Really, Martin, must you say these things?"

"Ah, I forget myself. Forgive me yet again, Sister. Once a Marine . . ." Obviously in pain, Storch blurted out, "I sent for you, McFadden. You have to get me out of here. These poor people . . . will suffer for helping me if I'm found. Can't let that happen."

Kneeling beside the laboring nun, McFadden asked her patient, "Who's looking for you? What happened?"

Grimacing as fresh dressings were taped in place, Storch spit out his words. "Wickes and his goons. He picked me to deliver the kidnap ransom in exchange for Rosario's ladies. He wouldn't let the general go. Sent me instead. I didn't want to do it. Wickes insisted. Said he couldn't trust anyone else. Told me to go naked. No way in hell I'm going to a gunfight like that. I went dressed with my Glock, McFadden. I'm not crazy."

"Did you know we got the women back?"

"Wickes knew that but he didn't say a word to me or the general. I figure that's why he told me the payoff had been moved up."

Puzzled, McFadden said, "Run that by me again."

The nun left the room with her helper, returning with a bottle of water. A grateful Storch gulped half of it and kept talking. "Wickes was working WITH the kidnappers. They were Pan-Pacific Security boys. He lined up some of his ex-military guys to do the snatch."

"Hard to believe, Storch. The group we hit at that fishing village was sloppy. We walked right through them. No security, no fire discipline, nada."

"Amateurs," snorted Preacher.

"Not the same team," replied Storch. "The ladies were handed off to locals. They were to hold them until the ransom was paid. Wickes has done this before. It's simple. Grab some rich kid or a wife or husband. Stash 'em in an out-of-the-way spot until the money is paid and then let 'em go. Next week, do it again. It's a cottage industry in Zambo."

"And you were completely innocent about this part of his business?"

Sighing, Storch rolled his eyes. "I'd have to take the Fifth on that."

"Must have paid well or you wouldn't have gone along with it."

"Hey, it's a living."

"Geez, you were Marine Recon Master Sergeant Storch. What the hell happened to you? Where's your pride? Your professionalism?"

"Spare me the ethics speech, McFadden."

"How did you end up here?"

Downing the remaining water, Storch winced in pain, gathering himself before continuing. "I really thought the hostages would be there for the switch like usual. I would give Wickes's guys Rosario's money and get the girls. Simple. Only I didn't see the women. So I asked these guys what was going on. They didn't give me straight answers. I got ready to back off with the money and then we got into it. Only they didn't know I was packing. I think I wasted one of 'em. But the other guy clipped me good. I played dead. Hell, I was as good as dead if it hadn't been for old José and the good sister here. After the OK Corral, I crawled a block and hid in a garbage pile. These two picked me up. I ended up here. End of story."

"Maybe your guys got greedy and decided to freelance," said Preacher.

Shaking his head, Storch said, "Nah. It dawned on me that Wickes figured he had to make it look genuine to Rosario. If you had showed up with his daughter and his girlfriend, there would be no reason to pay the ransom. Get it? We're talking five million American here. Like I said, Wickes moved up the delivery and had his guys take me out. The general thinks it all went south during the deal and my death was a consequence. Only I don't die so easy . . . and he's out his money."

"Okay," said McFadden, "I get it. Why send for me?"

"Who else could I trust? I want you to hide my ass until I'm well enough to bust Wickes's balls."

McFadden was shocked. "You want me to give you cover? Why should I do that?"

"Why not? I figure I've squared things with you by telling you this."

Lying back on his pillow, Storch's labored breathing slowed. Turning his back on the exhausted man, McFadden whispered to Preacher. "Check out what's happening outside. Make sure we're okay. If anything looks out of the ordinary, let me know."

Preacher slipped from the room. In minutes, he returned, saying, "Nothing unusual, but your truck looks out of place here. We should leave."

Nodding, McFadden reached down, tugging at Storch's sleeve. "You need a hospital. I'm not set up for anything like that at my house."

Groaning, right hand over his closed eyes, Storch pleaded, "You can't leave me here. If you take me to a hospital I'm a dead man. Believe me, Wickes has a long reach. Please, don't let me die here."

Conflicted, McFadden asked, "Where's the money now?"

Storch shrugged. "You'd have to ask Wickes, maybe Clemente."

Paling, McFadden leaned over him. "Clemente? Those two in bed together?"

"On occasion. Clemente has muscle and connections. Wickes

pays. They go back a ways. Sometimes a dirty job needs doing. Clemente will do it for a price."

"Clemente," said McFadden. "As if I didn't have enough problems already. Okay, Storch, we'll get you to my place. I know a doctor . . . ."

"No doctors," pleaded Storch. "Docs talk. Word gets around, I'm dead."

Studying the man's wounds, McFadden frowned. "I won't lie to you. You're in bad shape. Hell, you may not even survive the ride, but you've got to have a doctor look at you. I'll arrange it."

Storch dropped his objection. "Fine. Just get me out of here."

With Preacher's help, McFadden carried a groaning Storch to the truck and laid him in the back, a pillow of rags under his head. The little nun drew a blanket to his neck. "May the Blessed Virgin watch over you, Martin." He managed a feeble wave to his Good Samaritan as the truck pulled into the alley, headed across town.

At McFadden's, Eddie's nephew helped Preacher carry the semi-conscious Storch to the bungalow at the rear of the property. McFadden briefed Wolf and the team about their emergency mercy mission. Harboring Storch now put them even more at risk.

Eddie's widow assumed care of the new arrival's dressings, later awakening him for a bowl of soup. Preacher and the others divided up their guard duties for the night.

McFadden called Regina, got a recording, and left a message for her to call. Next, he placed a phone call to the doctor who had tended Shorty and without revealing details, told him he was needed again. Despite the physician begging off, McFadden insisted he come. Another phone call to Regina went unanswered.

Deciding against talking to the general, McFadden decompressed with a solo swim. Afterwards, he and Wolf looked in on their unwelcome guest. Storch was breathing peacefully. McFadden told Wolf, "Tomorrow we'll video his version of events, detailing Wickes's deceit and the ambush industry he's been running. It will be good insurance. Rosario should be interested to hear about that."

CHAPTER 57

Of the 179 species of snakes in the Philippines, fourteen are poisonous. Eugenio Clemente is the fifteenth—a viper, cornered and dangerous.

Mindful of the ticking clock, Wickes phoned McFadden early that evening.

"You're the last person I expected to hear from," said McFadden, grumbling.

Wickes offered an olive branch. "I apologize for my delay in conveying General Rosario's gratitude for saving his daughter and Frances Yadao. Brilliant work rescuing the ladies," purred Wickes. "The only downside of the operation was the most regrettable loss of my associate, Martin Storch."

Disguising his loathing for the man's blatant hypocrisy, McFadden growled, "Yeah, but don't forget the general's money. He said it was a sizeable sum."

"Yes. That also was regrettable. Always a gamble dealing with kidnappers. I'm just glad your crew was able to effect the rescue. Now that the smoke has cleared, my guess is the authorities might want to ask you a few questions about that hit on Clemente's top tier the other morning."

McFadden settled in a wicker chair on the porch. "Can't imagine why."

"Huh, might be something to do with your recent guests. They still about?"

"Am I my brother's keeper?"

"Don't play verbal games, McFadden. I assume they're still there. Rest assured, my lips are sealed. No matter. In addition to the general's thanks I'm calling about an overture I made to certain criminal elements who have been torching your community. I believe I can get them to cease this wasteful arson."

I'll bet you knew just who to contact, you sonofabitch. McFadden said, "That would be a great help to my neighbors."

"Glad to be of service. But we need a face-to-face to settle this."

Of course, thought McFadden. *Draw me out. Set me up like you did Storch.* "Who are we dealing with? Clemente?"

"Not directly. He's gone underground in the wake of the shootings. No one seems to be willing to say just where he might be hiding. You'd be dealing with one of his lieutenants who's been temporarily deputized to run things."

"I don't know. I'm leery of anyone but the big man himself making promises after what's happened. Besides, what's the angle for Clemente and his gang?"

A theatrical sigh escaped McFadden's cell phone. "This eye for an eye stuff is bad for business. No one ends up a winner. You game to take a meeting or not?"

"I'll need some time to think about that. I'd want Wolf with me."

"You have to move on this now. I don't know how long the offer will stay on the table."

Sensing urgency in his caller's voice, McFadden turned sarcastic. "What, Clemente and his crew have short attention spans?"

"That, and short tempers . . . and long memories," Wickes shot back.

Playing for time, McFadden said, "I'll talk to Wolf and get back to you."

"When? This won't wait."

"I'll talk to Wolf." He ended the call, thought of Wolf and the team. *Risky, but this just might work. Something's afoot. Let Wickes sweat.*

Evening brought with it rain, stifling humidity, and rising anxiety for Wickes. His outreach to a wary McFadden had been initially rebuffed. It was four hours until midnight, Clemente's deadline for bringing him McFadden's head. A wave of scenarios flooded his mind. *Where was Moises Castro? What was he doing? Has he turned on me? Does Clemente know?*

The cell phone buzzed, startling him. An unknown number flashed. Clemente or Castro? He picked it up, answered.

"You get this man McFadden?" snarled Castro.

Wickes bought precious time. "He's talking to his partner but I could tell he wants to meet. I'll call you with the where and when."

"You don't tell me. I tell you. And the time also."

"Fine. I'll pass that along when he calls me back." Daring a question, he asked, "What are you doing now? Have you finished your part of the bargain?"

"In one hour, everything will be done. I call you."

"Okay. Remember, I have to see for myself."

A malevolent laugh filled Wickes's ear. "Yah, I don't forget. You stay there. I send my man to bring you." The phone went mute.

I have no choice, lamented Wickes. *I'm a dead man if this doesn't work.*

CHAPTER 58

Clemente finished a bottle of rum and tossed the empty in a corner. Waving his pistol, he howled for more. Nameless and unsmiling, his teenaged watchdog brought him two fresh bottles and retreated.

Outside, a car door opened and closed. Footsteps sounded on planks spanning the stagnant tidal pool in which Clemente's sanctuary sat, one ugly shack amidst a thousand like it.

Womens' giggles, always a good sign in Clemente's world, floated down a hallway leading to his refuge. A rap on the door. Clemente raised his pistol.

Castro entered, followed by two demure girls, one-third Clemente's age. Sucking on his bottle, the gang boss eyed the visitors, slurring his words. "Whaa? You bring me schoolgirls, Moises?"

Smiling, Castro pushed the two forward. "You asked for women, Jefe. You will see these young ones are not little girls. Mama Selena sent them to you for your pleasure this night."

Leering at the young women, the drunken Clemente, pistol in one hand, the bottle of rum in the other, circled them. In lantern light, his heavy-lidded predator's eyes took on a glazed, lustful look. "Ah, Moises, you . . . think of everything. We'll see how well . . . she has trained these young ones. Leave us!"

"As you wish, Jefe. I will be nearby if you need me." Castro disappeared.

Laughing hysterically, Clemente howled, prodding one girl's breasts with his loaded pistol. "Ah, little one, do you think I will need him?"

Smiling despite her fear, she groped the sweating Clemente. "I don't think so," she whispered seductively. She led him to the big, sagging brass bed, her companion following. Playfully disarming Clemente, the second girl gently pried the pistol and bottle from his hands. She slid the weapon under the bed, out of reach. She withdrew a small leather pouch from a pocket in her robe. Distracted and breathing heavily, a rapturous Clemente threw himself on his back in the disheveled sheets. Giggling, naked, free of her robe, the nymphet straddled him, brushing her small breasts back and forth across his face. Drunken, defenseless, and ecstatic in arousal, he was no match for the two.

Her back to Clemente, the second girl emptied half of the contents of the pouch in the bottle of rum. Swirling the liquor, she turned, dropped her gown to the floor and offered the bottle to him. Clemente grabbed the bottle, took a long swallow and lifted the rum to the girl in his bed. She pretended to swallow greedily. He snatched it away, this time draining the bottle and calling for yet another.

Preoccupied with the giggling girl, Clemente did not notice her companion adding the remaining white powder to the fresh bottle. Offered more rum, Clemente grabbed the bottle and chugged half of it, splashing the remainder on his reddened face. Clemente's exertions sent the drug racing through his veins.

In ten minutes, coughing and confused, Clemente suddenly dropped the bottle, tried to sit up. His limbs did not respond. The first girl's weight held him down. Suddenly, the powerful narcotic, boosted by alcohol in his system, took effect, rendering him helpless. Locked in a strange, unsettling paralysis, Clemente could hear, could see, but could not react. Vaguely aware of the girls leaving his bed and hurriedly dressing, he saw Castro hovering over him, heard his voice but could only mumble incoherently in response. Another face floated into view. He knew the face but *from where*?

"Papa Manong," said Castro, "you remember Reynaldo

Nato? You spared his life once. Mama Selena is his woman. Did you know that?"

Stupefied, Clemente was confused, his memory fogged. *Who?*

Castro again, his face inches from Clemente's. "He has a gift for you."

Backing away, Castro filled the doorway, pistol in hand. Naked, sprawled on the bed, legs spread wide, his arms useless, Clemente could only watch as Nato lifted a linen bag from the floor and laid it between the gangster's thighs.

Nato gently untied the drawstring. "You see, Jefe, this bag?" A rustling sound, like paper scraping, caught Clemente's ear. "Do you hear that? What could this be? You don't know, eh?" Cramps worked their way into Clemente's legs, the muscles involuntarily twitching. "Ah, your body betrays you, Papa Manong. I must leave my gift to you. Pleasant dreams, Jefe. You have many souls awaiting you in hell, no?"

Clemente's lips moved, spilling gibberish and mournful sounds. Nato loosened the drawstrings, gently shook the bag, and stepped quickly from the bed, joining Castro in the doorway.

One minute passed. Nothing happened.

Nato took a step into the room but Castro held him back. "Wait!" he said. "You'll have your revenge. Watch."

Clemente looked down between his legs at the bag's mouth. The rustling noise began. A small green head with alert black eyes appeared. A snake, its tongue flicking about, testing the air. A silent scream caught in Clemente's throat. He wet himself. Reacting, the serpent's body coiled, then rose upright, the familiar hood spreading in an excited state. Clear of the bag, swaying to and fro, the curious cobra slithered between Clemente's legs, nestling against his wet, warm thigh. A spasm shook his muscles and the snake instantly reacted, sinking its fangs beneath his scrotum. The reptile recoiled, struck again. The cobra's venom sent its neurotoxin shooting through Clemente's blood stream. He could do nothing. His body aflame, his breathing and heart failing, death took him after twenty agonizing minutes. The snake coiled beneath his jowls, content to warm itself until the body cooled.

An hour later, Wickes was ushered into the shack by Castro. Staring at Clemente's grotesque stiffened body, Wickes shivered, shaking his head. "Philippine cobra, huh? Ingenious. But an awful way to die, Moises."

"Yes. He felt plenty fear and maybe much pain, eh. My man will call the police. They will find the body."

Backing from the deathbed, Wickes turned to Castro. "So you will be Papa Manong now, huh. How's it feel?"

Shrugging, Castro hefted the envelope the American had given him. "I want the rest of the money you promised."

"And you shall have it. You name the time and place."

"Tomorrow. I call you."

Wickes nodded. "I'll be waiting."

Pocketing the envelope, Castro added, "This McFadden. I want him dead."

Wickes was all soothing charm. "Of course you do. We both do. He'll meet with us to make the peace about no more fires in his barangay."

"I tell you where."

Nodding, the American said, "I understand. I will need at least one hour before we meet. McFadden is not a fool. He and his friends may be armed."

"As will my men."

"So be it. I must visit my bank to arrange for your money. At our meeting with McFadden I will give you the money, agreed?"

"Maybe you think McFadden will kill me first and you will get to keep your money, eh?"

Pretending hurt, Wickes said, "You've earned your fee, Moises. I'm an honorable man. I keep my promises. As far as McFadden's concerned, my money's on you. We'll do well together. Life is good, no?"

Wickes got into his car and drove away. He had an appointment to keep.

CHAPTER 59

Above a crowded street lined with electronics shops, food kiosks, sweatshops, and traditional medicine pharmacies, a trade in custom-made explosive devices shared the building with a ground floor noodle parlor and cell phone shop. One mistake by the top-floor tenant would have leveled most of the block. Neither ideology or terror were chemist Wei Chinn's forte—lethal, untraceable explosive devices were. His skills had been called upon by terrorists, political operatives, criminals, and estranged business partners. He was an invisible man.

Wickes had often called on Chinn's skills. His last device, packed in the luggage compartment of a scooter, had shattered windows and nerves at the Blue Orchid Hotel. Chinn crafted a bomb large enough to cause significant damage but small enough to spare human life. Instructions on where to place his explosive had been precise. The result was perfect. Wickes's company was awarded a security contract soon after. Today, however, the porcine American suffered three flights of stairs to purchase a device designed to kill.

The hard-shelled black briefcase looked innocent enough. Pleased with himself, the balding Chinese bomb maker opened the case, showing his handiwork to his visitor. "So, this is clever, don't you agree?"

Smiling, Wickes approved. "Yes. Magnificently diabolical, Chinn. You are the best at what you do. A masterpiece. Uh, just where exactly is the explosive?"

Removing rimless spectacles, the small man ran his hands over the case. "The entire container is lined with it. Tiny ball bearings are embedded throughout the material for maximum effect. Cover, handles, and interior. You cannot tell, yes?"

"Impressive, Chinn."

"Yes, it is my idea. Ah, and expensive."

"Worth every peso, my friend. A true craftsman. I appreciate such skill."

"Pay close attention. I explain again. There is no margin for error."

Mopping sweat from his brow, the American said, "I understand."

Centering the shiny briefcase on his cleared workbench, Chinn unlocked two clasps and opened the case. "So, you see. You open case, no problem." Taking several stacks of paper cut to currency size, he placed them side-by-side in the briefcase. "You fill with money, yes? You put real notes on top of each stack so it looks good. You must do this so that it looks authentic. Do not open wide like this again."

"I understand. Only open wide the first time to load the money, not after that."

"Good." Chinn shut the briefcase and snapped the clasps. "Next, only half open, not all the way, eh?"

Wickes nodded, sweat pouring down his back. "Okay, second time . . . only halfway open."

Chinn tapped the case. "Do not open next time, you understand?"

"Yes. I do not open the case the third time. Good."

Solemnly, Chinn glanced at his customer, then unsnapped each clasp, drawing out the moment. Lifting the lid to its upright position, he whirled on his stool.

"BOOM!" Wickes flinched.

Clapping, Chinn giggled maniacally. "Now you know."

CHAPTER 60

Summoned upstairs by McFadden and Wolf, the team listened to the two explain the situation, then watched a video of Storch's confession.

"Storch has been packed off to the Camp Navarro General Hospital," said McFadden. "He's in a coma. No one can get in to see him. Eddie's nephew says the army is pulling security on his room."

"Good thing you taped him," said Shorty. "Wickes know about this?"

Holding up the DVD confession, McFadden said, "He definitely does not know about this. But Wickes has contacts everywhere. He'll eventually find out that Storch survived. I hope the sonofabitch figures out it was me who brought Storch to the hospital. That ought to keep him guessing about how much I know."

"If he gets access to Storch he'll find a way to make sure he doesn't talk."

"I don't care, Shorty. This video is enough to hang Wickes. I've made copies."

Wolf claimed a chair, his feet propped on the railing. "Meanwhile, what's happening with Regina? You two talking?"

"We've been in touch. I've been dealing with too much stuff to spend time with her. I'm sure she feels it."

"You still in love with the girl?"

McFadden didn't answer at first. He got up, strolling the length of the screened porch. A light rain began falling. "Yeah, I gotta admit. I do love that lady. But this thing with her father is complicated."

Chuckling, Tiny said, "Ain't that the truth. Typical prospective father-in-law stuff. Plus, the guy's a sneaky bastard. Come to think of it, so were my first two fathers-in-law. You thought about showing the general this interview with Storch?"

McFadden shook his head.

"Maybe Tiny's right," said Wolf. "Might go a long way to fix whatever's broken with Rosario. He probably has a right to know Wickes screwed him. Could also go a long way to make Wickes's life miserable . . . which would please me greatly."

McFadden's cell buzzed. Taking the call, he paced apart from the group. Waving to hush the others, his brow furrowed. "Okay, I understand. This is a good thing, correct? Yes, of course, for us as well. Thank you for the call."

Dazed, McFadden sank into a chair, staring at his phone.

"Hey, talk to us," said Wolf. "Who called?"

"Eddie's nephew. The cop," said McFadden softly. He looked around the room, his mind trying to focus. "There's been a major change. Clemente's dead."

"Hallelujah. How did that happen?"

"Is it confirmed?" asked Preacher, leaning over McFadden.

"They have his body." McFadden looked at Preacher. "You were right. You hit him but the cops think he may have been poisoned as well. They suspect some infighting in the wake of Davido's death. Who knows? Doesn't matter. We've still got this other problem—dealing with Wickes. Now it looks like we'll have to deal with Clemente's successor."

"Hell, Sam, our quarrel was with Clemente," said Wolf. "Who's the new guy?"

"Don't know. But if Wickes is offering to broker some sort of peace deal it will have to be with the gang's new boss. Wickes claimed he could get them to lay off the fire bombings. Let's see if he can get the new top man to go along with it."

"Outstanding," said Tiny. "So what's the problem?"

"We'd have to take the meeting to work it out. Maybe it's a 'don't ask, don't tell' thing. Live and let live. Like Chicago City Hall and Capone in his day."

Wolf scoffed. "Yeah, didn't that one work out well. Do not trust these guys."

"If you guys back me up, it might be worth the risk to hear what he has to say."

"How about we take them both out and be done with it?"

"We'd be at war again. Look, I don't know Clemente's guy. This offer to stop the burning might be genuine. Have to chance it, Wolfman. Better to deal with Wickes—the devil we know—than one we don't. Besides, how would we explain wasting Wickes?"

Wolf was unconvinced. "I don't like it. Skip it, Sam."

"No can do, bro. I want to finish this. I need you guys covering my six."

Tiny said, "What the hell. I'm tired of living anyway."

CHAPTER 61

A cell phone shimmied across a nightstand, waking a fully dressed McFadden. A whistle brought Wolf to his side from the couch. The two pressed their ears to the phone. "McFadden here."

Wickes's tinny voice sounded nervous. "The meeting is on. One o'clock in the morning."

"What's wrong with daylight?" complained McFadden.

"Not my choice. You know Barangay Mercedes?"

"Northeast of the city, isn't it."

"That's it. There's a graveyard. Old Mercedes Cemetery. So-corro Street. Big acacia tree in the middle of the gravestones. Banyan tree on the south side. We'll find you. Bring a flashlight to signal your location. One o'clock."

"I'll bring a world of hurt if you or your man tries anything funny, Wickes. Just so you know, I won't be alone. And I'm coming armed."

"I figured as much. He'll have backup, too. Look, I don't want this to turn into a war, McFadden. For the record I'm not packing. I'm only the go-between."

"Most go-betweens I know prefer to meet in daylight in a lawyer's office."

"Can't be helped, McFadden. This guy is handling Clemente's business and he can't be too careful. You're not the only one he has to worry about, you know."

"Yeah, I feel his pain. Okay, one o'clock." He ended the call and stared at Wolf and the others. "Wickes didn't say a word about Clemente being dead."

"Maybe he doesn't know, Sam."

"Could be. Can't see the gang wanting to broadcast that un-til the new guy gets his act together. Still, it's odd."

"Not too late to call this off."

"Nah, I'm willing to see how things shake out."

Wolf shrugged. "Okay, your call. We'll back you. But meet-ing in a graveyard? We're dealing with a gangster who's appar-ently a necrophiliac to boot. Doesn't sound good. Not too late to call the cops, Sam. They could meet us there and bag the new Clemente along with Wickes."

"I'd rather have you guys in my corner."

"You know, Sam, this is like one of those B-movies where the heroes always decide to take on the bad guys by themselves. I always yell at the screen, 'Call the cops, idiot! Don't go it alone.' The people on the screen never listen to me."

"What can I say, Wolfman?"

"How about, 'Hey, officer, scramble your SWAT team' for starters."

McFadden stood, rubbing sleep from his eyes. Glancing at his watch, he said, "At least we've got a couple hours plus. Let's move."

The five dressed in black, boots, and facemasks rolled into caps. McFadden slipped four thirteen-round magazines in his pockets. He slapped a loaded magazine in his SIG Sauer and jacked a round in the chamber. Wolf and the other three loaded M4 Colt Commandos and packed spare magazines. "Hope we're not going to need those," said McFadden, holstering his handgun.

"Never bring a knife to a gunfight, Sam."

McFadden laughed. "Good point. Ready, gentlemen?"

Wolf shared a tube of black grease paint for camouflage. With fresh batteries in their headsets and two sets of night vision goggles from the previous rescue, they were primed for a fight.

Wolf tossed bottles of water in a small backpack and shouldered the M4. "Roger that. Let's go kick some Filipino gangster ass!"

"Let him get a few words out of his mouth first, okay?"

Tiny headed downstairs. "Yeah, like, 'Call a priest, please.'"

Eddie's nephew, the holstered .45 at his side, tears in his eyes, opened the steel gates as McFadden drove away. He locked the barrier, checked on his sleeping aunt, and took a turn around the walls, alert despite the hour. The pickup headed east through nearly deserted streets, Wolf in the cab, three of the team prone in the truck's bed.

CHAPTER 62

Slowing to a crawl, McFadden killed his truck's lights at the cemetery's western edge and snapped off the cab's dome light. Wolf opened the passenger side door and leaped out, scrambling into brush at the side of the road, his night goggles in place. Shorty and the others vaulted the bed and followed Wolf.

Forty feet down the road, McFadden turned on his low beams, bathing the road in dim light. Judging from the towering acacia tree, he had reached the center of the cemetery. He pulled over, killed the lights and engine, and got out, pistol in hand. His night vision glasses painted a clear picture of gray slabs and mausoleums standing in rows like ghostly soldiers.

"Wolfman, how do you copy, over."

His friend's reassuring voice came through his headset. "Lima Charlie. No hostiles in sight. Sit rep, over."

McFadden crept toward a low fence and vaulted it. "Heading to big bush, no hostiles in sight, over."

Moving quickly between aboveground graves, McFadden reached the acacia's massive gnarled trunk without seeing anyone. A sweep of the cemetery with his night vision lenses showed nothing but sleeping tombstones. Lowering himself to the ground, McFadden made another radio check with Wolf.

"Have you in sight," replied Wolf. "Pucker factor eight and rising. Everyone maintain radio silence." Three rapid clicks of static signaled their compliance. The team had moved into a rough L-shaped formation on Wolf's right. Hunkered down behind headstones, Preacher and Shorty commanded clear fields of fire despite the occasional vault. Closest to the road, Tiny anchored the kill zone by lying prone behind a broken obelisk.

"We have forty mikes until contact," warned McFadden.

Hugging the ground, mist moved across the graves like a gray blanket, adding to the unearthly scene. The rattling sound of a laboring truck cut through humid air. A van slowed, doused its yellow lights, and rolled to a stop near the fence, well past McFadden's parked truck. Tiny saw six figures exit the van and alerted the team.

"Roger," hissed McFadden. "Understand we have six in sight. Stand by."

Voices drifted across the cemetery. Five of the shapes slipped into the graveyard, the sixth stayed with the van, just yards from Tiny. Using a line of tombstones for cover, McFadden crabbed his way to a nearby tree and folded himself into the trunk.

"You're good," hissed Wolf. "I'm all over you. Contacts in sight."

"Roger, eyeballing them. Hold your positions."

The new arrivals wandered among the graves, working their way to the largest of the trees. They split again, one dropping back behind a sinking crypt, one dropping behind a slab of stone, and one crouching behind a twisted column of banyan tentacles. From the road another set of lights approached at high speed.

Likely Wickes, thought McFadden. The late arrival parked well back from the van and hurriedly shuffled to the gate. Judging from the man's bulky silhouette, McFadden confirmed the newcomer as Wickes. He was carrying a briefcase. After a hurried conference with the person hiding in the van's shadow, Wickes was pointed toward the big tree.

"Going in to show myself," radioed McFadden, pushing away from the rough bark.

"Wait one," hissed Wolf. "They're doing some sort of exchange."

In his lenses, McFadden studied the tardy Wickes balancing the briefcase on a sarcophagus lid. The fat man opened the case halfway, shining a penlight inside. For the briefest of moments McFadden stared at the face of the man at Wickes's side. The profile, illuminated for just seconds, galvanized him.

"Wolfman, you copy?"

A soft burst of static. "Go ahead."

"The guy with Wickes. I know him."

"Say again."

Calming himself, McFadden slowed his breathing, whispering, "It's the same guy who was driving the bike when Regina's friend was shot."

"You certain? Over."

Keeping his voice low, McFadden said, "Absolutely. Guy's name is Castro. Moises Castro. Remember the pictures Eddie's cousin the cop showed us?"

"Uh, roger that."

"He's with Wickes. This guy might be the new Clemente."

Wolf's voice was cold. "Let's waste both of them."

"Negative. Let's see what they're up to first."

"They're both dead men from where I'm sitting. Say the word."

"Wait one, over."

"Standing by, over."

Fifteen yards away, Wickes clicked off his light and shut the briefcase, locking it. He handed it to the shadow beside him.

Half-hidden by a concrete angel, McFadden flashed his light at Wickes's rotund shape. The figure next to Wickes stepped behind the go-between's body.

"Wickes! McFadden here."

"Ah, you came early. I told them you would. Bad faith, don't you think?"

"No harm in caution. That your guest?"

"Indeed it is. Do you want to meet face-to-face?"

"Close enough for me. No disrespect to the gentleman."

"Very well," said Wickes. "You want an end to the fires, correct?"

McFadden shifted from behind the statue. "Absolutely. Can he guarantee it?"

Two heads nodded. "He can. In exchange, he wants your assurance you and your friends will not interfere with his . . . ah, how shall I phrase this . . . certain activities of his."

Sensing slight movement to his right, McFadden turned that way. His goggles caught two fleeting shapes working their way toward him through the tombstones. "Tell your friend he has two over-eager associates heading my way. Advise these people to stop now or I will shoot both of them."

Wickes's bulk shifted in a hurried conference. The man beside him shouted an order and the movement stopped. Calling to the crouching figures, Castro lifted the briefcase, pointing to the van.

One of the stalking figures rose from behind a headstone, surprising McFadden with his close proximity. The summoned gunman took the offered briefcase and stumbled through the cemetery to the van where another figure crouched in the vehicle's shadow. The two got into the van.

Tiny crawled to a roadside ditch alongside the van to cover the pair. "I'm in perfect position. You want me to take them out now?" he whispered in his mike.

"Negative," radioed McFadden. "I want to hear what—"

The van erupted in a giant fireball.

CHAPTER 63

Tiny pieces of shrapnel ricocheted off gravestones like ten thousand bullets. Night was turned to day. Temporarily blinded by the brilliant light, McFadden was thrown off balance by the shock wave. Night vision gone, he backpedaled, fleeing the blast's heat. On the road, what remained of the twisted, blackened van flamed like a Roman candle amidst burning brush.

Acrid waves of burning rubber, nylon, oil, and flesh drifted through the necropolis, choking McFadden. Gripping his handgun, he tumbled into a sunken grave, the rough stone outline gashing his forehead. He crawled across wet grass until he found solid stone. Surfacing alongside a crumbling crypt, McFadden knelt against a pair of rusted iron doors. Two figures dashed past, stopped, turned, and shot. McFadden returned fire, moved, and fired again. Behind cover, Shorty dropped one of the shapes.

Preacher let a pair run past, drilling both in the back.

Running toward McFadden, one of the survivors sprayed bullets from two handguns, screaming maniacally, "You are dead man!" It was Castro, doubling back.

Raising his pistol, McFadden fired, hitting the gangster center mass with three shots. Pitching forward, Castro writhed in pain, refusing to die.

Wolf appeared from behind a chipped angelic statue and emptied half a magazine into him. "Maybe I ought to drive a wooden stake into this guy just to make sure." He helped McFadden to his feet. "Geez, Sam, you look like crap. What the hell was that all about?"

Gazing at the van's smoldering shell, McFadden mumbled, "No idea. A bomb of some sort. One second I'm looking at Castro and Wickes, the next second the world's exploding. I lost my night vision." He leaned on Wolf. "You had my six. Nice job."

Steadying McFadden, Wolf walked him toward the road. "You handled yourself well, considering. I was tucked against the tree when that thing went off. Lost my night vision for a bit, too. Picked up Castro searching for you. Followed him. Shoulda taken him out when I had the chance."

"Where's Wickes?" asked McFadden. The answer was a disembodied moan. The pair followed the sound to its source. Shorty stood over a singed, bloodied Wickes. The big man lay on his back, across a grave. His shirt shredded, his bloated paunch peppered with bleeding holes, Wickes looked mortally wounded.

"Help me," he pleaded.

McFadden ran his flashlight over the corpulent casualty. Wolf knelt over Wickes. "What was that explosion?"

Groaning, Wickes mouthed through bloody lips, "Help me. I'm hurt."

"I can see that," said Wolf. "Talk to me. Was that a bomb?"

"Bomb . . . I set a bomb to kill Castro . . . afraid he was going to kill us."

"You're dying, Wickes. I'll help you but you have to talk to me."

"Ohhhh . . . need a doctor. I'm bleeding to death."

"Yes, you are," said McFadden. "But we're too far out for an ambulance. Talk if you want our help. We know you set up Storch in the ransom thing. He told us everything. We know you took Rosario's money. You were in bed with Clemente, weren't you? Talk, you lying sack of shit or we're walking away! You'll die here."

Clutching Wolf's sleeve, Wickes pleaded, his eyes filled with tears. "It's not Rosario's money . . . not his."

McFadden leaned closer, his cell phone aimed at the wounded

man's heaving chest. "Whose money, Wickes? Whose money are we talking about? Rosario's money? We'll get you to a hospital but first, talk to us."

A wail escaped from Wickes. "Rosario and his brother skimmed the money . . . millions."

"How? From who? Clear your conscience while you still have time."

"Millions . . . from the . . . Saudis."

"Saudis? Don't bullshit us, Wickes. So help me, we'll walk away."

With an iron grip on McFadden's leg, a tearful Wickes cried, "It's true. The Saudis poured millions into public works and highways . . . supposed to help the Southern Mindanao peace initiative. Some of it went to senior people in the Moro National Liberation Front . . . so much money . . . government . . . people got greedy . . . Sonny Rosario siphoned off millions. Pablo got a piece of the action in return for protection and his silence."

"Is that where he got his millions . . . the ransom money? What about it?"

Gritting his teeth in pain, Wickes nodded. "Stolen. Doesn't belong to him. I'm dying . . . please, isn't that . . . enough? Get me to a hospital, please."

"Where's the ransom money?"

"I don't know." Wickes's breathing slowed.

"That much cash doesn't just walk away. What'd you do with it?"

"Don't . . . have it."

Sighing, Wolf raised himself on one knee. "He's lying. C'mon, Sam. Let's get out of here." He backed from the babbling man.

"Wait . . . please." Wickes fainted.

McFadden emptied a bottle of water on the unconscious man, reviving him.

"You win," surrendered Wickes. "My place. Taped behind Chinese screen . . . my bedroom. Please . . ." He drifted away.

Rifling through Wickes's pockets, Wolf found a set of keys and winked. Glancing down at Wickes, he whispered, "Lot of yapping for a dying man. He's not dying, Sam. He's in shock. Sorry to say, this bag of lard ain't hurt bad enough to die. Not tonight anyway. Let's get him to his car. Hey, where's Preacher? Tiny?"

Preacher straggled in, exhausted. "Tiny's gone."

"What do you mean, 'gone'?'" said McFadden.

"Gone. The explosion," sighed Preacher. "He was right there when it blew."

"No way!"

Pointing over his shoulder with his M4, Preacher said, "There's nothing left of him, Sam. He went up in smoke along with two of Castro's boys."

"Check it out, Wolfman," ordered McFadden. "Take Shorty."

Preacher stared back. "They won't find anything, Sam. Tiny's gone."

Wolf jogged to the van's smoldering chassis. Shorty limped to the road. Preacher watched their silhouettes searching amidst the dying flames. "Sorry, Sam."

McFadden raged. "Shit! Not Tiny. Not now. What happened?"

"I figure he moved in close to take out those two in the van."

Wolf and Shorty returned, their sooty faces grim. "Preacher's right, Sam. There's nothing left but . . ." He held up a twisted weapon and shredded harness.

"Okay, we'll figure this out later. Right now we have to move," said McFadden. "This asshole's coming with us," he said, pointing at the unconscious Wickes. "Let's get the hell out of here while we can."

Wolf lifted Wickes over his shoulders in a fireman's carry. "This is worse than carrying a log at BUD/S course. Damn, he must weigh at least a ton."

Preacher led Wolf across the cemetery's uneven ground with a flashlight.

Holstering his SIG Sauer, McFadden followed close behind the laboring Wolf. "You thinking what I'm thinking?"

Wolf grunted. "Wickes's place, right? So help me, Sam, if that money isn't where he says it is I am personally gonna put a flash-bang up his fat ass."

Wolf found the road. Ignoring the distant curious drawn by the firefight and explosion, they reached the parked cars. "Preacher, drive with Shorty and follow us. Sam, you ride with me." Wolf unloaded Wickes in the SUV's cargo space. McFadden patched the wounded man as best he could. He and Wolf led the way back to Zamboanga, a moaning Wickes their cargo, bloodied but alive.

CHAPTER 64

Feeding like frenzied sharks, Zamboanga's media gorged itself on "Clemente Heir Gunned Down in Cemetery" stories. Wickes's role was marginalized, his involvement misunderstood. The case's byzantine facts also eluded the city's overburdened detectives who were dealing with internecine warfare between various gangs. The vacuum created by Clemente's death and that of his successor had unleashed a war. Recovering in a city hospital, Wickes, claiming American citizenship but having no memory of the night in question, was mum about his relationship with Castro and Clemente. He asked for painkillers and a lawyer. He got both.

Questioned briefly about the possible link between the barrio arson and Clemente's gang, McFadden and Wolf answered honestly—up to a point. More alert interrogators might have connected the shootout at the café and the cemetery fight, but luckily for the two, only the fires were discussed. Preacher and Shorty stayed out of sight. Clemente's demise was not mourned at police headquarters.

"His death was convenient for many officials," reported Eddie's policeman nephew during a clandestine visit. "Certain debts were cancelled and many now breathe easier. Now might be a good time to consider leaving. While there is still some confusion among my colleagues about the circumstances," he hinted.

With Storch locked in a coma, Wickes recovering, and police chasing their tails elsewhere, Wolf argued for a confrontation with Rosario. "He needs a reality check, Sam. This guy has to know we have evidence of his complicity in this whole sorry mess. In my mind he's tied to Tiny's death. Tiny was family."

Waving a DVD copy with the Storch-Wickes confessions, Wolf said, "What's on this disk could break the case wide open." Suffering along with the others in the wake of Tiny's death, he slumped in a hammock, the disk on his chest. "We're withholding evidence, Sam. Not a good thing. Back home we'd go to jail."

"I'm not saying we don't use it, Wolfman, I'm just not sure how or when."

"So how do we explain holding the ransom money?" said Wolf. "That's even more troubling to me than the disk with the confessions. I'm beginning to think it might have been a mistake to take it from Wickes's house."

"We could bank the cash and transfer it to an overseas account," said Shorty.

The five argued back and forth for two hours, continued over lunch and went at it again during a visit to the dive boat.

McFadden had stashed the ransom beneath the floorboards of *Laticauda*'s hidden armory of shotguns.

On the stern, out of earshot of Sal and Andy, McFadden pitched an idea to Wolf while Preacher and Shorty listened. "What if we meet with Rosario, show him the video, and give him some time to think about it?"

"He'd call his contacts and we'd end up in an unmarked grave."

"What if we gave him an option?"

"Like driving to the police station and turning himself in? Can't see it, Sam."

"No, we tell him to make a big donation to the people . . . like that obscure little nun who saved Storch. You know," said McFadden. "Charities. Schools. Hospitals. He forfeits the money, gets good publicity out of it, and keeps himself out of jail."

Shorty leaned against a rail, arms folded. "I like my idea of keeping the cash."

"C'mon, Shorty. Be serious," scolded McFadden. "It's not our money."

"Tiny earned it as far as I'm concerned," said Preacher. His remark stung.

McFadden, about to answer, thought better of it and kept quiet.

The team's morale had bottomed out with Tiny's loss. A pair of seagulls landed in the silence, waiting for a handout. Wolf tossed a cracker overboard, scattering the birds. He watched them fight among themselves. "How about Rosario buys us out and pays for our tickets home?"

McFadden threw up his hands. "You serious, Wolfman?"

"Yeah. Who wants to spend the next twenty years rotting in a Manila jail? Look, the ransom is not Rosario's. Technically, it belongs to the government whether we like it or not. But that doesn't mean all of it has to be accounted for. Wickes must have used some of it to pay off his goons. Maybe the amateurs in the village got some as well. You hear what I'm saying, Sam?"

"I do," said McFadden. "How about this. We show the disk to the general, tell him to cough up the money to the government, and be done with it. He can put all the blame on his dead brother Sonny for all I care."

Shorty scoffed at the proposal. "So he gets a walk, huh? Then tell me again what Tiny died for?" More brooding silence descended.

To break the spell Wolf took another tack. "We could send copies of the confessions to the media and police. They can sort it out. Let Rosario worm his way out of that."

McFadden snorted. "Wickes could have a change of heart. What if he told about our involvement with the Clemente hit and the graveyard shootout? He might even throw himself on the mercy of the court and take Rosario down with him."

Staring at the deck, McFadden said, "We're screwed no matter where we turn. We should have called a TV station, had them meet us at Wickes's place, showed them where he hid the money, and then waited for the cops to show. That would have kept everybody honest . . . I think."

Wolf hugged McFadden. "That's brilliant, Sam! It's not perfect but it has a certain wild appeal to me. We could insist on anonymity. The TV guys might go for that."

"They wouldn't go to jail to protect their sources," cautioned McFadden. "They'd fold for the cops and you know it. To make that work we'd have to give the cops a heads up AFTER the TV people showed. That way the money would be in the open. To hell with Wickes. Let him talk his way out of that. He'd either give up the general or keep his mouth shut. Rosario's a big boy; he can deal with it. Remember, he's supposed to have all these friends in high places."

"You know he'd point the finger at his dead brother," said Wolf.

"I don't care. I'm willing to gamble on this angle." McFadden looked at Preacher and Shorty, who had remained silent. "What do you think? You guys in?"

"Sure," said Wolf. "They've always wanted to see the inside of a Manila jail."

"None of you has to be here when we do this," said McFadden. "You heard what Eddie's cop nephew said. You could fly out tomorrow. Be back in California before it hits the fan. Say the word. I can handle it from this end. This get-out-of-jail option isn't going to be there forever."

"You serious, Sam?"

McFadden, solemn, nodded.

Wolf shook his head. "Well, I'm staying. Your decision. Make the call, Sam."

"I will . . . with three exceptions. First, Shorty and Preacher take the pass and fly domestic to Davao City. From there, they follow the original ex-fil plan. It's a narrow window but a good time to make themselves scarce."

"Now wait a minute," said Shorty.

Wolf interrupted. "If you don't leave now you may lose your leg."

"Hey, I'm doing okay," he protested.

"No, you're not," said Wolf. "I've been watching. You were still hurting when you jumped from Sam's truck that night in the graveyard. Don't lie to me."

"Wolfman's right," said Preacher. "I'm good with leaving while we can. I'll cover Shorty on the way home, make sure he sees a stateside doctor."

"You wanna keep the leg, you go home, Shorty," declared Wolf. "You'll also have to talk to Tiny's daughter when you get back. Can you handle that?"

Both men nodded. There were no further arguments from them.

"Wolfman's right," said McFadden. "You guys and Tiny did everything we asked of you and more. Timing is crucial. You should leave while you can, agreed?"

Two voices answered as one. "Agreed."

McFadden propped a hand under his chin. "Second exception. I've been thinking about what you said, Preacher. About the ransom money. How you said Tiny earned it. How Shorty said we should sock it away in an overseas account."

"That was half-assed, Sam," interrupted Shorty. "I was just letting off steam."

"No, no, you were right. You gave me an idea. I wouldn't put it past Rosario to get back some—maybe all—of the money by claiming it's his. He might be able to pull it off. Before he has a chance to do that, I think we should lighten his wallet. I know a discreet banker who can do that for us. For a generous fee he'd set up a Singapore account. From there it would be easy enough to spread it around, open other accounts and eventually get it back to the states. Tiny's daughter could use the bulk of it. And we have expenses."

"All this the general would provide without knowing?" asked Wolf.

"Exactly," said McFadden. "I'm thinking a half-million would be about right."

"I like it, Sam," chorused Preacher and Shorty. "Do it."

"First thing tomorrow."

Wolf finished the conversation. "So, Sam, your plan to call the media about Wickes's ill-gotten gain. You said there were three exceptions."

"So I did. The last exception is: we're not there when the TV and cops show."

McFadden high-fived him.

CHAPTER 65

Wolf dropped off Shorty and Preacher at the airport. "Rosario bought your tickets home but don't thank him. He doesn't know it, remember?"

The three laughed. At the airport, Shorty and Preacher waited apart from each other until their Davao City flight was called. Wolf kept his distance to make sure they boarded without problems. He drove back to McFadden's by a different route.

Meanwhile, McFadden sent Eddie's nephew to post DVD copies of the confessions to various news organizations. With Wickes still in the hospital, he and Wolf drove to his gated community at midnight and used a passkey to revisit the recovering man's townhome. The two spent an hour replacing the remaining ransom money—minus airfare, expenses, and money wired to Singapore the previous day—in its original hiding place behind the Asian screen.

The next morning, they called the TV people with the promise of a major news scoop. Newspapers and radio were fed the same story. Glued to the television, McFadden and Wolf sat at home to watch the games begin.

A feeding frenzy erupted when the media invaded Wickes's residence. Called by the gated enclave's overwhelmed guards, city police followed the media's footprints. What had been a one-ring circus erupted into three rings of chaos with a soundtrack of shrieking sirens and a shouting media scrum.

A phalanx of shoving officers crowded into Wickes's home trying to shut down live, close-up shots of detectives arriving to bag millions in ransom taped to the back of a gold-leafed Chinese screen. Broadcast nationwide, the scene captivated an audience hungry for such sensationalism.

Cornered by cameras and microphones, the senior policeman on the scene retreated to a sofa, parsing his replies, doing his best to appear in charge. A flurry of questions flew at him.

"Did one of your informants tell you about this money?"

"Our sources say this is money from the Rosario ransom. Is this true?"

"What's the connection to Wickes, the man in the hospital?"

"Is it true Eugenio Clemente played a part in this crime?"

"Sir, sir, sir . . . can you answer why . . ."

A flying squad of uniforms fought to the besieged officer and hustled him away. McFadden was pleased. Everything was public, in the open as he and Wolf wanted. As expected, it wasn't long before two police cars arrived to escort them to headquarters for more questioning. McFadden carried his ace card: a single copy of the Storch and Wickes confessions.

At the station, he and Wolf were separated. During his interrogation, a cooperative McFadden surrendered the videotaped confessions to the lead detective along with a stern warning about guarding its confidentiality. The video genie was out of the bottle the following day. In possession of the mailed confessions, television anchors played the damaging recordings and hinted at official leaks. The media's accusations caused an uproar at police headquarters. No whistleblower was found but the paranoia in the department lingered.

CHAPTER 66

General Pablo Rosario weathered the initial wave of police investigators. Treated with deference at first, he grew defensive as more investigators called on him. His role in the affair came to light. Flanked by his lawyers, the retired general went on the charm offensive with sympathetic TV reporters and fawning newspapermen. A defiant Frances Yadao, clutching Rosario's arm during his initial media appearances, eventually locked herself in her cottage to avoid attention. Sequestered upstairs at the estate's main house, Ivy Rosario drifted through depression, a delayed result of the kidnapping and the accusations about her father.

Pursued at the Blue Orchid Hotel, Regina imposed a news blackout of her own, denying entry to journalists and cameras. Despite her efforts, a few enterprising tabloid reporters booked rooms to get to her. Pan-Pacific Security workers, unsure of their status and pay in Wickes's absence, abandoned their posts. News crews used the lapse in security to roam hotel grounds. Regina deputized a replacement manager and went back to her father's house to care for Ivy. The home's cosmetics of fresh plaster, paint, and new glass could not erase memories of the assault.

A new cook had been hired. One of the general's surviving bodyguards returned, wielding a cane in addition to his pistol. He limped around the grounds leashed to a new dog. Pan-Pacific Security, paid out of Rosario's pocket and reduced to one pair in an austerity move, covered the gatehouse and beachfront. The memory of the murdered housekeeper, Amihan, lingered. It was not the same.

To Regina, the house was more confining than ever. She returned as a stranger with her own questions. Her calls to Mc-Fadden were made in secrecy.

The following evening, after yet another dinner suffered in silence, both daughters and Senora Yadao sat with Rosario in the first floor's main room. Ivy's head lay against Regina's shoulder. The air was funereal, the mood tense.

Flanked by his lover, the general, cup of strong coffee in hand, sat facing his daughters. "I'm embarrassed that you have been subjected to these false rumors, my dears. Even I am not sure what story Wickes has told the police. The man will stop at nothing to save his skin. Such times we live in, eh? We may have to endure more duels with nosy detectives and their scribbling pens. I hope for better days when this is over. I doubt this situation will reach a courtroom."

Composing herself, Regina treaded lightly. "But what of his assistant's accusations? This man Storch claimed Wickes had been conducting kidnappings for several years. What horrid men, both of them, if it's true. Wickes was your friend."

Unruffled, Rosario played down the relationship. "An acquaintance, dear Regina. There is a vast difference between the two. Yes, we often played golf together, but that was strictly a business association. I do not call this man a friend. The questions raised by his associate's accusations are most troubling. I was as surprised as you at these claims."

Cradling a lost Ivy in her arms, Regina raised another uncomfortable question. "What do you say to those linking you with that monster, Clemente? They are writing horrible things, Father. How you knew of his crimes and how—"

Impatient, Frances Yadao waved the question aside. "Really, Regina, you cannot seriously believe what they are saying or what these people write. You of all people should know how badly television and newspapers can be when sinking their teeth into such a story."

Bristling, Regina shot back, "You ignore what others are saying because you do not want to believe that there may be some truth in what they say!"

"How irresponsible! Wicked!" Frances Yadao hurled her words across the room. "You must not talk to your father this way." She sat back, brushing her silk blouse, as if the outburst had spilled venom on the fabric.

Rosario raised both arms like a referee. "Please, my loved ones. We must not quarrel among ourselves at this critical time. We must have solidarity. I demand it from each of you until we can sort out what is the truth."

"It's this McFadden who poisons her childish mind," scolded Frances Yadao.

Before his daughter could respond, Rosario fastened his eyes on her. "Frances is right, Regina. You are not to have any contact with Sam McFadden. He does not have the best interests of our family in mind. He is not welcome here. Do you understand?"

She started to protest. "I have—"

Rosario was on his feet, his eyes fierce. "I forbid it! Do you understand?"

She meekly nodded, unwilling to fight her father in Yadao's presence. "I'm taking Ivy upstairs," she said. "She's tired. This is not helpful, to hear this."

"It's hard for all of us," said Frances Yadao, her voice icy.

The sisters robotically kissed their father's cheek, pointedly ignoring the woman at his side. When they were out of earshot, Frances Yadao turned to Rosario.

"How much trouble are you really in, Pablo? And please, do not speak to me as a child. I am not as naïve as you may think."

Reaching for her hand, the general said, "Naïve? I have thought of you in many ways, my darling, but never in that way." He rose, lit one of the foul-smelling cigars she hated, and threw open the French doors leading to the garden. "Tomorrow, when these dull-witted detectives come again to repeat their unimaginative questions, I will surprise them with a revelation, a discovery I've made."

Holding the cigar aloft like a conductor's baton, he announced, "I will tell them I have uncovered my late brother's perfidy. Though I may have to use a word they can understand." He chuckled at the thought. "I will tell them that Sonny had indeed skimmed Saudi money for his gambling debts."

Yadao smiled slyly. "Yes, everyone knows Sonny was a profligate gambler."

"As a senator of the people, he had access to the Saudi donation because of friends in the government. It's true, you know," said Rosario. "He was close to those who were in charge. Too many important heads sitting on influential shoulders will roll if they insist on pursuing this."

"Be careful. Those in power may sacrifice you if need be, my love."

"My dear Frances, I don't think so. My silence about their roles is the price for my freedom. 'Poor Sonny,' I'll say. 'He was tempted. Took the money to cover his debts and'—this is the key—'to cover his mismanagement of the import business.'"

At his side, she said, "How would you explain such sums in your possession?"

"Simple. I will say this was money from the business. I am part owner, after all."

Pulling him to her, Yadao kissed him. "Were I a detective, I would exonerate you immediately. Thankfully, Sonny cannot contradict you, my love."

Rosario stared at the setting sun, his arm around his mistress's waist. "Even if my brother were alive, who would believe him? Whose word would they accept? His . . . or the word of a soldier who has always served his country?"

A soft giggle. "You are so wicked, Pablo."

"Ah, so that is my appeal to you, eh? That I am wicked?"

"Yes. Wicked and passionate. To find that in a man is a ɕ thing."

"Well. Let us put the wicked aside for tonight and explore the passionate."

"As you say, my general."

CHAPTER 67

Mid-week, without being challenged by a bored sentry manning the door, a uniformed nurse exchanged pleasantries and entered the private room at Camp Navarro General Hospital where former Marine Recon Master Sergeant Martin Storch was recovering, guarded around the clock by military police. Later, the embarrassed guard would recall the nurse saying she was there to check the patient's vitals. Once past the gullible sentinel, the nurse injected potassium chloride in the IV line and left the room. Within minutes, Storch was dead. The masquerading nurse was never found. A hurried inquest listed the death as a "cardiac arrest brought on by massive sepsis resulting from previous wounds." Case closed.

With no relatives on record, Storch was given a military burial in a local cemetery with a voluntary honor guard from the base's American garrison.

"Smells like a rotten fish, Sam. Guarded round the clock and Storch suddenly dies? You've got to be kidding." On the screened porch, Wolf sat at a table field stripping one of the Berettas. Rubbing lubricant over each machined part, he spoke without looking at McFadden, opposite. "We're on Rosario's list. The old boy has to know by now that we skimmed some of his ransom money. Time to follow our guys and get out of Dodge."

'et us leave yet. Nah, it's Wickes's turn," said
ιe same maintenance on his pistol. "He'd be
∟shairs, not us."

₀ɯced down the oiled barrel. "Those two deserve
_ιι other. No doubt Wickes had a hand in taking out Storch. But Rosario's probably having coffee at his estate right now, planning how to take out Wickes and then us. You should call Regina and ask her if daddy's up to no good."

"Not sure this would be a good time to do that, Wolfman."

"You don't want to see your relationship go down in flames, do you?"

"No, I don't. I'm hoping we can ride this out."

"Might be your moment to put all your cards on the table, Sam. Get her to make a decision about her future with you. She'd be free. You two could ride off into the sunset with me tagging along to carry your luggage."

McFadden laughed. "And what if it doesn't turn out like that? Then what? Say she watches her dad go to jail for what he's done. How does that play? 'Hey, there's Sam McFadden, the guy who put my dad in jail.'"

"Trust me. Guys like Rosario don't go to jail. You just want to stay on Regina's good side."

Shrugging, McFadden said, "Damn right. That's why I didn't make a big deal about my role in any of this. Yeah, I want to stay on her good side."

Wolf tossed down his rag, took a long draw on his beer. "There you go, underestimating Regina again, Sam. Woman that smart has to know you didn't have a choice about the evidence. Even a blind man would have seen that."

Ignoring the lecture, McFadden rubbed oil on a spring.

Wolf kept at him. "It's a moot point anyway. You're poison to her old man, Sam. He's got her locked up on the family homestead and has hidden the key."

McFadden wiped his hands on an oily rag. "Now who's underestimating Regina? She gets out occasionally. She's trying to help her sister recover from her ordeal. Still calls me when everyone's asleep. Gives me the inside scoop on what's happening."

Wolf stopped polishing, looked up, expectant. "So, give it up. What does the lovely lady say?"

McFadden stared past his friend. "She thinks there's a deal in the works."

"I KNEW IT! That sneaky bastard is gonna walk, isn't he?"

"Probably. Must be all those high-level people in the food chain looking out for one of their own. Feels just like home, buddy." McFadden assembled his weapon and changed the subject. "By the way, we've got another set of divers who want to go out, courtesy of Regina. She runs the hotel from Camp Rosario most days. Anyway, she has a family looking for some reef time. With all this other stuff going on I figure it'll be good to get away and make some shekels. Whadaya think?"

"Pay the bills. Yeah, we can use the income. Firm it up."

"Will do. Can't leave town without letting the police know what we're doing, though."

"I'll be glad when that's over. I hate waiting. It cramps my style. Just so you know, I'm helping frame out the Aquino home today. Then I'm taking a well-deserved siesta."

"Appreciate your doing that, Wolfman. That means a lot to the neighborhood folks. It's been a month since the last house fire. Nothing's happened since Castro went down shooting. I hope that was the end of it. I'd be with you but I'm meeting Regina at the boat this afternoon."

"So she does get out. Tell her hello for me. Maybe she'd like to get Ivy out of the house for some beach time. Maybe dinner here."

McFadden snorted. "Not likely. Her old man would ground them for life if he found out they were seeing us."

"You know, I never liked the guy, Sam. Not since the first time I met him."

"You had a different take on him. Hey, I confess I didn't read him right from the beginning."

Wolf reassembled his pistol. "That's because Regina messed with your pea brain from day one." Whistling, he headed downstairs, chatted with Eddie's nephew and picked up a tool belt from the workbench. He rode McFadden's bike to the Aquino home to spend the day building walls. McFadden drove to *Laticauda* to busy himself planning the next dive trip.

Later, in T-shirt and shorts, he hailed the visiting Regina from the pilothouse catwalk. "Hey, lady, you want to tour my boat? Come aboard."

She came down the gangplank, ducked inside the main cabin, and greeted him with hungry, prolonged kisses. She followed him into the galley, nibbling his ears and neck. McFadden snagged two iced beers. "Too hot inside. Let's sit under the canopy." Regina followed him outside and sat next to him on the padded bench, legs curled under her.

"You look exhausted," he said.

She managed a wan smile. "I feel eighty years old."

"Don't look it. And thanks for the heads up on that family wanting a dive trip. We appreciate the contact. Should be fun."

"You're welcome. It'll be a nice diversion for you. Away from the city."

A cooling breeze rippled the harbor. They sipped in silence. "How goes the war on the home front?" he said softly.

Avoiding his eyes, Regina said, "I have more disturbing news, Sam."

"Oh, great. I haven't seen you for a week and you bring bad news."

"Can't help it. These past weeks have been miserable without you."

He reached for her hand. "Same here. Your father has drawn a line in the sand where I'm concerned. Sorry, I could care less about him but I worry about you."

"You know, I don't blame you for giving the police those video confessions."

"It was the best we could do under the circumstances. I felt terrible about doing it. Didn't want to hurt you, of all people. But it was important evidence."

"You're too honest, Major Sam. My, I haven't called you that for so long."

"Back to our first days together." He kissed her neck and shoulders. "Back when things were a lot less complicated. Okay, give me your best shot. What's the bad news?"

"I overheard father talking to one of his cronies."

"So much for the court's gag order. What did you hear?"

"It was Clemente's men who tried to burn your boat that night."

"We figured as much. He probably made the connection with my foiling the attempt on your life."

She shook her head. "That wasn't the reason. Father asked Wickes to have it done. He in turn hired Clemente's men to do the job. That way there would be no direct connection."

Confused, McFadden stared past her, his eyes focused on an incoming ferry. "Why? Your father and I were friends at the time. Why would he do such a thing? Did it have something to do with us?"

"Maybe. Remember my telling you he had his fingers in so many things? How he was so secretive about his dealings? How I said to watch out or he'd work his way into your business?"

McFadden gulped his beer. "Yeah, I think you said you didn't want my dream to be anything other than what I wanted it to be. You were being a loyal daughter but you were also trying to warn me."

She stood up to catch the faint breeze. "Clemente's men set fire to your dream so you would have to come to my father for financial help. He knew you were nearly out of money. The fire pushed you in a corner. You got his money in exchange for his taking over your original partner Felix Cataldo's 60 percent share of the business. Don't you see?"

From the corner of his eye McFadden saw Sal come on deck. He waved him away. "Okay, what you're saying makes sense. But how do I prove that? How would I even fight something like that?"

She faced him, her hands cupping his face. "You can't. It's all rigged. He has all these people who owe him something. The police, the judges, the bankers, even people in the government all the way to Malacañang Palace. He's going to force you and Wolf out of the partnership. He will buy out your share. He's going to take your dream away, Sam." Tears streaked down her face. She lowered her head in her hands. "I'm so ashamed. I'm sorry."

Stunned, McFadden held her close. "When . . . is this supposed to happen?" Shaking her head without answering, Regina sobbed.

McFadden stood, awkwardly trying to comfort her. Embarrassed that Sal and Andy had been drawn by Regina's crying, he shot a menacing look at them. Both heads disappeared down the hatch. From his back pocket he offered the only thing he had— the oily rag used on his pistol. Laughing through her tears, Regina dabbed at her eyes with the one clean spot left on the cloth. Soon both of them were laughing, the tension evaporating.

"I'd better get home," she sniffled.

"Wish you didn't have to go. I wish you could spend the night on board."

"Wouldn't that be romantic," she said, drying the last of her tears. "But Ivy needs me and I'd be missed at dinner. Command performance, you know." He walked up the gangway to her car, his arm around her waist. She got behind the wheel and leaned up to kiss him. "Stay safe, Plain Old Sam. I love you."

She drove away, leaving him more conflicted than ever about seeing justice done.

CHAPTER 68

Dusk was closing in with no break in the city's humidity. A dull gloom had settled on McFadden's house. Eddie's death, followed by Tiny's, had settled over the walled property like a cloud. Rose still cooked but had become more withdrawn. Her nephew stayed on, faithfully standing watch in turn. McFadden and Wolf at least had the luxury of a daily swim to relieve stress. One evening, they relaxed poolside after a contest of underwater laps at which Wolf, as usual, won. McFadden was turning steaks on the grill into medium-well charcoal.

Considering Regina's news of her father's treachery, Wolf took McFadden's retelling rather well. Surprised at his partner's docile acceptance of Rosario's impending coup, McFadden pressed him. "Not like you to take news like this so calmly, Wolfman. You're worrying me. Please tell me you're not thinking of doing something stupid."

"Define 'stupid,' Sam."

Spearing the steaks, McFadden growled, "You know what I mean. Getting your frogman on, as they say. Sneaking out after I tuck you in for the night. Dropping a grenade in Rosario's sheets when he's sleeping. Stuff like that."

"Have I thought about it? Yeah. Would I actually do it? No."

"It was gutsy for Regina to tell me this latest news."

"Yeah, it was. How can she live in the same house with this guy when she knows this is really what he's like?"

McFadden slapped the meat on plates, added baked yams and rice. Wolf stared at his steak. "Where did you learn to grill, Sam? Welding school?"

"Too pink?"

Dusting his meat with salt and pepper, Wolf shook his head and began eating. "We're in limbo here," he said between bites. "The longer we stay, the less we can expect a resolution to this mess. So, to answer your question about why I'm so mellow about Regina's latest, it's because it's more of the same. I'm not shocked at all. Rosario wants us out, pure and simple. Gone. He's sitting pretty. We got rid of Clemente for him . . . or at least got the ball rolling for whoever finally had the stones to actually take out Clemente. We broke the kidnapping and nailed Wickes with Storch's confession."

"So how come Wickes's rolling over on the general doesn't end it?"

"Sam, you're a babe-in-the-woods when it comes to understanding basic evil." Between mouthfuls, Wolf kept talking. "The almighty blessed Rosario with the perfect fall guy, his dumb-ass brother, Sonny. What a great cover. Everyone hears about how Senator Sonny skimmed the money, dumped it in the general's bank for safekeeping, and later conveniently got himself whacked. Rosario proclaims his innocence saying, 'I didn't know' and everybody buys it. Except everybody knows it's bullshit. It's the emperor's clothes. A game, Sam. They've all closed ranks and we're left on the outside looking in. At least we got some of Rosario's money before he could shut us down. It's life, my Boy Scout friend. Time to exit left."

McFadden chewed on his steak and Wolf's theory.

Taking the silence as a sign to continue, Wolf said, "So what if Rosario thinks he has us by the short ones? So he buys us out. So what? We get the hell out. Start a dive operation in Mexico, Belize, or Jamaica. We both know a dozen spots in the Bahamas where we could set up shop."

Breaking his silence, McFadden said, "So that's it? That's your solution? Strike the tents and leave?"

"Hell yes. You have a better idea? What do you need to convince yourself that it was a nice try? You had a terrific dream. It was worth a shot. Didn't pan out. Happens to the best of us, Sam. Look ahead, not back. If you look back what do you see? When I look back I see General Pablo Rosario gaining on us."

"I see Regina."

Pushing away his plate, Wolf threw up his hands. "Oh, great, my partner's a romantic. Face it. The lady's sticking close to home, Sam. She's got a basket case for a sister, a poisonous harpy sleeping with her father, and not enough courage to cut and run with the man she loves. You're gonna end up as a knight-in-waiting hopelessly in love with a nun-in-training. Makes for a great story but a lousy future."

"Cheap shot, bro."

Wolf didn't back down. "Guilty. I'm trying to give you a reality check here, Sam. I vote to leave. Start over. Move on." He got up, stacked the plates, and stomped off, leaving McFadden staring at the empty table.

CHAPTER 69

Zamboanga Harbor, four days later

Enraged, Wolf shouted into his cell phone at McFadden. "We're not going ANYWHERE, Sam! I'm telling you, NOBODY will sell us diesel. Yes, I've been to all the fuel docks. Yes, I've talked to them until I was blue in the face." He paused, listening to the questions. "Look, you don't understand. They won't give us any fuel! Yes, our cards are good. Are you listening to me? No, it's not that. Yes, I tried cash. To a man, they won't take it! Our tank is one-quarter full. We'd be lucky to get to Big Santa Cruz and back."

Calming, Wolf told McFadden, "Call Regina and tell her we have to cancel with that family who wanted to dive. We can't chance it. We couldn't even siphon enough fuel to make this work, Sam. We're being shut down. That sonofabitch!"

Footsteps on the pilothouse ladder interrupted Wolf's phone tirade. Sal's round face showed. Wolf barked, "What?"

Thumbing over his shoulder, the deckhand said, "Some guy come on board. Say he want to talk to you, Skipper."

"Okay, tell him I'll be right down." Sal disappeared. Wolf passed the news of his visitor to McFadden on the other end. "Gotta go, Sam. We got a visitor. I think I know who this might be." A pause. "Yeah, my thoughts exactly. Some lawyer with the paperwork from the general. I'd like to shoot the sonofabitch. What? No, not the lawyer . . . Rosario. Well, maybe his lawyer too. I'll call you back."

Ringing off, Wolf went below. It was a sober-looking bank messenger, not a lawyer after all. The visitor presented him with exactly what Wolf thought he was carrying—papers with Rosario's signature. As majority owner, the general had called the loan. After signing the papers, Wolf walked out on deck. When the deliveryman was gone, a timid Sal and Andy shadowed Wolf, asking what had just happened. He told them.

Apprehensive, knowing too much about the recent history between the general and their American employers, Sal and Andy wandered disconsolately throughout the boat, collecting their belongings.

Wolf tried to persuade them to stay. "Maybe this new owner will need crew to take care of *Laticauda*. You should wait and see what happens, guys. We'll settle up. Pay you what you got coming. You'll be all right."

He didn't believe his words and neither did they. But they stayed.

Wolf checked the tanks again to be sure. There was fuel enough to run the machinery for pumps, electricity, and refrigeration. The duo stayed behind when a subdued Wolf left in the pickup. He would not be back. The two Filipinos knew it, as did Wolf.

CHAPTER 70

From McFadden's house, mid-morning, Eddie's nephew ran to the building site where McFadden was helping a neighborhood crew raise rafters on the Aquino family home. Trading his tool belt for the bike, McFadden excused himself, arriving home to find Regina sitting under an umbrella in the backyard. Ivy sat apart, dangling her feet at the far end of the pool. She waved. He returned her greeting and leaned down, greeting Regina with a kiss. "This is a surprise. To what do I owe the honor of a visit from you two lovely ladies?"

A sad smile settled on her face. "Ivy and I have come to say goodbye, Sam."

He dropped into a seat, total surprise written on his face. "What do you mean, goodbye?"

Taking his hand in hers, she said softly, "I'm taking Ivy to America. We're leaving. We're going to Mother's."

"Why? When? For how long?"

She stroked his cheek, a look of ineffable sadness clouding her eyes. "We can't stay here anymore. There's something else I never told you, Sam. It's always been there but I've denied it . . . until last night. I finally confronted Frances and my father about it. They lied to me . . . again. It was the last straw."

"Can you talk about it?"

"How well do you know your Bible, Sam?"

Puzzled, he said, "Not as much as I should know, I guess. You know, stories as a kid. That sort of thing."

"You familiar with the story of David and Bathsheba?"

"Vaguely. Enlighten me."

Regina smiled maternally. "David seduced Bathsheba."

McFadden said, "That I remember. She was married at the time, right?"

"Yes. Her husband was Uriah the Hittite, an officer in David's army. To cover his adultery with Bathsheba, David had his general put Uriah at the front during a battle and then fall back, leaving Uriah alone. He was killed. Bathsheba was suddenly a widow but she was carrying David's child and he married her."

"Pretty cold, Regina. But what's the connection with your father?"

"Frances Yadao's husband was once my father's subordinate, a fellow officer. Father and Frances were lovers. Her husband found out about my father taking that Saudi development money from my uncle and confronted him. Father sent Frances's husband and his men into combat with the Moro guerillas on Basilan and didn't support him when they were ambushed. It was a disaster. The army investigated. That's one reason father took early retirement. He didn't want a formal finding to discover what he had done. Mother knew."

"About the defeat or the adultery?"

"Both. She knew about Frances since the beginning. At first, she stayed because of us. But after the massacre occurred she realized what had happened once she discovered the connection with Sonny and the money. She confronted Father but he lied about it. She knew. That's why she left. She wanted to take us with her. He threatened to fight her for custody if she said anything."

"But you've been visiting your mother ever since then. I don't get it."

"They worked out an agreement to allow us yearly visits with her. She would have had a hard time proving the charges given his connections."

Silent, McFadden sat back, absorbing the news. "Just when I thought it couldn't get any more sordid than it seemed, you tell me this. How long have you known?"

"When I turned twenty-one, Mother sat me down for a long talk. She thought it was time to tell me the truth. I had always known something was not quite right but she kept putting me off." Gazing at her sister cooling herself poolside, Regina said, "Ivy doesn't know. I'm not going to destroy her life with this. Sorry, Sam. I've been carrying this for a long time. But with all that's happened this year I felt it was time. I finally feel free."

"I think I understand why you have to leave. My gut tells me this is bound to get worse before it gets better. I love you, Regina. This is not over. You and I are unfinished business. I don't know how this plays out but promise me you won't forget me, please. Even when you've reached California, remember me."

"How could I forget you?"

"What are your plans?"

"We leave in two hours for Manila. From there, a flight to Los Angeles. We only have carry-on bags. Father thinks we've come to the city to shop. I didn't dare tell him."

"Your mother . . . you told me once . . . in Santa Barbara."

She nodded. "Yes. We've talked. Both of us think it's for the best." Reaching for both his hands, she said, "Ivy needs to get away. We can find help for her there. Mother knows many excellent people who can care for her."

"Ivy," soothed McFadden, "is experiencing something soldiers deal with. It's called PTSD, post-traumatic stress disorder, or something close to it. We all handle it differently. She's young, a wonderful young lady. I think this is the right thing to do. You'll be in my prayers."

McFadden kissed Regina's hand. "Perhaps I can see you both when I get back to the States. Would that be possible?"

She rose, put her arms around him. "Anything is possible, Plain Old Sam. I would love to see you. Please come."

"Nothing would make me happier," he replied. They kissed, his body pressed against her yielding softness. He walked the sisters to the steel gate.

Eddie's widow had come from her house to say farewell. He waited. "Goodbye, Rose," said Regina. "Please take care of Major Sam. Keep him out of trouble."

Showing a shy smile, Rose said, "Is not always easy with him."

McFadden walked Regina to the driver's side. "You may have been followed. He'll move heaven and earth to stop you."

She cut him off. "I thought of that. I have a friend who owns a dress shop. We'll park in front and go out the back. She promised to have a taxi waiting to take us to the airport. By the time he discovers we're gone it will be too late. We're only an hour to Manila. Once we're on the plane there will be no turning back. Come see us. I have so much more to tell you."

One last kiss and they were gone. McFadden climbed the stairs on leaden feet, grabbed a bottle of beer, and sat on the porch beneath a slow fan stirring Zamboanga's humid air.

Dusk was dropping its curtain when Wolf finally returned. McFadden could tell he had been in a bar. The two traded stories. Wolf rejoiced at the news of Regina's flight with Ivy. Rosario would rage at his daughters' flight and hold McFadden responsible but he knew Wolf would have his back.

CHAPTER 71

Another shoe dropped two weeks later. During a noon break in court proceedings, Burton Wickes disappeared. A huge explosion triggered under his lawyer's car vaporized the American and his attorney. The two ceased to exist. Glass from adjacent offices rained on a blackened crater deep in the street. An entire block downtown lost power. Choking smoke drove people from nearby offices.

Later that night, retired general Pablo Rosario claimed an assassination attempt on his life. Granted extra protection by prosecutors, he moved only in a government-supplied armored limousine when attending legal hearings. Without Wickes's testimony, Rosario's case stalled. A new prosecutor, appointed by Manila, flew to the city and hurried the government's attempt to bury things. Another half-month dragged by before word from the president's men ordered proceedings ended. A press conference sealed it.

McFadden and Wolf, in unofficial home arrest for the past

two months, watched the staged farce in the living room, the fans battling stifling air. Their limbo at an end, the two were released from further court appearances by summary judgment. Their passports were returned. Allegations relating to the cemetery shooting, weapons possession, and sundry other violations conjured by zealous government lawyers fell by the wayside. By design, the Clemente hit never registered on the court's radar.

"Didn't I tell you?" crowed Wolf, a celebratory whiskey in hand. "Did I not say this would all end up like a drunk pissing on a barroom floor?"

"What the hell is that word picture supposed to mean?" asked a relieved but subdued McFadden.

Wolf plopped down on the couch, saying, "I have absolutely no idea. It was the first thing that came to mind." Snatching the remote from McFadden's hand, Wolf muted the endlessly droning, self-congratulatory press conference.

Wolf hailed McFadden. "To my noble companion. Warrior, veteran, patriot, brother, helmsman, and diver extraordinaire!" They saluted each other with solemnity, collapsing in bitter laughter.

In the morning, the two quietly booked return tickets to California via Honolulu. Fearing hidden trip-wires in the court system, they added some of their own cash to the set-aside ransom money for the steep cost of last-minute tickets. There were errands to run, suitcases to pack, goodbyes to say. There was a final trip to the pier to say farewell to faithful Sal and Andy.

It broke Wolf's heart to see Rosario's hand already at work— the boat's name had been sanded off. The faintest of outlines showed only the letter "a." McFadden and Wolf gave away everything they owned. Eddie's policeman nephew was given a coveted prize: McFadden's SIG Sauer. Rose had first pick of McFadden's belongings, followed by the nephew. On their last morning,

McFadden presented their young watchman with two Berettas and the shotgun, a gesture that moved the young man to tears.

"Take care of the next tenant," said McFadden, pressing fat envelopes in each of their hands. *If Rosario only knew.* He smiled at the thought. Rose and her nephew, silent and heartbroken, promised to look after the home.

The pair left the way Wolf had come only months before, on Cebu Pacific Airlines. The stop in Manila was uneventful, their connection to Honolulu on time. When they lifted off, they grinned at each other. At the edge of Philippine air space, McFadden listened to Wolf happily babbling about plans to take him surfing. No stranger to the sport, McFadden had agreed to a one-week layover in Hawaii.

When they left Oahu the following week, McFadden was restless, replaying the last three years of his life. Other than a duffle bag in the luggage hold and the funds for Tiny's daughter, he had nothing to show for his Philippines sojourn. Wolf had even less. But life to the ex-SEAL was one continuous adventure. Zamboanga's episode had been a close-run thing but he pigeonholed it in a box along with memories of Africa, Central America, Iraq, and Afghanistan.

Waiting for them in Los Angeles was Shorty, his leg stiff but still attached and healing. The three found a bar and hunkered in a corner. McFadden gave an accounting of the ransom money now in five Singapore accounts and an equal number in Tokyo. The plan was to begin moving the cash to trust accounts in Canada. Tiny's college-bound daughter would benefit over the next two years.

"Preacher wanted to make it," said Shorty, "but his wife has him working non-stop on their lake home. He's more afraid of Colleen than he is of us."

Badgered for details about the outcome in the Philippines,

McFadden and Wolf gave the short version. Later, in the midst of a sea of hurrying strangers, the men exchanged the usual promises to stay in touch. Hugs were shared and then McFadden was by himself, a strange feeling in a city of millions.

CHAPTER 72

After making a phone call, McFadden bought a one-way ticket on the five-thirty Santa Barbara shuttle. Settling back in the plush blue seat, he composed a speech, reciting it one dozen times in his head. Arriving at eight that evening, he snagged a taxi and gave the Hispanic driver a scrap of paper with a Tunnel Road address in the hills of Mission Canyon. Forty minutes later, he stood at the foot of a curving driveway of paving blocks bordered with wildflowers and banks of evergreens. Floral scents perfumed the clear air. At the top of the sloping drive sat a stuccoed hillside home framed by a family of palms and cypress, reminding him of the Philippines he loved. Throwing his duffle bag on his shoulders, McFadden walked to a set of varnished teak doors set in large coral blocks. He set down the bag, took a deep breath, and pushed the doorbell once, twice.

A delicate, barefooted Filipina wearing a black skirt and pale pink blouse opened one of the tall doors. Greeting him with that familiar dazzling island smile, she said, "Good afternoon, Major Sam. Miss Regina been expecting you. Please to come inside." McFadden set his bag down in the spacious entry. Just beyond, sunlight flooded a wide room overlooking forested hills.

"Major Sam, you come this way, please." She led him down two carpeted steps and vanished. "Just plain Sam will do," he called after her. He was alone.

"Hello, Just Plain Sam."

Regina Rosario ran across the room and threw herself in McFadden's arms, burying her face against his chest. She sobbed. He stroked her hair, kissed her forehead, cheeks, and lips.

"Come with me," she whispered, taking him by the hand to a wall of glass looking over a backyard Eden. A wide concrete patio ran the length of the house, ending where a hillside rose in terraces planted with giant glazed pots overflowing with blossoms. Off to one side, a curving pool shimmered in the dying sun. She pushed a button and floor-to-ceiling walls of telescoping glass slid back, bringing nature indoors.

"Beautiful," he marveled.

Gazing at a pair of figures sitting at a redwood table shaded by a huge umbrella, he asked, "Ivy?"

Regina broke into a wide smile. "Yes, Ivy. And her Jimmy. He's just out of the Marines. Be kind to them both, Sam."

McFadden strode across the lanai. Ivy leaped to her feet, meeting him halfway. He enveloped her in a brotherly bear hug. She kissed him on the cheek, motioning to the young man. "Sam, meet my Jimmy."

The muscular all-American held out a hand. "Pleasure to meet you, sir. I've heard a lot about you." Eyes locked, the two shook hands.

"You treating this young lady well?"

Taken aback, the youth blurted out, "Yes, sir. Absolutely. Ivy's special to me."

McFadden slapped the man's shoulder. "Good. She's special to me, too."

"You're a former Marine, right?"

"Once a Marine, always a Marine, sir."

"Good people, Marines. Say, where's the matriarch of this operation?" he asked Regina.

A steady, feminine voice floated from the trees. "Matriarch?

You make me sound like an old lady, young man. I don't do 'matriarch.'" Regina's mother, white-haired but definitely not fitting a matriarchal profile, sauntered down the terraced hill, her arms cradling a riot of color. "Ah, the superman Regina raves about."

The young Filipina who greeted McFadden suddenly reappeared. Handing off the blossoms to the woman, Regina's mother shed her gardening gloves. "Mariana, I think we'll have wine out here, please."

She offered a hand to her guest. "So you are Sam McFadden."

"Guilty," he stammered. "How do you prefer to be addressed?"

The green-eyed, tanned woman rolled her eyes at Regina. "Oh, isn't he a diplomatic one. Call me Dorothy, Sam McFadden." Winking at her daughter, she added, "Or should I just refer to him as Plain Old Sam?"

"That works for me, ma'am—uh, Dorothy," he volunteered.

Brushing soil from her elbows, she declared, "We've been waiting. You'll stay for a late supper, Plain Old Sam. You too, Jimmy."

His arm around Regina, McFadden said, "I do believe I have time, Dorothy."

"That's a yes. I won't take no for an answer. And you're staying the night. You and my Ivy's Marine friend will bunk in the pool cottage. Twin racks, of course. You have your own latrine. Or, as Jimmy would say, 'head.'"

Clapping her hands, the gardener-turned-hostess said, "Everyone, join me for a glass of wine. What more could a mother ask for than to have her children by her side? I love you both. I also congratulate Jimmy for finishing his hitch in the Marines, for serving with honor, and for Sam McFadden's safe arrival. Cheers, everyone!"

As the sun dissolved into the sea, the five dined outside at a candlelit table set with linen and silver, under trees strung with lights, beneath a clear Santa Barbara night sky sprinkled with stars.

CHAPTER 73
EPILOGUE

Of the three SEALs who answered Tom Wolf's call for help, only Preacher Hackett and Shorty Severson remain. Finishing his Lake Superior home to his wife's satisfaction, Preacher now hunts, fishes, and attends occasional reunions with others from his years in the teams. Sensibly fleeing Minnesota winters, Preacher and wife, Colleen, spend time in a rented beach home on the Gulf. To unsuspecting neighbors, he is simply a good man, a helpful snowbird who admits to once being career Navy, nothing more.

Shorty, his leg healed, was called back to save the family farm in the heart of the country. Returning to work the land with his four brothers, he is as far inland as he could be from the sea. Shorty Severson is content, an odd phase in his life considering how many times he had risked going in harm's way.

"Tiny" Tim O'Neill's only child, a first-year college student, began drawing money from the trust fund under McFadden's watchful eye. In addition to his only child, Tiny left behind three ex-wives, multiple girlfriends, and a screenplay gathering dust in a San Diego safety deposit box.

Tom Wolf, retired SEAL team commander, keeps his hand in by working special ops for an off-the-books government intelligence arm. Staying close to Washington, DC, keeps him available and in the loop. His extensive list of contacts is constantly being updated. Occasionally he pursues projects for DARPA, the Defense Advanced Research Projects Agency, a science stepchild of Eisenhower's born in 1958. Wolf's latest assignment is split between drones and small satellites. He keeps a quiver of boards at a friend's house on Oahu's North Shore, returning during winter months to surf. The Wolfman routinely stays in touch with McFadden.

Retired general Pablo Rosario never got over what he called the "betrayal" of his daughters. He refused their calls and did not seek reconciliation. Framed pictures of his girls were turned to face the wall. With the help of an expensive team of Manila lawyers, he escaped all blame for alleged involvement in the Clemente-Wickes-Storch debacle. Considerably weakened politically in the wake of the scandal, Rosario saw his circle of influence shrink. Even faithful Frances Yadao, who at first remained loyal, finally deserted Rosario. Returning to Manila, she attempted to heal the rift with her first husband's family. Her effort failed but she did not return to Zamboanga, leaving Rosario on his own.

During his final court appearance, Rosario was shadowed by Eddie Delgado's nephew. The general's stalker fired six shots at point-blank range, killing him. Rosario's bodyguards riddled his assassin's body with fourteen bullets. The .45 caliber M1911 Colt used in Rosario's slaying was recovered from the sidewalk where Eddie's nephew fell. A loaded Beretta pistol was also found. The killer's motive remains unknown. Eddie's widow offered no clues.

In Zamboanga, General Rosario's creditors sold the *Laticauda*, renamed *Falcon*, to a Taiwanese shipping firm. Returned to an ignominious trawler role, the ship struck an uncharted reef in the Sulu Sea during a typhoon one year later and went down with all hands. The ship's grave, not far from the *Yogaku*, is unmarked.

In the fall, Ivy, finally healed of her demons, stood in the shade of her mother's spreading backyard trees and exchanged

vows with her Marine, Jimmy. Within a year, they made Dorothy a grandmother and Regina an aunt.

McFadden courted Regina under the watchful eyes of her
mother, finally winning approval to marry the Filipino-American beauty in his mother-in-law's garden. It was a small ceremony. Ivy served as bridesmaid. Wolf flew in to act as best man.
His hilarious, mocking toast at the rehearsal dinner the night
before kept everyone laughing throughout the meal. Laughter
and tears were Wolf's gift to the McFaddens. The new couple
live in San Diego and visit Regina's mother often.

In Zamboanga, the Kuratong Baleleng lives on. A new crop
of manoy and sandalo battle police and other gangs for control
of the city's barangays and streets. Their war will never end.

30078767R00151

Made in the USA
Charleston, SC
04 June 2014